LIVE WIRE

BROOKLYN BOYS #2

E. DAVIES

Publisher's Note: This is a work of fiction. Names, characters, places, and incidents are a product of the author's imagination. Locales and public names are sometimes used for atmospheric purposes. Any resemblance to actual people, living or dead, or to businesses, companies, events, institutions, or locales is completely coincidental.

Live Wire / E. Davies. – 2nd ed.
ISBN-13: 978-1-912245-31-4

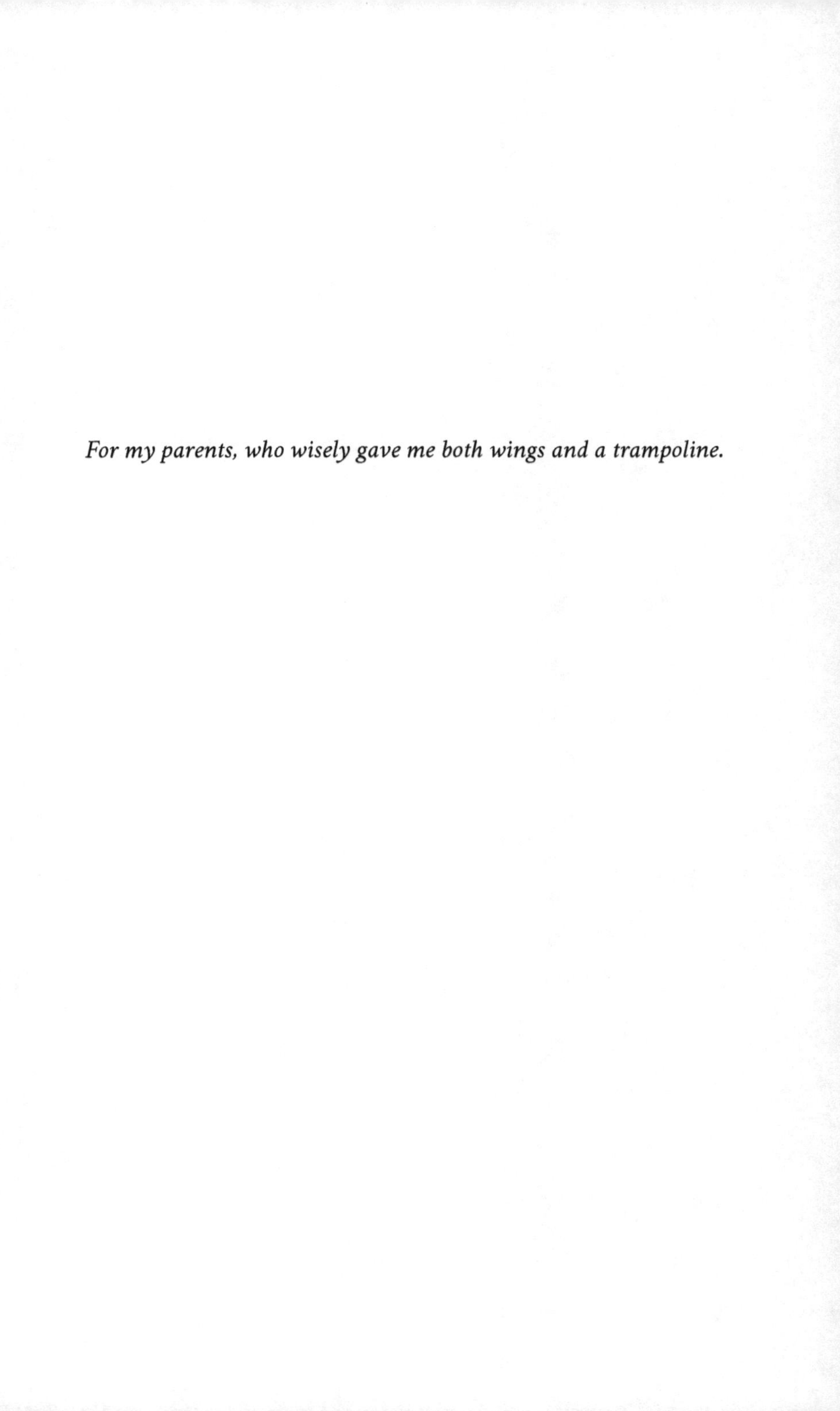

For my parents, who wisely gave me both wings and a trampoline.

"We really shouldn't be doing this."

Yet, as usual, I was pressed up against my bedroom door and my ex was kissing my neck.

Xavier was annoyingly good at foreplay. Which was, among other reasons, why we kept ending up in bed.

"I don't care," he reminded me. "And your boner tells me you don't care, either."

I knew—vaguely, in some rational part of my brain—that I always felt like shit after we slept together. But that part of my brain was packed away with the last of my bedding and picture frames.

If I looked over Xavier's shoulder, my life was contained in neat cardboard boxes. I should have felt sad, or angry, or... I didn't know, something.

Bittersweet? I could lay claim to that, but it was an apathetic kind of feeling. Not relief, like a sneeze you'd been waiting for all day, but the kind so far overdue that you'd already filed it away in your mind.

"You don't have to go," Xavier murmured, his hand curled around my shaft through my jeans.

It was hard not to remember how well he sucked my cock, too. After all, we'd fucked more often since breaking up than we had in the last few months of our supposed relationship.

There was a unique appeal to the forbidden—or at least sensibly discouraged. I'd never been good at denying myself pleasure.

"Fuck the rules," Xavier whispered into my ear, his teeth grazing my earlobe. However often he exploited my weakness, it never grew less effective. My knees and resolve weakened.

"One last time?" I murmured, my palms flat on the door at my sides. If he'd ever been much of a top, I might feel like prey. As it was, he was coaxing me into indiscretion.

"Cross my heart."

"Again? You said that last week." I pressed a hand on his chest, trying to figure out if I was about to dig my nails in or push him away.

I knew which option my dick wanted, but he didn't get a vote here. In the brain-body working relationship, my body had won every argument since the breakup.

It was time to ignore Downstairs Darren and use my brain.

"That was before I remembered how good your dick feels in my mouth," Xavier whispered.

Fuck, he was really fucking great at this. Heat crawled along my spine, and I knew I was blushing. I was rock-hard now, my toes curling into my bedroom floor.

The floor where he'd fucked me like a boring straight porn star just a couple weeks ago, the day I told him I was moving out.

God, thinking about that didn't improve my tight pants situation.

"What do you say?" Xavier whispered, his hand slipping into my pants. When I didn't answer, he added, "The magic word will do."

"No," I moaned, which made him pause and look at me in just as much surprise as I felt right now.

Apparently I *was* capable of using my brain sometimes. Huh. First time for everything.

And last time for something—letting him talk me into great sex that left me crying into a bottle of wine later.

"No," I repeated gently, a sense of finality rushing through me.

There it was: the relief I'd been waiting for. The breath of fresh air.

Xavier took a step back, his expression crestfallen. For a moment, I felt bad for causing that.

No, dumbass, I told myself. *His happiness is his problem. I can't give myself up to make him happy.*

"So we're... done-done?"

"Yeah, babe." I ran my hands down my face and then took hold of his hips to gently steer him away from my door.

When I opened it, Xavier huffed but accepted defeat. He looked around at my boxes and half heartedly offered, "Need some help?"

"Nah. Thanks, but I've got it."

I had a plan to move these last few boxes one trip at a time. Moving in Brooklyn was a real pain in the ass. I hadn't done it in ages, and I hoped I wouldn't have to again for a while.

No more dating roommates.

Xavier, about to be my ex-roommate as well as ex-boyfriend, took a shaky breath and walked out. It sounded like he was heading straight to his room.

It had been *our* room at first, but after we broke up, our last roommate got sick of hearing us fuck out our differences and moved out, so I'd taken the spare bedroom.

Definitely no more romance for me for a while. Safer for everyone that way.

I wasn't gonna fuck up anyone else's life.

1

ADAM

"So, how are things?"

I surprised myself with how closely I hung onto Dad's every word. Mom was off at her knitting circle, which meant Dad was taking the semi-monthly phone call.

They'd said to call every day when I moved out to my first place on my own—sharing a cabin in Knoxville with my best friend. But after I'd ended up leaving voicemails more days than not, we'd agreed that I'd call every week, and then they'd started missing *those* calls. Dad had summer fly-fishing trips. Mom had Bible studies classes.

Now I talked to them maybe once a month.

Which was fine with me, obviously. They were the ones who'd told me to get a job or join the military, and that the military would at least keep me on the straight and narrow.

A concern they'd particularly had when my boss turned out to run a gay ranch, and my roommate was so gay that my shirts didn't dare wrinkle around him. Moving to Brooklyn with him didn't look great, from their perspective.

"Oh, fine. Holding the wolves from the door?"

"Yeah, yeah. My new job is full-time. Nice to only have one job again," I admitted.

"Fine" was all I usually got from them, but at least they didn't worry that something had happened to me in the big city.

"Well, that sounds good. I'd better let you get supper on," Dad told me with a distinctly forced air of cheer.

I felt like telling them that Kev had moved out, but I didn't want them to suddenly get nicer to me—only to be disappointed that another gay man had moved into his room and freeze me out again.

The less they heard, the better. The fewer chances I got to hear what they thought, the better. Even if I was straight, just being around *those gays* was dangerous, in my parents' opinion.

"Okay. Take care," I said, trying to ignore my sinking mood.

"You too. Talk soon."

My dad hung up and I sighed, tossing my phone into my stack of pillows and crashing on my bed face down.

I moaned into my pillows and wrestled the biggest one before I rolled onto my back and glared at the ceiling.

At least I didn't have parents like Kev's. He may have just moved out, but he was still my best friend, if that didn't sound too middle school. His parents had kicked him out for real. Mine just heavily implied that if I ever came out as anything not straight, I'd be out of the Christmas newsletter until I changed my mind.

And there'd been some shouting sometimes, and a slap when I

earned it. But nothing that bad. Especially since I was effectively straight. Since moving out, I'd had plenty of chances to test that out at last. But I'd never quite needed to.

Not yet.

I glared at my phone and willed it to bring a date to me—any date—to distract me. I'd swiped right on half the Tinder profiles of Brooklyn, but they hadn't returned the sentiment.

There was some kind of gulf in my chest. My family and friends were safely on shore, and I was a raft being swept away to sea. Every call with my family emphasized that. Even Kev, now that he had a boyfriend he was living with, reminded me of everything I felt unsure of. Every Tinder marathon, too, was like cramming a square peg into a round hole—however hot the owner of said hole was.

Looking at my phone just reminded me of too much shit.

I left it where it was, the traitorous bastard, and headed to the kitchen to see if Darren had started anything for dinner.

My new roommate and I hadn't quite worked out a dinner schedule. He'd suggested cooking his own meals, but I knew he left early and got home late from work some days. I didn't like to think of him skipping a meal just to grab extra sleep. I'd done that myself too many times.

Darren was standing over the stove, humming along to the radio as he stirred a pot. That was a promising sign.

"Hey," I greeted and punched him in the shoulder gently to let him know I was there.

Darren jerked his chin in greeting. "Hey. I'm making gazpacho."

I frowned for a few seconds before I figured it out. "That's that cold soup stuff, right?"

"Yep. Tomato. It's good."

"Cold?" I pretended to shudder. "You New Yorkers and your weird shit."

"It's fucking hot." Darren didn't have to tell me that twice: he looked as roasted as me, in a muscle shirt and cut-off shorts that looked weirdly attractive. They didn't usually flatter guys.

Before I accidentally assigned a 1-to-10 value to my roommate's attractiveness and spent the next week drinking whiskey to forget it, I turned to grab glasses. "Ah, but you forget the secret weapon."

"Iced tea?"

"Bingo." I poured them and presented him with one, flourishing. "For the chef. Wait, if you're serving that cold..."

He grinned. "It's lunch tomorrow." Before I could pout, he added, "I have sushi being delivered."

Another thing I hadn't eaten much of before moving here. Learning to eat with chopsticks had been a point of simmering frustration.

"Oh, you're the best new roommate ever," I praised him, breaking into a grin. I liked sushi now that I'd learned raw fish could actually taste okay. New Yorkers were weird, but their food was good.

Darren laughed. "Only if you get it on a mug."

Before he moved out, Kev had bought me a Worst Roommate mug, and I treasured it. Making fun of him had made my days pass a bit quicker, and I'd worried that I wouldn't connect with Darren the same way.

No need to worry, apparently. Darren had been more than happy to laugh and joke around with me. He'd taken his part of the cleaning and housework seriously, and he made supper sometimes.

The only thing was that he was gay, but he wasn't bringing home guys all the time, so we hadn't yet had that conversation. Another thing Kev had taught me—mostly by verbally slapping upside my head—was that not all gay guys did.

"You all right?" Darren asked, his gaze way too perceptive.

Fuck. Now I had to cover. "Yeah, great," I lied, hopping up to sit on the counter. "You look good tonight. No homo, bro."

He chuckled. "None taken," he teased. "I'm out on a date later."

"Oh yeah? Me too." God, I had no idea why I'd even said that. Dumbass, I chided myself. I sure didn't—though with Tinder, maybe I could if I were lucky.

Couldn't let him be the only guy getting action around here.

"Well, then," Darren laughed. "You got a protocol for this?"

"I told you about the watermelon and strawberry code." He looked blank and I barely muffled my sigh. Kev and I had worked things out so well, too. How else was I gonna explain it? "Text me if you know you'll be out, and I'll text if I need the apartment or I'll be out, or vice versa." I waved a hand. "It gets complicated when both of us have dates, though."

"I know mine isn't coming home," Darren said firmly. "It's a first date."

"So?" I grinned. "Isn't that a perk of gayness? None of that *tell me about your life ambitions* shit, you just get straight to the good stuff. Haha. Straight."

Darren shot me a slightly annoyed glance—I knew how to read

him by now, and it was clear. "Not all guys work that way, you know."

I just liked getting a rise out of him. Out of most guys, really. I didn't even know why. I screwed around a little with girls, but with guys, this felt like the only way I could establish trust or have a deep kind of conversation without defending my sexuality. Joking was a kind of bonding, right? I respected people's limits—mostly—and didn't make shitty jokes just for the shock factor.

"Yeah, only the fun ones," I said and grinned. The doorbell went off. "Oh, sushi!"

"Wanna grab that? Tip's on the counter."

I swept up the bills and exchanged them for the meal when I got to the door. "Thanks," I added to the driver, who nodded once and took off down the stairs again.

One job I'd considered, but luckily, I hadn't had a car and thought it likely I'd crash a motorbike. Thank God for full-time work.

"Is it all there? Should be three trays," Darren told me as he shut off the stove and I brought the food to our tiny living room-slash-dining room. It was basically a sliver to the side of Darren's room, where the landlord had thrown in a cheap wall or two to make a one-bed a two-bed and double the rent.

Darren had graciously agreed to take the crappier room since he was glad to be out of his old living situation. I'd tried to go easy on him, knowing he was just getting out of a bad place, but teasing was in my nature. I wasn't gonna stop now.

"Three trays," I confirmed. "Grab me a beer?"

"You got it."

"And one for yourself, if you've had that kind of week."

"Boy, have I ever."

I frowned in concern. Darren looked stressed, after all. I might be a dick sometimes, but I could listen to him vent for a bit.

Sure beat my plans for later: sitting around refreshing dating websites and hoping that somehow, something would click into place.

Not just to get a date, but to *want* one. Something about a relationship appealed to me, but not all the time. I was kind of take it or leave it on the whole thing.

And it wasn't just me being repressed. I was almost sure of that.

God, I was a mess. I was glad when Darren came around the corner and started bitching about George, his contractor. It was nice to listen to someone else's problems for a change.

Stopped me from getting stuck in my own head, with no way out.

2

DARREN

One predrink with Adam later, I was ready to rumble and walking to Friction.

It had been a month since the breakup, and I was still single. I hadn't even tried to date since moving in with Adam, and that had to change.

The guy I'd met on Grindr had agreed to meet me at nine at Friction. If all went well, we wouldn't be there until closing time.

I was determined to break out of this slump. I'd been looking forward to this for a couple days now, trying to plan how to act and flirt and come across as attractive as possible.

On the other hand, Adam had asked for the apartment tonight, so I'd have to make sure my date lived alone or figure something else out. I didn't want to get kicked out of the bathroom for trying it on in there.

But that was a problem for later. First, I had to make sure I got along well with this guy.

Once I was inside the bar, I chose a spot where I could see the door, but I tried not to watch it. The nerves were kicking in now, making me second-guess everything from what I'd worn to my planned conversations.

Finally, I was getting back out there. It was a great first step, and the guy seemed cute.

I realized something was wrong when I'd been waiting ten minutes with no sign of him. Twenty minutes in, I ordered a beer for myself, and as I worked on it, nobody had approached me at the bar where we'd agreed to meet.

Except…

Holy shit. No way.

I pulled up the picture on my phone to double-check, but the obnoxious cleft chin and muscled frame was identical.

The guy had just walked in with *another* guy on his arm, and they were dancing away on the nearly-empty floor, giggling into each other's ears.

Did he just forget about me? Or worse yet, did he get a better offer and ditch me for it? That was starting to feel all too familiar in my life. The other guy *was* hotter than me.

I opened and closed my mouth a few times, not even sure what to say. "For fuck's sake," I finally muttered and turned on my stool to finish the beer.

At least he could have texted to cancel. Or did he want to wind me up by showing off his hotter date? In any case, I wasn't in the mood to buy into whatever the hell game he was playing.

I sent Adam a quick text. *What's the state of the apartment?*

I didn't get a response quickly, which told me what I wanted to know—he was probably busy with someone. Without another guy's place to crash at, it was gonna be a long night. I could always show up here a bit later, anyway—when it was too busy to notice or care about my date. That would pass the night.

I blew out a sigh and pushed the glass back with a nod to the bartender. Better get my ass to Bubbles before I said something to that prick that I'd regret later.

On the way out the door, the bouncer did a double-take. "You're leaving early."

It was just procedure, I knew. Better business to make sure there wasn't some asshole inside scaring customers away. But I could pretend it was friendly small talk from someone who cared.

"Yeah. Looks like I was about to get caught in the middle of a love triangle."

"Ohhh. That's only sexy in the movies, right?"

I grinned at him. "Oh, it can be sexy in real life, but not when there's more assholes than the dicks they deserve to get stuffed with."

He snorted and waved. "Have a good night, then."

"I'll try. Who knows—I might be back," I winked.

It took me just a minute to see myself to the diner next door, passing by the single lonely door between the buildings that I knew led up to the owner's apartment. Jared and his boyfriend, Shay, and I had all had a couple drinks together up there.

The diner was warm and friendly no matter what my mood was like every time I walked in. The bright red seats and menus cheered me up, and the smell of coffee and bacon seemed impossible to ignore.

Having Bubbles right next to Friction was kind of like the best part of being a kid, combined with the best part of being over twenty-one. You could go get hammered and then have a milkshake on the way home.

I spotted some familiar faces in one of the booths, thankfully, just as my phone went off.

Whatever fucking fruit will give me some privacy until midnight?

Orange you glad I'm a good roommate, I texted back, smirking to myself at the joke. I could see Adam rolling his eyes now. As much as I made fun of him, I did respect the strange fruit code he had.

At least Bubbles was always open, even if my love life and front door were closed.

I checked out the booths—a couple guys I knew hanging out in here. I picked the closest table and approached.

"I got stood up, and now my roommate won't let me go home until midnight." I sighed deeply as I draped myself across Billy's lap until he budged over enough that I could squeeze into the diner booth.

"Hel*looo*, bad day. Shots?" Billy offered. He always seemed to be hanging around here. Though his hair was silver, he dressed like he was still in his thirties, and he always had an opinion to offer. He knew the diner owner, Jared, even better than I did.

"Nah," I said with a sigh. "I want a clear head tomorrow."

"Oh, where's the fun in that." Billy shook his head. "Bad news. You're getting old."

I glared. "Don't remind me. Guess where I saw my date? Or rather, who with?"

By now, a couple of the others were wandering over. Shay, Jared's boyfriend, interrupted and gasped, "No. He didn't turn up with another date?"

Jared's boyfriend hung out here a lot now, especially when he was doing work that didn't require him to be in the studio or on location. The weather anchor was responsible for the weather channel's Facebook feed, and he did some cheesy weekly posts that everyone ate up.

"Got it in one." My mood slumped even further. "I saw him—I literally saw him dancing *with* the other guy, half an hour after we were supposed to meet."

"Did he think you just went home without him? Rude!" That was another guy I didn't know too well—I wasn't even sure of his name. He scurried over to the other side of the booth and slid in. He was becoming a regular here, too, but they came and went. It was hard to learn everyone's name, and after a certain point, it just got awkward to ask "what's your name" yet again.

"I dunno what he thought. Maybe he was trying to start a catfight. News flash, bozo: I don't fight over men. Or anything," I added, shaking my head. "Not enough time in the world for mind games."

"Preach," Billy agreed and toasted that with his mug of coffee.

"Hey, weren't you dating a guy not long ago?" That was the nameless guy. "That tall one?"

"Mark," hissed Shay under his breath with a meaningful look. He knew about the breakup, because I'd come straight here to drown my sorrows in a greasy dinner.

At least I knew Mark's name now. "Nah, it's okay," I assured him with a wave of my hand. "That was so last week. Well, last month now."

"Right. Fuck, time flies. Sorry." Mark winced.

I shook my head. "We weren't meant to be. He kept trying to make it work, but… we never clicked like we should have."

"You lived with him, didn't you?" Jared came meandering by, order pad in his hand, as if he didn't already know what I wanted to eat. "The usual?"

"Please." I leaned back into the booth and stretched my arms along it as I rolled my neck. "Yeah, we lived together for… a year? Maybe eighteen months?"

"And you broke up last month?"

"Come on," I scoffed. "We were only dating for a year. You can't tell me that's too soon to move on."

Jared raised his hands without saying anything and headed for the kitchen, yelling for Enrique to get his head out of his ass, put down the phone, and put the bacon on even if he only had fifteen minutes left in his shift.

Not saying anything was surprisingly nice of him. Normally he wouldn't be shy about letting me know I was being a dumbass.

"Okay, be honest. Pull up Facebook."

I eyed Billy but unlocked my phone and did just that. Before I could protest, Billy had my phone and was opening the search box, tapping on my phone.

"Top search result—so, your most recent search is…"

I didn't need to hear everyone else's snickers to know I was blushing—I felt myself turning scarlet. "Yeah, yeah, whatever." I snatched my phone back.

"Xavier, his ex," Billy told the others, folding his arms. "That doesn't sound like you're over him."

"I am," I grumbled. I tried not to wilt under the scrutiny. "I just wanted to make sure he changed his profile picture to one that isn't, you know, us."

"Mmhmm." Shay propped his chin on his fist, his expression amused. "Pull the other one."

"No, the other *other* one." Mark made the obvious joke, but we all laughed despite our groans.

I sighed as Jared brought the coffee pot to fill my mug. "I just don't get why nothing ever seems to work out."

"Stop forcing it," Shay told me. His gaze flitted up to Jared, and a fond smile crossed his lips. "When it's right, you'll know it."

I pretended to gag, and Jared pretended to spill the coffee in my lap. The squeak I gave while covering my privates made everyone chuckle.

"Gross and romantic we might be," Jared told me, "but it's my diner. Put up with the lovey-dovey eyes or shut up."

I held my hands up in defeat. "Fine. Make everyone else jealous, why don't you."

"Speaking of jealous..." Billy was suspiciously busy on his phone. "Huh. So Xavier's seeing someone already."

"I know—" I broke off and gave him a guilty look.

"Aha! You *are* Facebook stalking him." Jared pointed the pot at me. "That way lies danger. There's nothing about him you need to know."

"Why? Do *you* know something? Has he been in here?" I asked, eyeing Jared. We'd met at Friction, after all. No doubt he'd picked up the new boy toy that way. Just because I followed his accounts meant nothing.

Jared snorted. "He has, but still... unfriend him if you can't resist."

"Okay, now I need to know."

Billy was always a reliable leak. "If you must know," he said in a confidential stage whisper that probably made the kitchen pots rattle, "I saw him yesterday."

"And?" I just wanted to check that he wasn't obsessing over me, that was all. After moving out, I'd blocked his number just to make sure I didn't give in to temptation. Who knows how much he might have been trying to reach me?

"He *did* ask if you had a boyfriend. I said I had no idea—I don't keep tabs on people," Billy claimed, which was as outrageous a lie as ever. "But you're clearly not meant to stay friends if you're here checking in on each other."

"We can stay Facebook friends," I protested, folding my arms. I hadn't come here to be made fun of after getting stood up. "We haven't slept together—we haven't even talked—since I moved out."

"Holy shit, a whole month without screwing him." Billy raised the hand that wasn't holding his phone and waved it in the air. "Praise the Lord."

I laughed despite myself. "Oh, shut up. It's more self-control than I showed for like, three months of living together post-breakup." Since moving in with Adam, my self-esteem had risen considerably. I knew perfectly well that wasn't a coincidence.

"It says here he's going on a trip to that Sand and Suds party with the new boy. The one in Hawaii."

"Yeah?" I knew the one he meant. One Hawaiian resort held its own circuit party squeezed between major Pride event weeks. Xavier had been talking about it for months—ever since last year's drew such a big crowd that it had appeared on all the gay social media outlets.

"I bet he's paying for his new boy toy to go. Look at him—totally a student." Mark leaned in and scoffed. "He's not even as hot as you," he told me.

It didn't help. "Oh, great. So my ex left me for someone younger, too. A sugar baby. I'm not even hot enough to be a sugar baby," I lamented.

"Technically *you* left *him*," Shay reminded me. "And a good thing, too."

"Sure it was. Good." I tried not to think of him on the beach in a Speedo with some hot new arm candy. If someone else could actually connect with him for more than an hour at a time, they were welcome to have him. It was better for me and my life that I wasn't in that situation.

Hawaii, though.

"I was talking to a couple guys at the bar last night about it," Billy told us. "It's just next month now. The resort's doing a drawing. You bitches better not win," he warned us as we all reached for our phones. "Those tickets are mine."

"Do they pay for airfare?"

"Hell, yeah. And a seaview room, and all-inclusive meals *and* drinks."

Shit. That sounded like the trip of a lifetime. I wondered how much it had cost Xavier. Even Hawaii would have gone wrong if he'd paid for me to go. The fights we would have had? Unbelievable.

Despite telling us we better not win, Billy was trying to motivate us to enter. "Go on, do it," Billy encouraged everyone, elbowing us all until we did. "You never know until you try."

I smiled to myself. Yeah, you never did. Trying never worked out in the end, but if I just gave up, he was right—nothing would happen.

"Imagine if I won," I said with a snort of laughter. "I'd have to avoid Xavier all week. Awkward."

"*Awkward*," everyone chimed in together to echo me.

As Jared dropped off my hangover special and I dug into the greasy deliciousness, my mind started to wander. If I did happen to win, a week on a beach would be a great stress relief break after all the shit that had happened to me lately.

Get real, loser, I told myself. *It'll never happen.* Still didn't stop me from daydreaming, though.

3

ADAM

This was my chance. I'd always grabbed chances with both hands and wrestled them like a pig in a mud puddle, but this time? I just couldn't.

Finally, I had the house to myself until midnight and Grindr installed on my phone.

For months, I'd been debating it. Not that I was seriously thinking about going gay, but the part of me that was curious… well, that part had whispered in my ear.

I was young, single, and in Brooklyn, far away from anyone who gave a shit who I screwed.

So why did I still hesitate, even with a safe, blank profile?

I hadn't been able to use Grindr before now. Kev had constantly started new Grindr profiles, so I never could have found and blocked all the new profiles. Eventually he would have spotted a profile five feet away and asked too many questions.

The first thing I'd done after Darren moved in was block him. I still didn't have my face on my profile, or half my vital statistics. It hadn't stopped a couple guys from messaging me anyway.

But every time I opened one of their messages, I got the jitters.

Not because I didn't want to try it out. Whether I wound up being gay —or bi, I guess—I was happy getting my dick into anything, really.

But as I glanced at one of my new messages and my heart did that now familiar flip flop in my throat, I figured the time had come.

Why not invite a guy over? Just once? We never had to see each other again. The guy who'd just messaged was five hundred feet away. He could be here in minutes.

I could finally figure out which side of the fence was greener.

"Okay," I breathed out to steady my nerves. I'd even cleaned my room earlier while Darren got ready for his date. Made the bed, vacuumed the carpet.

It looked good, and I looked good. I'd gone for the farm boy look —it worked well on me.

"Now or never."

I opened his message and sent a quick response.

Down for fun now if you are.

His response was almost immediate.

Your place?

There was a map icon, so I clicked that to send him my location. Then, I settled back on the bed, biting my lip and patting my hair into place.

This was crazy. In today's world, I could find a guy in ten minutes flat. Why the hell had it taken me eight months?

I choked back the adrenaline rush by breathing deeply and imagining how good it would be to get off.

Crap. That was the other part. What if he expected me to suck his dick? What if I sucked at sucking dick?

And then there was the part of me that had never admitted to what I really wanted out of sex with a guy.

The doorbell rang and I nearly jumped out of my skin. My hands shook now as I raced for the door, then reminded myself I was home alone.

Jesus. Calm down, Adam. He's not going anywhere.

I didn't know if that made it better or worse.

"Hey," I grunted and nodded as I opened the door. I didn't know what was supposed to happen now, so I moved and talked slowly, letting my drawl buy me time.

He was pretty good-looking. Dark hair and eyes, and bright white teeth that flashed in a smile. Smooth-shaven, and warm brown skin that looked soft despite the baking heat of August.

The kind of guy who could make you relax with a wink, and who could have his pick of guys at a bar—even I could tell that.

What the hell was he doing on Grindr? Wasn't it just for desperate losers like me?

"Hey," he answered and stepped inside. "You're hot. That's a nice surprise."

I smiled, shoving my hands in my pockets so he wouldn't see them shaking. "You too."

"You here alone?" He glanced around, clearly keeping his voice down.

"Yeah. Yeah, my roomie's out for a while." I managed a jaunty grin.

If there was one thing I was good at, it was faking it. I sure as hell never let them see me sweat.

"Great." He winked, and just as I'd predicted, my knees melted.

I wanted this. He seemed nice, and friendly, and… well, just nice. So why was I so nervous I could hardly breathe?

"My room's there." I pointed. "Want, um, coffee or something?"

"No, thanks. Just you." The guy's boldness took me aback, and I realized I didn't even know his name.

"I'm Adam."

"Ricky." A silver chain swung out of his shirt when he pulled his t-shirt away from his neck, catching my eye and mesmerizing me for a moment.

Then, he pulled the t-shirt off.

"O-Oh." I laughed, hoping it didn't sound as shaky as I felt. "Shouldn't we talk about what we want? Before we get into it?"

I sounded like a virgin now. Fuck.

"What do you want?" It wasn't even a smartass response—Ricky just took that on board.

"Are you a… top? Or bottom? Or do we just suck each other off?"

Ricky grinned. "I like it all." There was a certain swagger about him that reminded me of myself. It was kind of embarrassing, but in response, I just dialed it up.

"Yeah, bro. All right. What do you wanna start with?"

Ricky gave me an odd kind of look for a moment. "Don't tell me this is your first time."

"What? Dude," I scowled. It wasn't even a lie. I'd had sex with plenty of girls. It was just fine. I didn't mind it. I might not have had gay sex, but I sure as hell wasn't a virgin. "Harsh."

"Just sayin'," Ricky answered, raising his hands but still smiling.

When he headed into my room, I had no choice but to follow. He was sitting on my bed, so I sat next to him. He reached out to touch the back of my neck and I couldn't help it—my shoulders rose defensively, my breath catching.

"You're so new to this," Ricky murmured. "So am I. You don't have to be ashamed of it."

"What?"

"What?" Ricky laughed. "I've been with girls before. I just downloaded Grindr because I thought... well, I live and work around here, I see a lot of gay guys..."

"They seem to have it easy, don't they?" I brightened up. This was not going anything like I'd expected. "I know. That's what I thought. So, wait—you're saying you haven't been with a guy either?"

Ricky looked defensive for a moment, but then he sighed and lifted his shoulders in a shrug, a smile playing around his lips. "Guilty. So, what do a couple clueless guys do?"

"I dunno." I snorted and folded my arms. "Kiss?"

But when Ricky leaned in, I found myself tensing up again, turning my face away. I didn't know how I wanted to start this, but apparently it wasn't with a kiss.

"You know what?" Ricky said, clearing his throat and slapping my knee awkwardly. He stood up. "Maybe this isn't the best time for either of us."

"Yeah." I cleared my throat, rubbing my face. I didn't want to push myself into doing something dumb just to prove anything. I had nothing to prove, right? I could take it at my own pace. "Yeah, that's probably right."

"I'll head out, then." Ricky grabbed his shirt and walked for the door.

I found myself staring after him, wanting to call him back. Not because I wanted to fuck, but because I wanted... something else. I wasn't sure what. Hell, if he'd asked me to cuddle and watch Netflix, I would have.

"W-Wait." I couldn't stop myself.

Ricky paused and looked over his shoulder. "Hm?"

"I... If you wanna go find someone else to hook up with, you know, don't let me stop you." I dug my nails into my palms, hating that I sounded so damn... needy?

Ricky wandered back and leaned in my doorway. "Or?"

"I dunno. We could watch Netflix or something..." I trailed off. "And not chill?"

It took a few moments, but then Ricky smiled. "Yeah. You know what? What the hell." He came back into my room and closed the door, his thumbs in his pockets. He was way more casual now, smiling instead of pulling cool guy faces. I liked this version of him better already.

My heart was fluttering with pleasure, and it was kind of a new feeling. Even though I didn't want to sleep with him—I was sure of that now—I wanted to lean against him and crack jokes about a dumb movie and get to know him a bit. There was something familiar about him, too.

"Whatcha wanna watch?" I grabbed my laptop and scooted over

on the bed, rearranging pillows to make space for him. We had a couple hours until Darren was allowed back, if Ricky didn't want to leave early and find someone else who was better at hooking up than me.

"I dunno, I like dumb horror movies."

"Yes!" I high-fived him and patted the bed beside me, and when he sat, I didn't flinch away this time. I elbowed him as I pointed out my Netflix selection. "Here's what they've got."

"I've seen most of those," Ricky told me, and then pointed to the screen. "I've never seen Snakes on a Plane, though."

"Fuck, yeah." I snorted with laughter. "I've seen everyone joke about it, but not actually seen the movie yet. Let's do it."

It was way easier than I'd thought to settle back into the pillows with him, our sides comfortably resting against one another. He cracked just as many jokes as I did, so neither of us got pissed off that we were talking too much throughout the movie.

Maybe we could be friends. Hookup-to-friends? Who even did that?

Me, apparently.

A couple hours and a couple beers later, we were jostling each other around as the movie ended, pretending our hands were snakes and trying to stuff them in each other's clothes—and weirdly enough, it felt platonic, but it felt *nice*.

I'd never messed around with a guy quite like this before. I'd always worried that he might think I was gay, or worse, someone else around us might think that. But just like that, I was with someone who knew my great big stupid secret, and everything was okay.

"Man, I feel kinda dumb," I finally said as I shut the laptop, swatting his hand away one more time.

"For what?"

"For… I dunno, hyping this all up."

"Trying to hook up with a guy?" When I nodded, Ricky smiled to himself. "Yeah. Yeah, I've been scared about it for a while," he told me. His voice went quieter and wavered. "I… I didn't know who I was. Still don't, probably. I got hung up on trying to label it instead of just… rolling with it."

"I guess that's kinda where I'm at," I admitted slowly.

God, what the hell was I doing? It was worse than confessing to a priest or something, because he could see my damn face. Sure, Brooklyn was big, but if he lived nearby…

Relax. Not everyone is out to get you now. And he's got just as much to lose.

It wasn't a healthy way to think and I knew it, but it calmed me down for now. Still, the moment was gone.

"My roommate will be back soon, so…" I stood up and headed for the door.

Ricky's lips parted for a moment, but then he shrugged. "Yeah, sure. Wanna swap numbers?"

Swap numbers? That would mean hanging out again, and talking to this guy who knew I was too much of a coward to even try fucking one guy. "Yeah," I said, injecting some enthusiasm into my tone. We swapped numbers, and thank God, he didn't try for a hug or a kiss or anything before he left.

"See ya," I raised my hand, holding open the apartment door for him. After he left, I bumped my head against the door and stayed there for God knows how long. A neighbor's door banged so loudly it sounded like it was next to me, and I jumped. Fucking sound-proofing here sucked, too.

I'd better text Darren and then think up a good story about a girl or two that would keep him from asking too many questions. I hated lying, but I'd hate telling this particular truth even more. I wasn't ready to talk to myself about whose pants I wanted into, let alone him. I didn't owe anyone anything, much less him, the truth about who I dated—or brought home to fuck and ended up watching a fucking movie with, like a lame-ass coward.

Like a nancy boy, the voice in the back of my head that sounded strangely like my dad whispered.

That made my mind up: a little white lie never hurt anybody.

4

DARREN

Okay, maybe I was stalking Xavier a *little* bit.

It wasn't like I was still into him. I don't think I'd even been into him for the last few months we'd been together, let alone now. But hearing that he'd gotten together with some other guy—even younger than me, and no doubt less screwed-up—had put a bee in my bonnet.

We still followed each other on Facebook, Instagram, you name it. We hadn't actually been in touch, but I'd seen his newly redoubled efforts to post gross couple photos, like he wanted me to see them. He'd always been the type who needed to show off the man on his arm. That had been good for my ego at first, but now?

Shoulda known I'd end up the next ex-boyfriend to whom he had to prove something.

Wait, was that a photo of them in his living room? It looked different now—bright and cheery, but also so hipster. There were even fairy lights strung up in the background, and this was not fairy-light season. It was fucking August, not Christmas.

New upholstery on the couch, new cushions, and even new curtains. He'd found himself an interior decorator or something.

And here I was, splitting the world's narrowest living room with a roommate who seemed to barely tolerate me, and had only let me come home at eleven last night—and who'd still managed to score, when I'd failed at even having a date of my own.

Wait, *our* stuff was gone. No rug we'd hand-picked at the market on our trip to Mexico together. No vase from the yard sale near his parents' house upstate. Not even the stuff I'd bought him, like the hand-woven wooden star that had hung above the mantelpiece.

He was erasing me from his life, and he wanted me to see. I wasn't going to sit around feeling sorry for myself, then. I was going to show him that I'd moved on—and show all my friends at the same time.

"You up?" I called out, rapping once on the wall between our rooms as I emerged from my makeshift bedroom. The wall between my room and the hallway, and the hallway and living room, were both decidedly flimsier than the other walls. That, plus the stupidly narrow living room right beside my room, made it obvious the landlord wanted twice the rooms for twice the rent.

"Hnnngh." Adam's response could have meant anything from *I'm jerking off* to *I've been awake for hours*, but at least I knew he wasn't asleep.

"I'm running the vacuum in a bit." The guys at Bubbles were right: I needed to move on, and I was gonna start by making the most of this new place. "And I'm redecorating."

What I got in answer was another grunt, and then Adam surprised me by poking his head out of his room. "Need any help?"

No arguments or complaints about me changing things so soon

after I moved in—just matter-of-fact. That took me aback. "Uh. No, not right now. I gotta figure out what we're gonna do first."

"Make the living room look bigger?" Adam suggested. "Turn it into a ball pit?" He ambled for the kitchen. "I'll do the dishes, then."

From the impression I'd gotten from Kev, Adam was lazy, but he hadn't seemed like that to me at all. He was willing to do his share of the work.

"One of those things is not like the other," I said with a laugh. "How the hell would we have a party in a ball pit?"

"The real question is: why wouldn't you?" Adam shook his head. "Not enough imagination."

"I'll show you imagination," I threatened with a laugh as I grabbed the vacuum cleaner to drown out his response.

One whirlwind of cleaning later—Adam handling the kitchen, and me the other common spaces—we crashed on the couch with iced tea, and Adam finally asked the question I'd been hoping he wouldn't.

"Spring cleaning itch? It's August, you know."

"No," I hedged. He raised an eyebrow and looked at me, and I sighed. "Fine. I just want to make the space I live in… look nice. I spent a while living in a kinda crappy place, and now he's cleaned it up, and it looks really fucking nice…" *But I guess I wasn't impor-tant enough to clean up for. Maybe it's true: once you live together, you stop putting in the effort. Like I said, I just need to stop living with boyfriends.*

Adam was smiling knowingly. "Ahhh. So you're trying to one-up him."

"Am not." I worked my jaw around as he gave me that infuriating grin, and then I finally sighed. "Okay, fine. Maybe a little. But I was out talking with friends last night and they said he's seeing some new guy."

"Asshole." Adam scoffed. "Bet he's not as good as you."

A glow warmed my chest, and I tightened my grip around the cool glass. I wanted to squeeze him in a hug just for that little moment of solidarity. He didn't have to take my side—we weren't even that good friends yet—but he automatically had. "Yeah," I agreed. "Definitely can't deep-throat like me."

Adam turned a funny shade of red and I nearly choked on my iced tea. "Did not need to know that," he sputtered, grabbing a pillow and shoving it at me like he wanted to start a pillow fight.

I laughed and drained the rest of my glass, then put it on the floor, tucked under the table where it couldn't get knocked over. "Careful what you start there, mister."

"I don't start anything I can't finish." He raised a brow in a challenge.

Fuck, that shouldn't have looked so hot. He looked like he was daring me to do it—and my mind immediately raced to what else he might dare me to do.

I knew it was stupid to fantasize about your straight roommate going gay, but Adam was hot, and he had the kind of personality I liked: a lot more complex than he let on. And his heart was good. He might try to hide his generosity, but I knew about it. Kev had told me he took care of this old lady's garden beds for free, and didn't want anyone to know. I'd made a mental note not to tell Kev any secrets, but I was glad I knew that about Adam.

"Fine!" I smacked him first, lightly, on the chest—and I got thwapped on the side of the head for my trouble. "Oh, it's on!"

"Come at me, bro!"

I swung with all my might and the thin little cushion made a sadly quiet thwapping sound as it hit his shoulder.

A few fast-and-furious minutes later, we were laughing uncontrollably. He slid off the couch to the floor but kept taunting me, so I kept it up and straddled him, knocking his pillow out of reach.

"Oh, you bastard!" Adam squirmed under me, trying to get the pillow back, and I grabbed his arm and pinned it down. Then the other arm.

I came to, realizing I was riding my roommate—sweaty, hot, and grinning like a loon. And I was happier than I'd been in days, maybe months.

Also, he had a semi, and so did I.

Fuck.

I tried to blame the body contact—it had been so long since I'd gotten laid, after all. Even longer since I'd smiled while I did it, instead of growling Xavier's name and cursing him out while we fucked like animals.

Whoa! Not what I needed to think about, even remotely, while our dicks pressed into each other's thighs.

I rolled off him and tried for a casual grin, but from the look we exchanged, we both knew damn well what the other one had felt. "You're good," I breathed out.

Almost instantly, Adam snickered and said, "First time a guy's said that to me."

"Not the last, I bet." Then it hit me: I was flirting with my straight roommate, my fingers still holding the memory of being curled tightly around his wrists. I could way too keenly remember my knees digging into the carpet, my dick so close to brushing his.

I was getting hard now. Fuck. I had to stop it before he noticed. Even straight allies had their limits.

Adam just grinned, casually sliding a hand down to pluck at his sweatpants like nothing had happened. "Man, that was an adrenaline rush."

"Yeah," I breathed out, seizing on that excuse. He was giving me an out, and goddamn, I was taking it like I'd never taken a guy, hard and fast—

Fuck.

It was one of those moments where you just know you're gonna be jerking one out to it later. You store it on that *guilty spank memory* shelf in your brain, in a box that you don't open until your next *long* shower, and try to act like nothing happened, but goddamn, your whole body can't wait.

"Yeah," I hastened to cut off all thoughts by distracting myself with speech. My tongue was clumsy and thick in my mouth, and my lips tingled as much as my fingertips with the urge to roam across his body.

Okay, Operation Look Like My Life Is Together was suddenly way more urgent. It wasn't like Adam would ever say yes if I tried to sleep with him, but that would make our relationship permanently awkward.

I'd moved here to get away from permanently awkward.

Adam, goddamn him, just got up and seemed to shrug it off. He acted like no boner-touching had happened as he bent over to pick up the cushions.

Oh, yeah. Damn my traitorous eyes, but they went there. Just for a second. He had a nice ass, and gray sweatpants were the perfect way to show it off. Irresistible, just one glance.

I was proud of my self-control when I managed to *stop* looking. I headed to the window instead, tugging and readjusting the blinds until all the slats were straight. Half of them were bent or wonky, so it gave me a minute to get my dick under control.

"So, you still into this ex?" Adam said it so casually that it shattered any hope I might have had that he actually cared about the answer.

Not that I hoped he did. I knew better than that, and besides—as I'd already established, trying to get with Adam would be an epically stupid idea on every front.

"No. God, no," I said with a laugh.

"What's the story then?" Adam crashed on the couch and stretched his feet out on the coffee table.

I looked around the room, but there wasn't anywhere to hide. I took the armchair instead of sitting next to him, trying desperately to get some space. If I felt his body heat right now, even with the less-than-fantastic subject of Xavier up in the air, I was just gonna get a boner. This time, I don't think I could have stopped it.

Which was really the problem I'd had after Xavier and I had broken up—not being able to keep it in my pants. Desperation, in other words. I had to knock that shit off, one way or another. Fewer inconvenient boners meant fewer stupid decisions.

"Well," I hummed, drawing my legs up beside me and folding my arms, "I dated him for like, a year. We moved in together. I was never really happy around him."

"Just didn't click?"

I nodded. It was humbling to admit it now, but I needed to. "I was trying to force it, and it wasn't working. For a long time, I thought I was just screwing up a good thing… but it wasn't a good thing for me, or it wouldn't have taken so much effort, you know?"

Adam was already nodding. "Yeah. I know."

I didn't stop to ask how. I didn't want him biting my head off in the middle of our bonding moment, after all. "So, yeah. We broke up and kept living together for a few months, and I… well, we kept sleeping together."

Adam hissed through clenched teeth. "Duuude."

I was blushing. My cheeks heated up, and my shoulders rose as I tried not to get defensive. "I know, I know. Stupid idea."

"Why'd you do it?" Adam was throwing everything at me now. Tact was not his strong suit, but hot damn, he had some balls to be asking.

Still, weirdly enough, I didn't mind talking. Maybe because I'd tell him literally anything to distract us from *that awkward boner moment*. If he was exploiting it to satiate his curiosity, I didn't care. Anything besides letting my brain dwell on the other implications of the word *satiate*.

"Because, uh… He's hot, and I didn't respect myself?" I half-smiled and stared at his feet on the coffee table. If I looked at him, I might do something like get teary, and he wasn't the hug-it-out type.

Adam surprised me by grabbing me by the arm and hauling me closer. The armchair and couch were that close together, our living room was so tiny. "Hey."

I went when he pulled me, and I found myself wrapped in his arms. Just like that, the tension and stress and fear I'd been holding in my body—everything from *will he respect me if I cry?* to *how much can I say without sounding like a loser?* just vanished.

Adam hugged me tightly, and everything else disappeared besides his strong arms around me. Fuck, the hole in my chest just ached that much more as I let myself hug him.

Adam was such a decent guy. Why couldn't I find someone like him? Someone kind, rugged, stubborn, and smart enough not to take life too seriously? Most importantly: someone who was into me and not just using me because I was there?

"Thanks," I finally mumbled and pulled away, surprised at how much calmer I already felt.

Adam offered me one of those mysterious little smiles I couldn't quite interpret. "Welcome." I could tell by the way he stood up that he was pretending none of that had happened, letting me have my pride. "Want a beer?"

"God yes." I meant that with every fiber of my being. If it meant we were good, and we never had to bring up any of that again, I wanted a beer *so hard*.

5

ADAM

Shoot me now.

Not only was my boss in a bad mood, but half my coworkers were shirtless, sweaty, and turning on thoughts in my brain I thought I'd left behind in many socks under my bed years ago.

"Think I can sneak off for a smoke break?" That was Paolo, out of breath as ever. How the hell he managed to do this work with lungs like a factory, I didn't know.

I heaved another bag of soil out of the truck flatbed and shook my head. "If you risk it, it's on your head."

Our boss, Henson—we called the ex-Marine by his surname—was sitting in the truck cab, talking loudly about costs on a project on his phone. He tended to spend his days driving between job sites, delivering supplies and making sure nobody was fucking around. It was like my parents had threatened—I was at boot camp. Only I didn't have to pretend to be straight and I wasn't locked into it for life.

With a job like this, hard work was its own reward—not a punishment for not being a good enough son.

Still, being yelled at for nothing I'd done wrong had me frustrated, itching under my skin for some kind of relief. Not getting laid in like six weeks, whatever I'd told my roommates, sure as hell didn't help. But ever since I'd gotten these hare-brained ideas about wanting to try it with a guy, I hadn't been able to either act on them or shake it off.

Leaving me in limbo, a state I was way too familiar with. Like life was edging me. So not fair.

"Fuck it, I'll wait 'til he's gone." Paolo was jittery, but I clapped his shoulder.

"You'll get through. Come on, help me move these around back."

By the time we had the truck unloaded, Henson was raring to go. "You boys got the bed clean? Good, 'bout time." He had a sprawling twang to his voice, a kind of unplaceable accent he claimed was from moving around to a million Army bases as a kid. "I'm taking off for the east town site. Don't call me, I'll call you."

"Yessir." I knew the rules—respect him and he'd respect you, mostly. Might call you a lazy asshole a few times just to make sure you didn't sit down on the job, but he'd treat you fairly. I could deal with that.

Henson stomped back to the truck cab and took off, peeling out onto the street without a backward glance.

"Phew." Paolo moaned in relief. The homeowners were rarely around, and neither were their neighbors. Nobody to report us if we took a couple minutes off here and there—especially in the August heat. "Did you hear him saying he's gonna have to cut back some hours?"

"Yeah." I sighed. That meant less money for someone on our crew, but the client was refusing to expand the budget even though the work had expanded.

Today, we were all going home at noon. Henson had said there was no point wasting money paying us to try to work when Brooklyn was hotter than the devil's asshole. That would help with his money worries, at least.

The work was hot and miserable, but I didn't dare complain. It was steady work except when stuff like this happened, Henson paid us pretty well, and I didn't have to scrounge together hours between three or four different part-time jobs anymore. I even had days off now and then. And I was getting experience and contacts, learning how it worked.

I daydreamed about starting my own business. That was where the money was. My dad had done the same—as a lawyer rather than a low-paid landscaper, but still. CEO was where it was at. Maybe I had years to grind to get there, but with a vision, I could work towards it.

"Come on," I told Paolo. "Get these last couple bags around back and then you can smoke. And I could use the little boy's room."

The homeowner had left us the keys to the in-law suite. It was a huge place for Brooklyn, big enough to have its own cottage in the garden. They wanted an electronic keypad and a separate entrance installed, which meant it was probably an Airbnb. They also didn't want *our* type clattering through their precious clean house with our muddy boots.

I wasn't about to go tattling on him for smoking around back of the cottage. It was cool and sheltered and out of the sun, we could keep our water bottles chilled in the mini-fridge, and we could take a piss in the middle of the day.

Bliss, compared to some job sites.

"Fucking mood he's in," Paolo mumbled under his breath, the sound of his voice catching my eye. As he heaved a bag over his shoulder, it took a second for me to look away—some dirt had spilled out of the corner of the plastic, sticking to his sweaty back.

There was something about a man's body—sweat-covered and smooth—that had always grabbed my eye. From PE classes until now, I'd never been able to shake the fascination.

I'd thought my failed date with Ricky would take away the urge to touch, lick, bite, *fuck*. Nope. Darren had gone and made it a thousand times worse. Now that I'd felt a man above me for the first time, his weight on my legs, leaning over me... It was all I could think about.

Darren, cheeks flushed and hair wild and gaze triumphant, his fingers curled around my wrists, pinning me to the ground.

My cock painfully hard, betraying me as it rose. My own stupidity in not wearing underwear under my sweatpants, and my moment of panicked, mortified realization that he'd felt it.

And then the realization that I felt the hard line of *his* boner trapped against my thigh, too.

He'd liked it every bit as much as me, but that was just a physical reaction, I was sure. He hadn't given me a second look after he'd rolled off me and joked around. He'd answered my questions about Xavier a little too well, showing me part of himself that he never would have if he'd known how I felt.

I was safe to talk to, a straight guy who couldn't screw with his dating life, and I wasn't going to betray that trust. Especially now that I knew living with me was such a desperately-needed safe space from living with someone who kept coming onto him when he felt down.

I might be a dumbass about emotions, but doing the same would be the kind of thing that made Kev slap me, and unlike my parents had done, for a damn good reason. Especially when I knew nothing about my own attractions or how deep they ran, I wasn't gonna toy with him like that.

"Hey," Paolo grunted, dropping the bag onto the pile. "I'll grab a smoke first, you fill up the new bed."

I'd love to fill a bed with Darren, though. Just once. Just to see what it was like.

I needed to stop thinking like this, or I was gonna get turned on again, and waiting until I got home and in the shower would be murder. "Sure."

I tried to distract myself by hauling a bag of dirt over to the bed and ripping it open, but the manual labor was so easy it came on autopilot now. As I mixed up the fertilizer and soil in the Henson-approved ratio, my mind had all the time in the world to wander, so wander it did.

Straight to the visual of Darren, sweaty and flushed-cheeked, telling me that I'd been good—and that it wouldn't be the last time a guy told me that.

And my dick liked it. Way more than I wanted to admit.

Why couldn't I have liked him as a buddy but not a sexual fantasy? Or even the other way around, a hot roommate I didn't care about? But no, I had to like him *and* want to get in his pants.

And worst of all, I had to have that weird hangup about just getting it on with some other guy instead. One thing was for sure: there was something about Darren.

Because when he'd looked down at me, for that half a second before he rolled off me, I'd been madly hoping that he leaned down to kiss me. Unlike my reluctance to let Ricky touch me, I'd wanted Darren's hands up my shirt, down my pants...

I was hopeless.

Seeing Paolo wander toward me again, looking exactly like he'd just gotten fucked—that was how he always looked after he'd been desperate for a cigarette—did nothing to cool me off.

"Shit, you worked fast."

Had I? I blinked and looked down before realizing I'd mixed up the entire bed while he'd been gone, way too caught up in trying not to let my thoughts run out of control. It was too damn hot to be sweating over anyone, let alone my stupid crush.

"Take ten," Paolo told me and waved me toward the cottage.

I already knew exactly how long my break would take, and how hard it was in my pants. "Yep." I headed for the door as fast as I could without arousing suspicion. The only one aroused here oughta be me.

The bathroom door was barely closed before I had my dick out of my pants. My heart raced as I braced my hand against the wall next to the toilet, my fly undone and one hand closing around my hard shaft.

Goddamn, it felt good to be out in the open air instead of hiding away, the life being squeezed out of me.

I refused to think of the parallels. It was just a hard-on, not a permanent life decision based on flimsy evidence, a desperation to get laid, and a stupid fantasy.

"Fuck," I breathed out, squeezing my eyes shut as I called the image back to mind. It came way too readily—Darren's beautiful eyes squeezed shut, his lips pursed, making a noise of exertion as he struggled to keep me down on the ground. Was that how guys decided who was on top? A wrestling match? I'd be into that.

He wore enough short-shorts, and I'd seen him shirtless. I could picture almost every inch of his body as I visualized him riding me. What was his dick like? Elegant or cute? Dusky red or pale pink? What did it look like bobbing in the air as he thrust his body up and down, his eyes glazed, his lips parted in pleasure?

What would my name sound like spilling from his lips as he held me down on the living room carpet and we cried out so loud the neighbors heard?

Fuck. *Fuck*, I came hard, but at least my aim was right. No mess to clean up as I flushed, tucked myself away, and tried not to think about how goddamn deep this hare-brained idea had suddenly gone. *Eight inches deep,* my immature sense of humor supplied, and I snorted a laugh.

That was it. One way or another, I needed to find a guy I clicked with and get this out of my system. How the hell I was gonna do that without Darren finding out was another matter, but it seemed like the only crazy solution to all of this.

And that way, I could be sure I wasn't just using Darren because he conveniently lived with me. I wanted to throttle Xavier for doing that to him and making him doubt himself, so how the hell could I justify doing it myself?

No, Darren deserved a good guy, someone sweet and caring and way less screwed up than me. Someone who was sure of what he wanted in life.

With that stupid edge finally taken off, I had a job to get back to.

6

***

DARREN

Monday was never my favorite day of the week, but this week was especially not.

As always, the job was running over-time and over-budget, and the foreman wasn't happy about it. That was the only small mercy —I didn't have to break it to a homeowner directly that they'd been sold a place with tin foil and strings for wires, as so often happened.

"You're shitting me," was George's only response when I let him know the news: there was rust at the bottom of the main panel. That meant probable water leaks, and it explained why two electricians had already rewired the meter and failed to fix the problem. Idiots hadn't even done the most basic of safety checks.

Nothing failed to surprise me anymore, though. It seemed like honest tradesmen were getting harder to come by these days.

"Sorry, man. You can see for yourself." I jerked a thumb toward the cabinet.

"I can't believe nobody even looked…" George trailed off into a grumble before he rubbed his face. "Whatever. We've got a guy coming in to do the sink tomorrow. We can knock out that wall for him to take a look."

I nodded. "I wouldn't rewire until whatever that leak is, you've fixed it."

"Gotcha." George sighed and offered his hand for a shake. "Appreciate you actually using your brain and helping us figure that one out. I was about losing my mind."

I grinned. "Yeah, a lot of guys don't seem to," I agreed. "No problem. Call me up when you want it rewired and I'll check it out again, huh?"

I preferred working as an independent subcontractor, flitting between companies as they called me up. Once I'd finished training and an apprenticeship, it hadn't taken me long to establish a name as a no-bullshit guy who would do the job right the first time.

In my mind, there was more money that way than trying to fleece people out of money in short-term swindles like neglecting to check for basic maintenance problems. That built long-term relationships, and those were worth more long-term than getting paid for the same job twice before they found out what you were up to. Plus, I could sleep with myself at night.

"I'll call," George promised, and I nodded as I headed out to my van.

Driving this thing in Brooklyn was always a headache, but there weren't many jobs that I could attend without a van. I didn't have the luxury of taking all my supplies on the subway.

My phone rang, and my heart leapt. I had a gap just now, before lunch. I tried to stick to Brooklyn so I could minimize driving time—if it was a job site nearby, I could squeeze in one more job and get some quick cash.

"Hey, Darren here."

"Darren Spencer?" The voice wasn't one of my usual buddies, and I didn't have the number saved. Sometimes homeowners passed my info on to each other, though.

"Speaking."

"This is Mario from Two Palms. You entered a prize draw we recently held…" I got all lightheaded as I dropped into my car seat and closed the door. I tuned out the rest of the sentence, but I got the gist of it: he was trying to tell me I'd won the tickets.

He was kidding. No way. This had to be one of those scams where they tried to sell you a timeshare. "Me and how many others?"

"One guest, man. Two tickets. One has to be you—we can't allow transfers, I'm afraid—but you can choose any guy you want to go with you, if you don't have a boyfriend. You never know, you could both get lucky here…" Mario trailed off suggestively.

"Am I seriously—are you serious? Are you kidding?" My voice rose, and a smile spread across my face. No way. He sounded serious as hell. "What's the catch?"

"Well, as the terms and conditions of entry said, we'd like to use your name and image in promotional materials. If your plus-one is comfortable, both of you—but just you would be fine, if he's not."

"Oh, my God." It was sinking in. "When?"

"The first week of September. Do you wanna hear more about what's included?"

"Sure." My voice was faint as I leaned back in my car seat and tried to catch my breath. I'd never won anything in my life, and after my awful bad luck at dating, I sure as hell hadn't expected this to be my time. My only good luck was the kind I worked my ass off to make happen—steady work.

Billy was gonna kill me. I tried not to giggle at the thought.

Business-class airfare for two—well, I'd never flown anything fancier than economy, so hell, that was a win.

A room, of course, for the week.

Meals and drinks and excursions all included.

The only price? Having my story all over social media. If I were the type to want sponsorships and whatnot, that would be perfect, but I wasn't.

"We're expecting a lot of influencers to turn out."

"Influencers?"

"You know, the guys on Instagram with a thousand likes on all their pics. Tastemakers, they're sometimes called."

"Sorry, I'm not one of them." I laughed quietly. "But I can pose for photos."

"Perfect. We can work with that," he said.

I zinged the seat back even further, trying to catch my breath and not just bounce out of my skin.

"Flights from JFK all right? Your location was down as Brooklyn, I see…"

I'd deal with any damn airport if it meant free flights. "JFK's fine." Was this my life? Was I making all of this up? I was gonna wake up and find out it was Monday morning, wasn't I?

"Do you need to get the time off, or can I make arrangements—"

"I can be off whenever I want," I interrupted him with a laugh. "Contractor perks."

"Mmhmm." He was clearly taking notes. "And do you know your plus-one?" Mario sounded hopeful.

Shit. My brain ground to a halt. I was gonna need someone to come with me. While Billy was an obvious choice, he also wouldn't wanna go without his best friend, Jackie. I'd never seen him talk about a vacation without her.

I didn't have a boyfriend, obviously.

Mario correctly inferred the meaning of the silence. "If you need time to ask a friend, how about I leave you my number?"

"Y-Yeah, that'd be good. Gotta make sure he's off," I fibbed lightly. I didn't wanna be that single loser who'd entered a draw for tickets for two, after all.

I barely managed to take down his number without my hands shaking, and then I promised to call him back. I hung up and stared at the roof of the van, abruptly realizing how damn hot it was in here. No wonder I was about to pass out.

The blast of warm air in the face when I started up the van didn't help. I grimaced and waited it out until the A/C kicked in before I opened up the vents again.

Shit. There was one more problem: I was gonna see Xavier and his new boy-toy. And I was gonna be the single loser who had to bring a platonic friend. The last thing I wanted was to be the asshole who looked like he was still hung up on his ex.

It wasn't that I hated Xavier or wanted him to be unhappy—like most of my exes, it was one of those complicated situations where I wanted the best for him, but if he *were* jealous of my new life and *did* realize that I was way too good for him, that wouldn't be the *worst* thing ever.

The other, much bigger problem, was what I'd done on Instagram after my marathon tidying session of the living room. After a trip to the thrift store, a little tweaking of the lighting situation, and waiting to make sure Adam was busy getting ready for work, I'd…

Well, I'd posted one little photo on Instagram. Our glasses on the table in the foreground, the cozy living room in the background. Two glasses, to be precise. And a caption that just read *#blessed*. If anyone—by which I meant Xavier—chose to interpret that as me having some action of my own, that was up to them. It was a tiny lie. I could write it off as a single date, or even me being happy with my roommate situation—and I was.

Except now Xavier was gonna ask about it, and admitting I'd failed to find another guy when he'd gotten some perfect little interior decorator was just embarrassing as fuck.

I wasn't gonna find a boyfriend in time for the trip. It was two weeks away. That was hardly enough time to get a haircut, much less a meaningful relationship. The only other solution was… well, to fool Xavier into thinking I'd moved on to bigger and better things. Which meant finding someone to fake it with me.

I slowly sat up as the van cooled off, and then mentally set a course for the apartment. I'd have enough time to drop by and eat lunch on my way to the next job site.

Who did I know that was single, hot, willing to fake it, and not a mutual friend of Xavier's and mine who might spill the beans?

"Oh." My jaw fell open as my solution—my salvation, really —hit me.

Surely to God he wouldn't wanna do it. There were a hundred reasons it wouldn't work out, from his job to the fact that a straight guy would never wanna be surrounded by a couple hundred gay guys for a week.

But there was no harm in asking, right?

"No way."

Adam's tone was awed, though. It was a *what the fuck* kind of no way, not a *go fuck yourself for asking* no way.

"Yeah way," I laughed. I'd gotten home to find Adam had made lunch, which was sweet of him, but I was suddenly too nervous to eat the ham and cheese sandwich in front of me.

Adam was giving me a funny look, and I swallowed hard. Suddenly, I was worried I'd offended him. "I just figured, you know… if anyone else wanted to go with me to Hawaii, you might."

"Why not some buddy from Friction? You know, like, a million guys."

Adam had taken about two seconds to sniff through my alibi of thoughtfulness and figure out there was another reason at work.

I felt myself turning red as I set the sandwich carefully down on the plate again. "So, a bunch of people I know are going. Nobody I know well. But they've already got flights and rooms, of course…"

Adam folded his arms and waited for me to say it.

Why were my palms sweating so much? Fuck, it was just one little sentence. *I want to show him I've moved on.* "And, uh, my ex is going. Xavier."

"You wanna make Xavier jealous." He smiled smugly, and as much as I wanted to disagree, he wasn't *entirely* wrong. I couldn't bring myself to do it.

I covered my face with my hands and braced my elbows on the table. "Oh, God. A bit. Don't judge me."

"Okay."

"What?" I yelped, looking up at him. "I mean—what? Wh-What?"

It had been that easy?

"I get a free trip, I get to be arm candy—and if gay guys want me, that's, like, a compliment. And you get to leave that shitty ex in the past where he belongs." Adam shrugged, like it was obvious. "Why not?"

I opened and closed my mouth a few times, lost for words. Whatever layers I thought Adam had, he suddenly added another whenever I wasn't looking.

"I... I mean..."

"Thanks, is what you say," Adam told me with a grin and a wink. "For saving your bacon and looking good on your arm so Xavier will be overcome with regret. Do you want him to cry?"

"No!"

"You don't even want him to regret treating you like shit a little bit?" Adam held his fingers an inch apart and then slowly narrowed them.

I was laughing despite myself, covering my face again. "Fuck, I should have known you'd be a dick about it." Honestly, it made this a lot easier to navigate, and I was thankful for it.

Adam clicked his tongue. "Luckily, you like dicks." He snort-laughed.

"Okay, you cannot make those jokes," I groaned. "You'll blow our cover."

"Oh, I'll blow it good."

"Fucking shoot me now." My appetite was back, though. I tried not to make eye contact as I took a bite of my sandwich, but when I looked back at him, he was licking the rim of his drinking glass —and not even in a sexy way.

I lost it as I struggled to swallow my mouthful and laugh out loud at the same time, covering my mouth with one hand and flipping him off with the other.

"See? We're like an old married couple already," Adam proclaimed. "Call back that guy and tell him I'm in."

This was going to be a long-ass week. But somehow, I had the feeling it was also gonna be one of the best weeks of my life. I hoped to God I was right to trust Adam to help me out with this.

"I will," I promised. "As soon as I'm done with lunch."

"Oh, yeah. Stuff yourself right now," Adam ordered, and I had to ignore the heat that crawled from my dick straight up to my cheeks at hearing him say those words. Fuck, he was hot, but that was the risk of this: my dick or heart doing something dumb because of what we were pretending to be—an Instagram-worthy couple.

But that was the brilliance of it all: enough guys had open relationships that I could sleep with whoever else out there to make sure I kept my dick in my pants around Adam, and nobody would question the fact that we were together.

Adam was a solid choice. For some strange reason, he seemed to want to help me out, and he got a trip out of the deal. For once, picking the straight guy was the *safe* bet, not the stupid one. But only because all of this was fake.

No way could anything form between us and destroy yet another friendship. My heart couldn't handle it—and neither could my wallet. Moving was expensive, destroyed my work schedule, and felt like ripping my life apart one stud at a time.

I was here, and I was here for good. I just had to make sure this whole crazy stunt stayed under control. No pressure, right?

7

ADAM

Only once Darren left for work did it occur to me that I might not
be a total genius.

I'd won myself a free trip to Hawaii with my roommate, and I was
helping him out of a pinch. What was more, my ego got a boost—
if he thought gay guys would find me hot enough to be his fake
boyfriend, I felt pretty damn good about that. And I got to
socialize more with gay guys and figure out how all this even
worked... all well away from home, or anywhere that anyone
cared who I was.

But the catch was obvious: I had to pretend to be Darren's
boyfriend in public.

It sounded easy, right? Along the way, I'd get to figure out
whether I was really into guys, or if all I wanted was to bust a nut.
And I wouldn't break anyone's heart in the process, or get halfway
through sex before changing my mind and tossing someone out
on his ass with blue balls.

Nothing could go wrong, except for everything that could
possibly go wrong.

"God, I'm a moron." I stacked up our plates and then faceplanted onto the table, tangling my fingers in the hair at the back of my head.

Suddenly, the pressure was on me. If Darren wanted to show Xavier that he was happy and blissful in love, my usual attitude was not gonna fly. I had to figure out how to act *lovey-dovey* in public—and around a bunch of gay guys who could sniff out one clue that I wasn't all that and a bag of chips.

But I didn't want to back out. Not for a second. I had to help Darren out, and besides—it was so wildly different from anything I'd ever done. It was a challenge and an opportunity all rolled into one. I'd never backed down from either.

If there was a word that fit me, where better to learn it than an island full of guys who were into guys? Drinking, water sports, and coming-out stories—it was gay summer camp for grownups.

Okay, I was starting to feel like a genius again. The time off was gonna be easy: Henson would be glad to see a reason to give someone fewer hours and save costs on the rest of this project.

Just in case, I'd better call him.

I dialed and let it ring a few times, chewing my knuckle as I waited to get through.

"Yeah?" Henson's gruff voice barked at me the moment he picked up.

"It's Adam. I've got a request—solution, really."

"I like one of those more than the other."

I wasn't wasting time—or giving him time to grouse at me. "You know you were saying you need to cut back our hours for this project? Well, I need a week off..."

Henson sounded interested. "Go on."

"If it helps you out, I'd really appreciate the time off. It's in a couple weeks."

"Sure."

No questions, no arguments? Goddamn, he must be having a really lousy day. "Thank you, sir. I'll confirm the exact dates with you tomorrow."

"Great. See ya." Henson hung up like that, leaving me staring at my phone. If I didn't know him, I'd be afraid he was pissed off at me now, but he was actually probably happy to react like that.

Okay, that was one obstacle cleared. Darren was going to be at work until late afternoon, so I had a few hours to myself.

I'd actually been considering job-hunting to find a part-time gig and fill some hours if the landscaping job got cut back. It had only been a few months since I'd gone full-time there and cut out all the other work, and I'd really been enjoying not going from job to job all day long.

But I couldn't really pick up a new job now, right before taking off for a week to Hawaii. That didn't look great on the resume. Better wait until I got back, then.

"Oh, shit." While I was at it, I really should tell people what was going on. If any photos got taken—Darren had mentioned something about being put on social media...

I swallowed hard. That could mean my family found out. But the chances that anyone from Knoxville who knew my parents was attending were almost nil. Anyone who wanted to tell them what I was up to would also have to admit that they'd been there for a week of hedonism too. That would make my parents run the other direction before they could even finish their sentence.

But Kev was gonna kill me if he found out from someone else what was going on. We were best friends, despite the way we joked around about not being able to stand one another after living together.

I started with an easy introduction.

Did you hear Darren's news??

YES! I think he texted everyone in his phonebook lol. Lucky bastard!

I bit my lip. How the hell was I gonna say this? Tact was not my strong point. *He needs a +1 and asked me...*

No answer for a good minute—just long enough that I was almost worried.

Then I got a phone call. Before I could even say anything, Kev stage-whispered: "You. Are. Shitting. Me."

"Where are you?" I laughed as I remembered: probably at school. I was proud of him for having the guts to leave behind his highly-paid but risky hustling career to pursue a new life path. He'd caught up on prerequisites with summer school, and that semester was just wrapping up. The main counseling training program would begin in September. Wait, had he just walked out of class? "Dude, don't skip class for me!"

"I—you—my *straight* best friend gets an invite to *the* biggest *gay* party of the year? I skip class for that!" Kev hissed, his voice finally rising to a normal tone. His voice echoed like he was pacing a hallway. He could be so overdramatic sometimes. "Bro!"

I laughed at my own word on his lips. Kev wasn't the kind of guy to say that, but we'd picked up a little of each other's speech. "Bro, I know. But—do you know about him and Xavier?"

"Darren's ex? That bruised dickhole?"

I winced at the painfully specific insult, my hand creeping down to squeeze myself reassuringly. "Yeah, that one."

"He's not—they're not getting back together, are they?" Kev's voice rose to a squeak. "I will take the subway right over there and—"

"No!" I hastily reassured him. "No, man, no way."

Kev breathed out a sigh that rattled through the phone. "Phew. What about him, then?"

"He wants to, you know, show him he's moved on."

Kev hummed. "That's always how you know someone's moved on," he murmured sarcastically.

I found myself weirdly defensive. He hadn't seen Darren talk about Xavier the way I had. Darren knew damn well that he wasn't a good version of himself around Xavier. If he missed the guy, it was probably just loneliness because he didn't have another boyfriend. Which brought me into the picture.

"So I'm gonna pose as his boyfriend. Under no circumstances are you to tell anyone else it's fake, though," I added hastily, before he got any ideas.

Kev huffed with amusement. "Yeah, word will get back fast. Everyone knows everyone. Except you…"

"Exactly." I was the bulletproof choice.

I'd heard lots of names thrown around when Kev was talking about his buddies at the gay club and the diner where they all seemed to meet up, and even the thrift store sometimes. Still, I'd never met most of them. Kev hadn't had them over to visit our crappy little place.

Well, it was looking nicer now, and I was gonna meet them all.

Maybe. Or maybe he'd keep me hidden away until the trip. We hadn't actually discussed that.

It was kind of disconcerting to realize how much I was hoping he introduced me to his other friends and started the charade early. Like I wanted to be important to Darren. No, I reminded myself, that wasn't it. I just wanted to make sure this pretense was good and solid.

That was all.

"That's genius!" Kev approved. "Even if you *break up*," I heard him air-quote the words, "after the week's over, it'll just look like you guys didn't work out. Especially if you keep living together, on good terms."

"He cleaned and then rearranged the whole living room yesterday," I informed him. "And I think he got a slipcover for the sofa. He's going all interior decorator since finding out that Xavier's new guy is one."

Kev chuckled. "Yeah, he's *sooo* over Xavier. Poor guy."

My shoulders were tense and my jaw ached, but I didn't say anything. "Yeah. So, now you know. If he announces it on Instagram or wherever, you can't yell at me that I didn't tell you."

"Look at you, learning to communicate like a real friend!"

"Fuck off," I told him, laughing as I hung up. A few moments, I got a text that just read, *xox*, and I shook my head but smiled as I responded with a single *o*. No need to send Kev kisses and make things weirder.

That was everything, wasn't it? All I had to do was pack and wait for my flight to paradise.

Plus learn how to be a jealousy-inducing hunk on Darren's arm, but that couldn't be hard, right?

My traitorous ears didn't tell me that Darren was opening the front door. Britney Spears was playing too loud to hear it.

So he was greeted with the sight of me shimmying back and forth to Toxic, mumbling the words along as I did so.

I don't even know how long he stood there, silently shaking with laughter. I had no idea he was there until I spun around and caught sight of him, shrieked and jumped into the air, nearly kicking my laptop off the coffee table.

"Fucking fuck! Darren!" I shouted, slapping my laptop closed to keep it safe from me, and to kill the music.

Darren was leaning against the wall with one hip, the stance emphasizing his slender form. For a guy who did pretty physical labor, he was lean and flexible.

Right now that slender body crumpled into a heap on the floor as he dissolved into laughter.

"Fuck off," I swore at him, folding my arms as my cheeks heated up. "I'm trying to—I need to blend in!"

Darren desperately tried to stop laughing, covering his mouth with both hands now. He couldn't quite look at me without bursting into giggles. "I—I can see that. Yes. You're right," were all the words he could manage to choke out between his stifled laughs.

I stomped to the kitchen to get myself some damn water. I muttered under my breath as I poured myself a mug and chugged the first mug, then refilled it. If I was just gonna get made fun of for all the stuff I didn't know and wanted to learn…

"I'm sorry." Darren came to the kitchen doorway now, flicking the lights on to catch my attention. "I just didn't expect you to… try so hard to fit in."

"Of course I'm gonna," I grunted, not looking at him as I headed back out to the couch. "If I stand there like a lump when your people's songs play…"

A quiet giggle slipped out of Darren's mouth, but we both pretended it hadn't. "My—yes. I'll introduce you to my people's songs. But only if you tell me why everyone in country music is sad."

I couldn't very well tell him off for stereotyping me when… well, all of that had just happened. Instead, my lips curled into a smile. I could finally see the humor in the moment. It had to have looked pretty funny to him.

"Hey, to be fair, I never claimed to be a good dancer."

Darren held up his hands in a *fair enough* gesture. "No. And not all of us are, so hey. Way to smash stereotypes," he congratulated me. "Did you make more iced tea before you, uh… did whatever that was?"

I snorted. "Yeah, there's a pitcher in the fridge. Knock yourself out."

"Fuck, yeah."

I couldn't help but notice he was all sweaty and dusty, and when he got up, there were a few fibers of insulation on the floor. "Dude, no fiberglass in the nice new living room," I scolded him.

Darren laughed. "You're telling *me*? That's rich."

Okay, maybe I hadn't kept this place in great shape before he'd fixed it up, but now I wanted it to look nice. It had to fit the charade, after all. "Am I doing it right?"

"Very well done. You're now a house-proud gay," Darren called out. "And I'm grabbing a shower."

While he did that, I opened my laptop, quickly muting it before it could begin broadcasting the results of my musical research again. I'd found a playlist of gay songs, and I was glad to hear I already knew most of them. Camp, cheesy, classic kinda stuff. It wasn't gonna be too hard to fit in at parties there. I'd heard Kev rave about enough movie stars that pop culture was no problem.

There was still just one problem: my own history. If someone asked, I was gonna freeze up like a rabbit in headlights, and that wouldn't help keep up our appearance.

"Okay," Darren said briskly, and I nearly jumped out of my skin again. Not from being startled that he was there, but because he'd walked around the corner dividing his crappy bedroom from the long, narrow space of the living room. And he was wearing only boxers.

He had abs. Good abs, too. And toned legs, and a little treasure trail of hair that disappeared into the waistband of his boxers, and…

That was way more information than my brain could process all at once. I shorted out for a moment and just gaped at him. To cover up the sudden *yes* my brain was throwing at me, I gestured at him and raised my eyebrows.

"What?" Darren retorted. "If we're together, you've seen me naked lots of times. You'll have to deal with this, minimum. You'll see me in less at the pool parties."

"Pool parties? Less? Wait, am *I* going to be in less?"

Darren picked off the bits of insulation from where he'd been sitting and then crashed beside me on the couch. "Okay, I think you need a 101. What to Expect When You're Accepting... my hand in fake-boyfriendship."

"Boyfriendship?" I scoffed. "Is that even a word?"

"It is now." Darren got up again and started pacing.

I could see his dick through his boxers. Well, the outline of it. But it was poking down his leg, trying to make a break for it, and if he just stood at the wrong angle, there was gonna be a wardrobe malfunction.

Why the hell was I holding my breath for just one glimpse? I was fucked in the head, wasn't I? You weren't supposed to want to see your friends' bits.

"Hit me with it." *The gay 101, not your dick,* I barely resisted adding, because that would lead to me explaining what the hell I was thinking about, and he didn't need to know that.

I adjusted myself, promised myself I'd get laid with the next girl on Tinder desperate enough to swipe right on me, and tried desperately to keep my eyes on my roommate's face.

How the hell had this become my life?

8

———

DARREN

Adam was gonna have to get over his sudden attack of shyness. Most straight guys I'd met didn't really care about seeing guys half-naked. Probably because they'd had less fear of walking into a locker room and joking around with buddies. I wasn't out in high school, but I was constantly afraid someone would find out—especially a straight guy.

Now here I was practically throwing myself at him, and I didn't feel a lick of fear. After our wrestling match when he'd shrugged off his own reflex instead of blaming me... hell, it was nice to be able to do this. I didn't worry that he felt like I was hitting on him for real. That just reaffirmed my instincts: we needed to set ground rules to make sure the whole plan went smoothly.

"So, you're my new boyfriend. Congratulations." I slapped his shoulder. "We met when I moved in with you."

"Are you sure? He won't find that suspicious?"

I laughed, suddenly self-conscious. "Hello, no. I lived with him for months, he'll believe it." I clapped and sat up straight. "I know. I went out on a date and you got jealous, and when I came back…"

"One thing led to another." Adam still looked self-conscious, but he was doing pretty well. Most guys would be laughing and making awkward *no homo* jokes right now.

"Bingo. So we can be brand-new boyfriends. Still have that tinge of awkwardness." I eyed him and then took his hand.

Adam's hand felt like a board at first, but then he relaxed and clumsily shoved his fingers against mine until he managed to hold my hand.

"Okay, that was the worst hand-holding ever." I groaned under my breath. He clearly wasn't used to showing affection. And I could understand that, but we only had a couple weeks to get comfortable with each other. "I'm gonna bring you out to see my friends once before the event, right?"

"Right. I was gonna ask about that." Adam looked intent. "Do I need to be on Instagram?"

"It's probably better if you aren't." I shook my head. "You'll be my nice, down-to-earth, Southern boyfriend. Mama's boy type, not a vain, up-in-his-Facebook kind of guy."

Adam snorted. "I can be vain."

"A little vain is okay. Especially if it means no plaid on this trip." Adam looked disappointed, and I gasped. "No. You weren't thinking of it, tell me."

"Nooo," Adam dragged out the word.

"So, we're hitting the thrift store to get you gayed up," I told him. "God, this is gonna be a lot to get done in two weeks."

Adam nodded. "And once we're there? Just, you know, holding hands and looking cute?"

"We'll have to kiss if we see Xavier," I warned him. "My friends will be cool with it if you're a little uncomfortable with PDA. Some guys are. But…"

"The point is to make him jealous of what he's missing out on." Adam looked determined, like a man on a mission. "Do we gotta practice?" Nobody had ever had to screw up their face that much to kiss me before, and I swallowed a sigh.

Just until the end of the trip, I reminded myself. *Then I can find someone who* wants *to kiss me.* This was not great for the ego.

"Sure. That's a good idea. Doesn't have to be yet, though," I told him and let go of his hand, heading for my bedroom to grab a pair of pants.

Much less awkward if I did pop an unexpected boner. Skin-to-skin contact had done that to me before, not that long ago.

"So if someone else starts flirting with you," Adam said, wandering into the doorway and leaning there. No personal space. God, this was about the only time that would come in handy.

I shrugged. "Some guys have open relationships. Some sleep around together or separately. But this new into a relationship, and what with the whole thing of…" I trailed off.

"Trying not to be available so he can worm his way back into your head?"

Ouch. For a guy who presented himself as not very perceptive, he was a little too smart sometimes. I huffed a laugh. "Yeah, something like that."

I stepped into pants and zipped them up, then grabbed a shirt. It was hard not to remember Xavier peeling this same shirt off me, whispering to me about how we needed to do this one more time. For old time's sake. Maybe I should grab some more clothes sometime soon—just so I wouldn't be wearing things Xavier would remember. New, better clothes to go with my new, better boyfriend.

"I'd be too jealous, anyway." I didn't miss the way Adam kept watching me, like he was practicing how to look at me. He filled up the doorframe with those broad shoulders and his broad attitude. It was hard to describe his ego, but he had a sort of self-confidence that led to him taking up space in the world. Wherever he walked and moved, he didn't shrink into himself or even tuck himself around other people.

He made other people move for him, and it was maddening how appealing that was. In the right guy, I'd even find it hot.

"Of… other guys?" I filled in as I buttoned up my shirt and glanced at him.

Adam nodded. "In a brand-new relationship? Hell, yeah. You're mine and only mine."

Fucking fuck, I was glad I'd just put jeans on, because my body was reacting to those words. Adam still stood there, looking at me like he had every intention of fucking me, his arms folded as he radiated that stupid self-confidence. How the hell did he do it? Get under my skin so easily?

My skin prickled with heat, and my body flushed with the need I was getting awfully familiar with. "I, uh… yeah." What a stupid answer. I couldn't come up with any other words, though. I had to fight through layers of *he doesn't mean it* to make my brain function.

"And the minute Xavier looks at you, I'll show him that."

I stifled a giggle at the thought of Adam bending me over and taking me then and there, in an animalistic display of *my territory.* Probably better than lifting his leg to do it. Okay, shit, I lost my composure and let out that laugh now.

"What?" Adam glowered and moved into the room, striding toward me. "You don't think I can do it?"

"Are you gonna rub your cheeks on me, like a cat—" I started to tease, but I didn't get a chance to finish that sentence.

Adam grabbed me by the hips and pulled me into him, crushing me against his body and sliding his arms around my waist and back. If I wanted to get away, I couldn't have.

I didn't want to get away.

I wanted to get closer, to crawl inside his clothes, to fucking ride him on the floor without shame or a second thought. My higher-level thinking was gone.

All that was left was need.

I gasped, and I didn't even have time to say anything before Adam crushed his lips against mine. It was a clumsy, awkward kiss at first, but we got through that stage in about two seconds flat.

Then he had me gasping, my knees buckling, as he licked into my mouth and sucked my lower lip. His tongue darted along mine, his hand closing around the back of my neck.

I'm gonna die. By the end of the week, I'm gonna come home and jump on Grindr and take home the first half-decent man I see. Oh, God, if I even make it to the end of the week.

"See?" Adam smirked obnoxiously, and I was torn between wanting to roll him over and fuck him until he couldn't manage that smug look one second longer, and wanting him to do just that to me. "He'll never suspect a thing."

"Okay, that'll fool him." *Fooled me,* I wanted to add. I swallowed hard and slapped Adam's chest to get him to loosen his hold. "You might break a rib, though."

"No, that'll happen during the water sports."

I felt my eyes go round as plates as my jaw dropped. Then I nearly choked on my laugh as it occurred to me that he meant water-skiing, not golden showers. "Okay, Gay 101 is back in session. Get your ass back to the couch," I ordered.

It made something inside me glow. I didn't fully understand it, but I loved that he actually obeyed without an argument. What would it take to get him to do that in bed? He'd be a bratty bottom, the kind who needed breaking in...

Nope, I was *not* letting myself go there. That was the line between this fantasy and reality. And if I started thinking that way, I was only gonna get my heart broken *and* make things a living awkward hell for us.

I'd done that once already. I didn't need to repeat my mistakes to learn from them.

I giggled again as I headed to the kitchen to grab us both iced tea.

"Seriously, what?" Adam exclaimed. "You can't keep holding this over me, dude."

"Sorry. You're just so vanilla sometimes," I told him, fighting to keep the laugh in. "Watersports and water sports," I paused between the two words, "are very different."

"What's the other one?"

"Uh... so, you know a golden shower..."

Adam burst out laughing. "What? Are they actually—are people gonna—what kind of trip *is* this?"

"Oh, it's not a fetish week," I assured him hastily. "But there's probably people who are into it. There are like a hundred different fetishes. Some of them you might recognize, some you might not."

"Like what?"

"Harnesses?"

"Duh. Pride Parades in big places like here have them." Adam huffed.

"Stonewall? Poppers? Friends of Dorothy?"

"Uhh… kinda?"

"You know what?" It occurred to me that I wasn't gonna be able to impart a lifetime, or even a few years, of cultural references and knowledge in two weeks. "Let's tell them you just came out."

"Perfect," Adam agreed.

"And that way my friends won't get suspicious. Nobody would think you're gay right now," I said with a chuckle. "Maybe we'll tell them you're bi. Even that might be hard…"

Adam's annoyance was like a flash thunderstorm in the summer. We got them sometimes over the city, clouds that built suddenly and scattered as quickly as they'd come. It was probably more of a thing where he came from. Maybe that explained him.

"Dude, don't make fun of me for being straight."

I resisted the urge to say, *Welcome to my life, imagine how high school was*, and just nodded. "Fair enough. For the next couple weeks, you're not, anyway."

Adam still scowled, and I couldn't figure out what I'd said wrong. He wasn't the kind of guy to believe straight people needed a pride parade of their own to celebrate several thousand years of being the norm. So what the hell was getting his knickers in a twist?

I couldn't work it out, so I let it go. Trying to interpret someone else's moods and act accordingly was the first step on a dangerous road. I wasn't walking that again.

"It's not your fault you're not in my cultural bubble," I decided to go with. That much was very true. "Hell, even Kev had some adjusting to do when he got here."

Adam grunted and nodded. "This is a crazy-ass idea. It's a good thing I'm getting a free vacation out of it, you know."

I grinned and clapped his shoulder. "Appreciate it, man. I don't know if I said that before, but... I'm glad you said yes."

That did the trick. Adam slowly brightened up. "You are? I mean, you must have tons of other friends..."

Nobody I could count on who was single and wouldn't let word slip to someone who might tell Xavier. But I didn't want him to feel like my last resort, because that sucked. "Yeah, but I want someone who'll make him jealous," I winked.

Adam puffed up. "Yeah?" He even deepened his voice a little, and I don't think he realized he was doing it. He just subconsciously butched up in response to my compliment. It was kind of adorable, actually.

If only it weren't for the minor straight thing, I was growing to realize that he'd be exactly my type.

At least I had a few weeks to pretend, right?

9

ADAM

Treasure Aisle was surprisingly quiet on a Saturday morning. Everyone in the gayborhood must still be recovering from their hangovers and grabbing brunch.

I was beating the crowds to the thrift store. I'd picked up a thing or two from my best friend and ex-roommate, such as when the thrift store tended to restock its best stuff. Saturday mornings, he'd be down here looking for fancy teacups. I had a look when I passed the aisle, but the only ones I saw were chipped. I never knew how chipped was good in his eyes—he liked to repair cracks and chips with gold glue, and he'd spend hours on one cup—and what was unfixable. Kind of like me.

Wow, I wasn't even hungover and I was having a self-esteem attack already. Small wonder, when my task for today was so big. I had to figure out what clothes looked gay enough for our vacation. Darren had taken one look at my closet and declared none of it useable.

Since I didn't have the money to splash out on brands like Kev, that meant picking the racks here.

I desperately needed a fashion adviser. I kept my eyes peeled for someone to ask for help besides the store staff, who looked pretty uninterested in helping out an unfortunate straight-curious guy.

"Shirts first," I mumbled, grabbing a basket on the way past a rack. I could handle that. That was the easiest kind of shopping.

The usual stuff I bought wouldn't work, I knew that much. What did gay guys wear? Tighter clothes, I knew that much. Maybe instead of sizing up, I should go for something that clung to my body better. That would make me look hotter, too, and I needed all the help I could get.

I was doing okay on acting gay—kissing Darren had proven that kissing transcended gender boundaries. It had been pretty fucking hot, if I did say so myself. Darren had looked surprised and pleased with my performance. He didn't have to know that not all of it was acting.

If I was fucking hungry for the taste of another guy on my lips, he didn't need to know that. It would only make this thing between us way fucking awkward. It had been so good kissing him that I still remembered it, days later, but we'd never mentioned practicing since then. Obviously Darren thought I was doing fine on that front.

I just needed to look the part now.

A Hawaiian shirt caught my attention, but that didn't seem very gay at all. Subtler than that, then… but still bright. No more cargo shorts. Something nice for shoes, too. How would I coordinate a week's worth of outfits? I was gonna have to get Darren to check them out ahead of time.

"You want to stay away from plaid."

I'd been staring at the rack for so long that I hadn't noticed anyone walking up behind me, and I nearly jumped at the voice. It sounded like a guy's voice, raspy but newly broken-in.

"Okay." That was a reedier voice, soft and shy. "Like this?"

I stepped out of the way and glanced over, trying to listen in on the fashion lesson without being too obvious about it. Both guys looked young, and they were both shorter than me.

"Yeah, that's good, but it's plain," said the older one of the two. I was pretty sure he was gay, but aside from his voice, I wasn't sure what gave me that impression. Then I saw it as he stretched to grab a shirt near me—a tattoo on his hipbone that looked like the male and female gender symbols and another line all squished together. That seemed pretty gay, right? "Try this."

He looked plain but well-dressed, like he could fit in anywhere— the workplace, a cocktail party, wherever. That was the kind of look I needed.

"Oh, that's bright," said the other guy. Was he a guy? He was dressed pretty androgynously, in two layers of shirts despite the heat. Definitely not suitable for Hawaii. "How about this?"

"We'll go with that. Grab a few more."

I tried to spy on the prints he chose, keeping an eye on which shirts the other guy's advice made me put back. For the life of me, I couldn't see much difference between the ones the guy giving advice chose and the ones he rejected.

Fuck, I was screwed.

"Oh, that's really straight." The guy laughed and waved his hand. "Get it away from you. The rest of them are fine, we'll go with those. Nice job. Until you figure out your style, thrift stores are the place to go. It's cheaper if you realize you're not really into that style after all, you know?"

Okay. Stripes were straight, that was the sum total of what I'd learned. Except—there were other striped shirts in his arms, and those weren't too straight?

Now was the moment, but… for once, I didn't have the guts to talk to someone. I couldn't bring myself to ask for help, or even go, *Does this look straight on me?* and make an ass of myself to make a joke. As the two of them headed for the cash register, the adrenaline spike of anxious excitement faded. I was really no closer to figuring out what would work, was I?

What had stopped me from saying hello? Aside from not wanting to go, *Hey, you look gay, can you help me get dressed?*, which sounded like a dick move. Maybe it was because they were strangers. God, I was getting too used to a New York City pace of life if that ever stopped me making conversation with someone I didn't know.

No, it was all my ego. I just didn't want to look like an idiot in yet another way. I didn't know anything about the gay world, as Darren had so painfully reminded me. Nobody would possibly mistake me, in his eyes, for gay or bi as I was now. Especially not in these clothes.

That wasn't just a jab at my sexuality, which felt so much in flux right now. It stung my pride, because what grown man didn't know how to dress well? Living somewhere like here, I only felt it more acutely. You could tell the people with jobs in the city—Manhattan, especially. Even the creative types had their own dress code.

I was just that slob in dirt-stained, holey jeans and a t-shirt. No wonder I'd had such bad luck with my dating life. Hooking up once on Tinder was one thing—but my second-date rate was batting a zero.

Okay, feeling sorry for myself was not going to help me. What I needed was to do research. Maybe if I headed to Bubbles myself and watched people in the diner, I could figure out what gay men wore. It wasn't like, an all-gay diner, but I knew Kev and his friends hung out there a lot. It was also next to the gay bar. Where better?

After a morning of taking notes, I could come back here and take a shot at buying something that would help me blend in with the crowd.

Not just for this week, either. If I could get guys to look at me twice when I came back home, that might not be such a bad thing. And the first step was to go where they were.

My heart racing, my palms sweaty, I stepped out of the shop and made a beeline for Bubbles.

***

"Hangover special, please." I ordered automatically from months of hearing Kev casually mention it. The place was cheerier than I'd expected. And… well… less gay.

I didn't know what I'd expected, really. Tina Turner and Cher posters? A disco ball?

This was a retro, yet cheerful place: potted plants lining the windowsill, bright red upholstery and menus, a central bar with a cash register and stools.

They'd found me a seat at the counter instead of the booths, since it was busy. Fine by me—I could observe people all over without being too obvious. I already had a notes file created on my phone.

"Coffee with that?" the waitress asked, scribbling already.

"God, yes." I grinned. "Black?"

"You betcha." She filled my mug without missing a beat and headed back to the kitchen.

I held the mug by my fingertips, wanting the warmth but resisting it at the same time. It was too hot outside at this time of year, and as soon as the sun rose above the tops of the buildings, Brooklyn was gonna be a scorcher again today. I was a little chilly in my shorts and t-shirt, but I'd make up for it by baking later.

With my order placed, I could set about my real mission.

The only problem was that everywhere I looked, guys were wearing different things. Some were in baggy shorts, and others in skinny jeans. Some guys wore blazers even at this hour, and others had on what must have been pajama shirts. There was every color and print except Hawaiian—and, I observed, very few plain stripes.

That was a start. *Prints, not stripes,* I noted on my phone.

When I started to have more luck, it was almost subconscious. I'd never really taken the time to just look at people's styles and see what appealed to me and what didn't. Now that I was paying attention, I quickly learned that I liked jeans more than slacks, and I liked how tighter shirts with the sleeves rolled up showed off forearms and pecs. I had both of those in spades, so that seemed like a safe bet, too.

Oh, hello. This guy knew what he was doing. He drew all eyes when he walked in, strode up to the male waiter on duty, threw his arms around him, and kissed him.

A few wolf-whistles later, they broke apart and the waiter flipped everyone off. "Cold coffee for all of you."

"I'm all out of singles, but thanks for the show." That was an older guy with bleach-blond hair and a smirk. He definitely looked gay.

Was it bad to judge people like I was doing today? I didn't want people thinking I was straight because of how I dressed, after all. Which was weird in itself—I'd always stubbornly clung to the word like armor. Truth had nothing to do with it. Protection was what I'd been after.

Now, though? The more Darren laughed at me for being straight, the less comfortable I felt with the word. It felt like an attack on me for being too cowardly to talk about it, or even kiss one damn guy.

"Hangover special." The guy who ducked under the kitchen window caught my eye, and I his.

If I could've seen myself in the mirror behind the counter, I'm sure I would have been pale as a ghost. I tried not to fall off my stool, but I lost my balance a little.

"Whoa. You okay there?" The well-dressed guy, who looked kind of vaguely familiar, took a seat next to me and patted my back to help me stay up on the stool.

"F-Fine, thanks."

I looked back at the kitchen, only to find him still staring at me through the window. There was no doubt about it—it was Ricky.

Think of the devil and there he was, dressed in a polo shirt with a stained white apron, looking... well, nothing like he had on my bed in my apartment.

He didn't stay frozen for long. "Two more coming up!" he barked, maybe for his own benefit and maybe for the waiters'. Like that, he was back to work, and I tried not to be ten times more aware of the clattering dishes than I had been before.

Maybe this wasn't such a big neighborhood after all.

I turned back to the guy who'd just rescued me from an embarrassing crash off the stool. "I like your style," I burst out with, desperate for anything to distract me from thinking about cuddling with the chef while my waitress dropped off my breakfast.

"Why, thank you." He smiled and held out a hand. "Shay. I'm the owner's boyfriend."

"Ohhh." I shook hands and grinned, nodding at the guy on the other side of the diner. "Adam. He's the owner?"

"I hope so, or I just kissed the wrong man." Shay winked. He seemed perfectly comfortable as he flagged down the waitress, asked for the usual, and thanked her.

I dug into my breakfast, swallowing the hundred questions that occurred to me. How the hell everyone here seemed to know each other was near the top of the list.

"I wish I could dress better," I admitted. "I'm kind of on a mission to do that."

"Hey, just making an effort goes a long way, Adam," Shay told me. He didn't seem to be making fun of me, either. "Start paying attention and you'll notice what you're drawn to. Make sure you've got the basics, and then have fun with accessories."

"Do you work in fashion?"

He shook his head and smiled. "TV. But everyone talks to me about it." Oh, shit. I was talking to a movie star? As I blushed, embarrassed not to have recognized him, Shay waved a hand and added, "Weather anchor. My shtick is dressing well."

"Oh, that's smart. I know there are anchors—female anchors—who wear, like, the same dresses?" I'd read something about that online.

Shay chuckled. "Yeah. They have pretty strict rules on what they can wear. No cleavage, a certain length, no green, no distracting prints… most guys get away with the same three boring suits, but I try to have a little fun."

I nodded. "Have I seen you on TV? Or Facebook or something?"

"If you ever watch TV for the forecast," Shay said with a grin. "And I post a lot on our weather channel's page. We do a weekly love report…"

That was it! I sat up straighter. "Yeah! The love spot report or something, right?"

"Yeah!" Shay grinned. "I get a lot of people who say they love it, but I always wonder if people actually use it."

I snorted with laughter. As far as I remembered, it was a little Facebook thing where he posted the best date locations based on the weather that week—indoor or outdoor locations, for example. "Why don't you get people to send in photos? Some cute couple pic in the location of the week?"

Shay paused and then set down his mug as his plate of food arrived. "You know, that's actually a great idea. I don't know why I didn't think of it. My boss will love it."

I brightened up. It made me feel good to come up with a smart idea now and then when most of my day job involved shutting up and hauling heavy things around. "Yeah? Cool."

"You got someone in mind? You could kick things off," Shay suggested with a wink. "A lovely lady or gent who wants a moment of fame?"

I was about to say no when I caught myself. Shit, I couldn't go ruining the illusion now. My hesitation did the trick, and Shay grinned, leaning in.

"Oho. I see."

"We're just—it's new—we're figuring it out," I stuttered, glaring when he winked. I was blushing now. Fuck. At least it would make this all sound authentic. "Yeah. Sort of."

"Well, I'll put out the call in public. No pressure," Shay told me and grinned. "What's their name?"

My heart fluttered. God, I was nervous. The guy was gay, so it wasn't that. But it was the first time I'd ever said this—even if I was just pretending.

"Darren. He's Darren."

Shay paused and eyed me for a few moments. "Say… Adam and Darren… he doesn't come here a lot, does he?"

"I think so."

Shay gasped. "No way. He's not Darren, uh… Spencer…? Oh, my God." He set down his knife and fork. "He dropped a hint the other day, but we—you're seriously?"

I nodded, and I tried not to feel miserable for how delighted he looked. He was obviously happy for Darren, and here I was just pretending. In a couple weeks' time, we'd "break up" and everyone would feel bad for us. We were leading them all on. Was this really worth the ego boost for Darren?

That was the other important thing I'd forgotten: I didn't like lying. I'd done it too much before, and I'd nearly fucked up my life the first time around.

What the hell was I getting into doing it again?

"I'm so happy for him! And glad to meet you," Shay told me with a broad grin.

Oh, fuck. If this felt like a long breakfast to endure pretending I was actually the light of Darren's life, it was going to be the world's longest week.

85

DARREN, ONE WEEK LATER

I cast one more critical eye over Adam, trying my best to turn off the part of my brain that reminded me I found him extremely fuckable right now.

More importantly, other guys would think the same, and they wouldn't think he was just the straight guy who lived with me and —for some crazy reason which probably mostly meant a free Hawaiian trip—was helping me look like less of a loser around my more romantically successful ex.

"What the hell are we even doing?" I covered my face. My laugh turned into more of a groan. "Oh, my God."

Adam rested his hands on my shoulders. "No second thoughts. I bought all these shirts for you, you know."

I grinned and leaned into him for a hug, trying not to notice that he smelled nice. "Yeah. You did a really good job, too."

"Thanks. I look fine? I've been looking on Instagram and stuff for ideas."

I loved him a little bit right now. He was really taking this seriously—way more seriously than he had to, or even than I'd expected him to. "Really? Well, dude, you look fucking hot. You should keep dressing like this after we're done."

Adam frowned at me. "What?"

I waved a hand up and down, indicating him. "That's hot to everyone. You don't think girls like a guy who knows how to dress?" Linen shorts, nice boat shoes, a button-down short-sleeved shirt... he was a sight for sore eyes in a sea of frat boys who dressed in t-shirts and baggy denim shorts.

Adam hummed and waved off the compliment, grabbing his keys and heading for the door. "I dunno. It feels so stiff."

"Not after you get it hot and wet," I told him and smirked as he figured out what I meant. I clattered my way down the stairs as Adam kept up with me.

He groaned and swatted my arm as he pushed open the door to our street. "Oh, dude!"

I grinned and sailed past him through the door, leading us down the street toward our little enclave of stores, restaurants, and nightlife. It was so nice to live within walking distance of all this stuff, saving us the subway ride to Manhattan. "What? I mean, the humidity in Hawaii."

"That wasn't what you meant, you dirty bastard." Adam snickered along with me, though. "Man, I can't wait to see what everyone thinks."

The reminder that all my buddies who were going out tonight were going to meet him was a jolt back to reality. "Right. So if they start looking suspicious, just remember..."

"We just got together, and I just came out," Adam interrupted. "I remember. Relax. We've got this."

For once, his confidence was nice. It was reassuring to be swept along in his wake as we headed for the diner together.

Bubbles was pretty busy, filling up with people who wanted to kill time between predrinking and heading into the club. They must do a killer business most nights. The club was open every day, and the diner was 24/7. I'd never seen either completely empty. A symbiotic relationship, just like Adam and me.

"Are they all over there with Shay?" Adam asked as he pushed open the door. I had to crane my neck over his shoulder to see where he pointed, but then I nodded.

How had he known Shay? Did he recognize him from TV, or was he suddenly the poster boy of the local LGBT club? Knowing Adam's tendency to throw himself into the deep end, it wouldn't surprise me.

I put my arm around Adam's waist and kissed his shoulder. His cologne was delicious and noticeable for the first time as I crowded up behind him like this. "That's them. Showtime." Then, I slapped his ass—just lightly.

Adam looked surprised but not displeased. He walked with a certain extra sway to his hips, showing off his assets, as he approached the table.

I'd never seen him look more in his element.

"Hey, I'm this guy's new boyfriend, and I need bacon."

Adam was greeted with a wave of laughter, and then the introductions began.

Should have known he'd get along with them. He was obnoxious sometimes—on purpose, I was sure of it—but he could also slide into any situation effortlessly. Outgoing covered a lot of bases.

Finally, we'd all made room in the booth, and we'd gone through the easy basic conversations—what Adam did for work, what our plans for Hawaii were, and when we left. We'd stuck with light meals since we were all going out dancing. The hangover special was great, but too much food to dance on.

"You'll never believe who was here last night." Billy leaned in and waved, catching my attention. "Xavier."

Beside me, Adam scowled. It was definitely not a faked expression, either.

Charlie rolled his eyes a little bit, but I grinned. I knew he didn't really come here for the drama. He was way past that phase in his life, even though he was pretty much the same age as the rest of us —mid-twenties to mid-thirties. I was on the lower end of that at twenty-six. But losing his boyfriend years ago in an accident had given Charlie perspective.

Even my lips turned down as I grimaced. "Ugh, I hope he isn't out tonight. Was he cruising for another guy already?"

"No, he brought the new boy. *Totally* a jealous clinger." Billy rolled his eyes. "I wouldn't let him within a hundred miles of me."

Somehow, that didn't surprise me. Xavier wanted to be needed. When it had become clear I didn't need him as a boyfriend or emotional support, he'd wanted to be needed sexually. If he found a guy who could meet that need, good for him.

"Huh," was all I said. "They still going to Hawaii?"

"You bet. Sorry to be the bearer of bad news," Billy added. "But it's all heat, no spark."

"What?" Adam frowned. "There's gotta be a spark."

"No way." Kev interrupted, slinging his arm around his best friend's shoulders. "You know the relationships that are, like, all sex and no real feelings?"

I nodded and held back my grimace. I knew that all too well. For some people, it was perfect—but for me, it was all I seemed to get, no matter how hard I tried. And when I did find a guy who had feelings for me, I did something to screw it up. It had been true since I'd come out, and I didn't expect my luck to change now.

"You two are way better suited," Billy concluded. "You're obviously into each other."

I blinked at him. We'd been there for, what, twenty minutes? Thirty? Were we doing that good a job of getting along already? We'd been touching each other more around the apartment, but aside from that, we hadn't even practiced holding hands again.

"Oh, your body language says it all." Kev—who was the only one apart from the two of us who knew the truth—leaned around Adam to talk to me. "You aren't hanging off each other like you've got something to prove."

"Well, that's probably down to me," Adam muttered. I could feel what he was trying to awkwardly shoehorn into the conversation. Fuck. I would have elbowed him, but there was no way of doing it without all eyes turning to me. I just had to swallow my trepidation and let him totally clunkily work in our backstory.

He'd neglected to tell me that he was an awful liar.

"I came out not long ago, so yeah. I'm still not used to... all of this." He laughed thinly, his first sign of nervousness since he'd arrived.

He was met with a round of congratulations and approval, which seemed to take him aback. I tried not to blush as I nodded, keeping my tongue firmly bitten. The average gay guy didn't just walk up to a new table of guys he didn't know and go *hey, I just came out*. Not unless he was looking for a boyfriend.

Kev's lips were twitching. He mercifully managed not to laugh, though. He just grinned and clapped Adam's shoulder. "Always knew you had it in you. It'll get easier from here out."

Charlie finally interrupted. He looked less bored now that the conversation wasn't all gossip. "Tell me, what are you guys doing in Hawaii, anyway? Give me more details."

I owed him a drink sometime.

As Adam tried to remember the themes for each day of our resort stay, I supplied the ones he was forgetting. All pretty standard stuff, but that reminded me to finalize our costumes. A few of them were going to be skimpier than Adam was probably expecting.

It was way too much fun to see him blush when he realized how little he'd be wearing. Then, he'd seemingly remember that he had a hot body and he'd swell up with excitement and tell me *let's do it!* He was really too cute sometimes.

The conversation moved on to someone else's gay cruise experiences, and I half tuned out as my thoughts wandered.

I felt kind of bad that Adam was having to go through this awkward socializing experience, but goddamn, I was grateful that he'd thrown himself into this without looking back. He could have refused to meet my friends here, or turned down the whole thing.

Why? That was the only thing that kept bothering me. It wasn't like he didn't get anything out of it, but... he did seem to be so on board with this that I didn't really understand it. Hell, he'd gone and kissed me like no man ever had, just to prove that he was gonna be able to do it.

A tiny part of me wondered if maybe… just maybe…

No way, though. Adam wasn't subtle. He was definitely not the type to test things out without going loud and proud about it, was he? He was in-your-face.

Kind of like "striding into your bedroom and grabbing you to kiss the life out of you" was in-your-face.

I rubbed my head and tried to ditch all the worries. It didn't really matter *why* he was doing it. If it was for a free trip, great. If he wanted to see what it was like to kiss a guy, at least he wasn't leading me on to do it.

"Oh, my God. You should have seen it." I'd missed half of the story Billy was telling, and I only tuned back in to hear, "He was riding that dick like it was the last one in town!"

"On your bed?" someone exclaimed. "Oh no, she didn't!"

Billy shrugged. "I was gonna kick them out. They didn't even ask first, you know? But then I realized that I was getting a free show. They were into it. And they said sorry afterwards, and left quarters for the laundromat."

I grinned as I leaned into Adam. These were the kinds of stories he was gonna hear at unexpected moments throughout our coming week together. He'd better get used to it now.

"No good deed goes unpunished," Kev concluded. "But, man. Get a lock for your bedroom door."

"That's never happened before."

I shook my head. "At least Adam and I don't have to worry about that anymore, huh?" I grinned at him. "No more stupid watermelons."

Both Kev and Adam exclaimed at the same time.

"He's still using that?" Kev elbowed Adam. "Man!"

"It's convenient!"

"And strawberry. I don't get that one," I added, just to wind them both up. It was kind of funny to see the best friends bantering.

"Strawberry is *don't come home for the next hour or two.* Just a short watermelon."

"Oh, like the sock on the doorknob?" Billy cottoned onto what was going on first, and then the whole table was paying attention. "Smart."

"Watermelon means the whole night," Adam added, glancing at Kev. "And not to worry about you."

"Or come punching out his boyfriend," Charlie said with a smirk.

I gasped. "What? I have to hear this story."

"Not right now, you don't," Adam told me, even though Charlie was snickering. "I think we should get ready to get down in the club. Before they get busy."

We all agreed, and it took a couple minutes for everyone to get their bills sorted out. Once that was done, Kev waved me on ahead and grabbed Adam to sit down for a minute.

I figured he wanted advice or a chat or something. I wasn't offended—they were good friends, after all, and I didn't think Adam had many of those. He sure hadn't mentioned any to me.

"See you in a bit," I said instead, and headed out with the rest of the group to Friction.

As we stood around, waiting for our IDs to be checked, the guys crowded around me. "Oh, my God. Dude, he's hot."

"He's so into you, too." Billy winked. "He kept looking at you every time you said anything. He was a little nervous, though. He gonna be okay tonight?"

Oh, crap. I hadn't even asked if he'd ever been to a gay bar before. "Fine, fine," I said, waving it off. "He's tough."

"I'm glad for you." Shay hadn't said much, but he did say that. "I'm heading to bed."

"Aww," we all said, but Shay wouldn't be talked out of it. He glanced at the apartment door—I'd hardly noticed it before this one time when I hung out with Jared after his shift and talked. Since then, I'd been over now and then for a beer, but not often. And, once, when I'd needed him to come downstairs and sort out an argument going on downstairs between Kev and a now-fired waitress.

The apartment up there was Jared's own private retreat, and I wasn't sure if he saw me more as a friend or a customer, so I tried not to intrude. Shay was definitely a friend, though, if only a casual acquaintance.

"I won't be much longer," Charlie agreed and hugged Shay with a smile. "Night, then."

"Thanks, man." I half-hugged him, too, and clapped his back. "For getting Adam in some decent clothes."

Shay blinked at me. "What? I didn't do that."

"Oh. He mentioned your name and I just assumed you'd met at Bubbles and… I dunno, rescued a helpless case. He did that all on his own?"

"Yeah." Shay laughed. "Man, I'm not great at telling what works on you white guys. I'd charge a lot more for my consulting services if I did."

I laughed and shrugged. "Fair enough."

"All I told him to do was trust his gut instinct. Same thing I've said to all of you."

My style hadn't really changed, but then again, I hadn't been looking for advice.

Shay was following my train of thought. He winked. "Obviously, he was just ready for a change. And so were you."

That was about right. Unfortunately, not the kind of change everyone else thought it was. I half-smiled and raised a hand. "I sure was. Good night, then."

After Shay disappeared into the door between Bubbles and Friction, we filed into the club, one by one.

I got Adam a beer along with my own, and then I waited for him to come in for what might just be his first-ever gay bar experience. Charlie was waiting for Kev, too, but he seemed content just to hang out at the bar and people-watch, so I didn't disturb his happy place.

Now that it had occurred to me that maybe Adam was enjoying this a little too much, I didn't feel quite so sorry for him. But how the hell was I gonna ask?

Are you bi-curious? Straight, with air-quotes? Do you already sleep with guys? Why the hell does that make me feel so jealous?

I had no right at all to be jealous of the people he was for-real dating. But, if it was an option…

It's not, I told myself. I had to be firm about that rule—so fucking firm that I was stiff as a board. Otherwise, I was just gonna get my heart involved, and… that never ended well.

Listen to my gut instinct, Shay said? That worked better for clothes than boyfriends.

I could throw away a shirt that didn't make my eyes look good, but I couldn't just ditch a boyfriend who made my heart feel small. Even now, all of this was happening because I had something to prove to that ex.

What a mess my life was.

ADAM

"Dude. What the hell have you gotten yourself into?"

At least Kev waited until everyone else had left Bubbles before grabbing my arm and starting his intervention.

"I'm fine," I assured him quietly. I didn't want anyone overhearing and reporting back to someone who might know Xavier, after all. For the size of Brooklyn, there were still only two degrees of separation instead of one, like Tennessee. "It's only for a couple weeks."

Kev folded his arms and eyed me. "I know you better than you think," he told me. "Something else is going on."

"Nothing's going on." I tried for my absolute best neutral face.

Kev snorted with amusement. "Sure. That's definitely the face you make when nothing's going on."

"There's nothing."

"Nothing is blushing now."

My face was indeed heating up, and the more conscious I was of it, the harder I seemed to flush. Damn it. I tried to ignore it and think about cold things like Antarctica and Kev's chill right now. "Nothing at all."

"The more you say it, the more I believe it."

I folded my arms and stuck out my jaw, fully aware I looked petulant, but also completely unwilling to admit to him the extent of this little project.

It felt like one of those foam figurines you got from the dollar store and dropped into water to grow eight hundred percent overnight. Suddenly, instead of a funny little idea to help Darren out and get a free tropical vacation, I was clinging to the frame of my closet in the face of a tornado.

"Okay, dude." When I didn't answer, Kev relented first. "I just want you to know that if you're experimenting, I'm happy for you. Everyone does it sooner or later."

"Years later than most people," I scoffed. That wasn't quite admitting what was going on, was it?

"And we came from somewhere different than many of the people around us," Kev told me quietly. "It's a thousand percent okay to figure all that stuff out later—or now." He pointedly nodded at me. "Whatever your parents have to say about it. Fuck 'em."

"What? Nah, my parents are okay," I mumbled, even quieter than he'd been talking. I really didn't want to talk about this where anyone might overhear. Besides, people would start wondering where we'd gotten to if we didn't get back to the group soon.

Kev didn't quite manage to swallow his derisive snort in time.

"Nah," I told him. "They're not like your parents."

Kev's parents could go rot in hell, as far as I was concerned. Any parents who threw a sixteen-year-old out to fend for themselves, knowing full well what that meant they'd be forced to do, could burn in the fiery brimstone they believed in, and the sooner the better. I only wished I'd known him earlier, so I could have helped him out back then.

"No, but yours ain't that much better." Kev touched my arm. I'd almost forgotten how touchy-feely he was.

I shook my head again. "They didn't stop talking to me." The more I insisted, the less I believed myself. Kev's words were getting under my skin. "They're just… busy with life. And they wanted me to grow up straight 'cause it'd be easier on me, and then they can get grandkids, and… you know."

I hated the look Kev gave me—the knowing sympathy. I hated even more that my gut twisted in response, my cheeks heating up. Whatever arguments I gave him, I knew the facts, and I knew what it looked like. If I told him more about growing up with them, he'd only dig his heels into his side of the argument.

But every kid got smacked around a little to keep them respectful. I hadn't suffered from it. I still jostled my friends around and roughhoused without, like, freaking out. I sure didn't feel abused. And I had more support—sort of. But I hadn't gone through what Kev had, that was for sure.

"I could use some advice." I kept my voice and face solemn, drawing his attention. "What's the best pillow for biting?"

Kev smacked my shoulder and pushed me out of the booth to stand up. He had to throw his weight against me two or three times before I let him shift me. "Oh, get out of here, asshole."

"I'm serious! A puncture at an inconvenient moment would throw off my mojo," I kept teasing, not letting it go. "If I drown in down, would that be poetic? Just for the rhyme?"

"I'm not gonna let you wind me up," Kev said. "Even if you're on my team now."

I smirked and pushed open the door, holding it for him.

But instead of getting offended or telling me off, Kev just beamed and sailed through the doorway, did a pirouette, and offered me his arm. "May I have the pleasure of escorting you?"

"As long as you're not doing *that* kind of escorting anymore." I wasn't sure how to take his arm, but I awkwardly wrapped my hand around his bicep and glared around us at anyone who might look in our direction.

Those few moments where I'd held the door and instead of being insulted, he'd drawn on something inside him that I wasn't sure I had access to, and then seamlessly taken the man's role in offering me his arm? All of that felt like a whole new kind of nonverbal language that I barely spoke.

I was still kind of reeling as we walked into the bar. Whatever else happened, I was glad that Kev saw through me like this. He wasn't going to take my defensive reflexes at face value, and the more he did that, the more I saw them for what they were: an artificially constructed attempt to protect myself.

From what? Intimacy? Compassion? Love? Vulnerability?

I had no idea. God, I hoped this time at the resort would help me figure that out.

By the time we rejoined the group, they'd found a corner of the dance floor. I knew how this much worked, at least.

Kev immediately glued himself to Charlie. Right away, Darren sidled next to me and slid his arm around my waist. He held a drink in a plastic cup in his other hand. "I was gonna get you a beer. Next round's mine."

I grinned. "Oh, I get free drinks out of this?" Over the music, no way would anybody hear. To them, it just looked like we were flirting as I draped my arm over his shoulders and leaned into him. "You never mentioned that."

"Perks of the job," Darren told me with a wink.

If I was gonna do this, I was gonna do it right. I rested my chin on his shoulder. "As long as you're not just trying to get me drunk." As I talked, my warm breath tickled his neck. That ought to make it hard to focus.

I heard Darren's quick intake of breath. Mission achieved. "I wouldn't want to cross any lines," he murmured back, which wasn't the flirtation I'd expected.

"Oh, honey," I snickered, picking up the lingo around me even faster than I'd expected, "I don't think you could find a line if you tried. Not even a tan line."

"More than I needed to know."

"I'd argue that's exactly what you need to know." What the hell had gotten into me? I wasn't just making it look authentic for his friends. "What if someone asks? You should know these things."

I'd barely had a drop to drink, but I found myself unwilling to let him go. I wanted to turn him on. I was playing with fire, and fuck, I liked it.

Darren let me go and swigged from his cup as he gave me a wink. "You're trouble," he told me, turning his back to start dancing.

I laughed. He was making me work for it, and I kind of liked it.

It wasn't the weirdest thing ever to be here. It was like a normal club, except guys were grinding on guys, and nobody seemed to care. Honestly, that was kind of liberating. I stopped looking at every guy twice to figure out if he was gonna give me trouble for hitting on the wrong guy like I would if girls were around.

Over the next hour, I quickly figured out that everyone hit on everyone at a gay club, and nobody took it particularly seriously. In fact, it wasn't much longer before a guy was approaching *me*. I knew for damn sure he wasn't hitting on anyone else, because he was making direct eye contact.

What do I do now? I couldn't look away. Instinct wouldn't let me. I knew he wasn't a danger, but would he take no for an answer? What if I kind of wanted him to flirt with me? I was finally being accepted—not just accepted, but *wanted*—in a space for and by gay men.

Whatever the hell I was, that felt good to me. Another piece of evidence for the *probably not straight* theory.

And then an arm slid around my waist, and Darren's cologne hit my nose as he rested his chin on my shoulder. He didn't turn his head to talk to me—he was looking at the guy over my shoulder. I grew hot under the collar as I realized what was going on: he was scaring him off and asserting his claim.

The other guy smiled and raised his cup in a toast, and then he melted into the rapidly filling dance floor. I probably couldn't have picked him out again. A lot of guys here looked similar.

Except Darren. He would have caught my eye even if I hadn't known him. He looked good tonight—as always—in skinny jeans and a t-shirt that barely seemed to hold him. It was the simplest outfit, but it made his ass look great, and it made me want to rub his pecs like he was doing to mine right now.

Even if this was fake jealousy, Darren had not only noticed me, but he'd noticed the other guy looking at me, and he'd come to protect me. That made me feel all kinds of high on life.

"Thanks for the save," I said, sliding my hand along his arm to rest over his. It wasn't even too weird being held from behind like this. Thankfully we were around the same height, so there was no awkward leaning up or down to do.

Darren grinned. "I didn't come off too strong there?" He rubbed my chest lightly. "Didn't want you accidentally hooking up with anyone. Just look away from someone if you don't want him."

"Oh." I blushed. I'd never even thought of what to do in that situation.

"It might not work in the straight world, but gay guys are better at reading those signals. If they don't get the hint, just shake your head. Saying no works, too." Darren patted my chest, and I wished it didn't feel like such a platonic, buddy-buddy coaching session.

Which meant I wanted him to be showing me these things as… what? A romantic interest? A boyfriend, for real?

Fuck, I was screwed.

"Thanks," I said again, and laced my fingers with his, not letting him let go of me yet. I leaned back into him just a little as I swayed with the music. "You know, you're pretty hot when you get possessive."

"You think so?" Darren growled. "You ain't seen nothing yet."

For all his words, he still sounded playful. God, I wished he realized what was going on in my head. But if he did, he probably wouldn't be saying these things. He obviously wasn't into me, and if he knew how much I was enjoying this, he'd pull back. But I'd have given my left hand (not the right—it had important uses) right now to hear him say it to me for real.

"Yeah?" I purred. "Are your friends buying this?"

Darren laughed quietly. "Hell, I almost am."

"Good." I stopped just short of pushing it further. We had plenty of time to kill together over the next week before we even left for the damn vacation. Making it awkward wasn't gonna help anything.

I remembered all too well what Kev had told me before: relationships could be transactional. I didn't want him to feel like he had to choose between turning me down and getting help showing Xavier that he didn't deserve Darren. If he thought he needed to date me to get that help, it would put him in a shitty situation. I wasn't about to do that.

But…

But the need that had crept into my very bones while I wasn't looking? I didn't know how else to satisfy it. It wasn't just a need to be seen as gay, but that was part of it. It wasn't a need to feel attractive, but that was part of it, too.

It felt more specific. Like I needed something from *Darren*, not just any guy.

So I put all my reservations to one side in my brain as I let go of his arm at last. I turned in his hold to put my arms around his shoulders. "You know what would convince them even more?"

Darren's gaze flickered to my lips and then back to my eyes, like he was waiting for permission. "Are you sure? You're comfortable with—"

God, by trying to respect me, he was overthinking this. Would he ask me this if he knew I was into guys?

I didn't give him a chance to waffle. I just leaned in to press my lips hard against his, just once. Then I pulled back and hissed, "Yes."

Darren's laugh was trembly. His arms tightened around me, and he pressed close. Suddenly he was breathing quickly. We hadn't kissed since that one time in his room last week, and we hadn't even talked about it. Looked like we were about to follow up on that now.

"Starting to feel like you're an exhibitionist," Darren whispered.

I winked. "No comment. You wanna kiss me or not?"

"I'd love to." Darren ran his hands slowly through my hair, and my knees weakened. Fuck, he was good at this. I could already tell, and I hadn't even given him the chance to warm me up last time. He was holding me like I was the sexiest man in the room. Hell, he *looked* at me like I was. Any hesitation I'd felt was gone.

And then he kissed me, closing the distance between us quickly, in one rush of breath. Our lips met, and warmth flooded me. My hands curled into the back of his shirt. We swayed together in the half-light of the club, and my chest thudded to the beat of the dance music that drowned out all other sounds. All my doubts and worries were washed away right along with them.

I just kissed him, letting him suck my lower lip and explore the tip of my tongue with his. He was showing off for his friends—and, hell, probably for the other guys around us. And I liked it.

I wanted to be possessed by him. Pretending to be his arm candy was tapping into something much deeper that had suddenly started to form, and now I couldn't shake the thought: I wanted to be his.

As we kissed, I lost track of time and what was an appropriate length of time to kiss. I had no idea how it worked in this kind of place anyway, so I trusted him to know whatever I needed to know. If security came to pry us apart, I wasn't sure I was willing to let go.

I could picture doing all the dirty things the guys around us were doing. Some were grinding on each other in a slow, sensual rhythm, and others were groping each other. It was hard to spot in the crowd, but if you paid attention, you could see a hand slip under a shirt or down a waistband.

We didn't go that far. Plenty of time to show off later, I figured. I wasn't going to rush this. I was just savoring my first real kiss—last week's had just been proving to him and myself that I could do it. This one was for real.

When Darren finally pulled away and we separated, I grew very aware that I was hard. Fuck. That was getting to be a real pattern around him.

"You do that a few times next week and everyone will believe it." He gave me a casual grin and nodded at the bar. "Getting another beer. You want one?"

"Sure." I welcomed the chance to adjust myself while he was gone and cool off while I carefully avoided eye contact with any other guys nearby.

After we rejoined his friends, danced a little more, and had another beer each, we didn't talk about it any more than that. I had the sneaking feeling we weren't going to—that was also getting to be a pattern.

Even when we finally walked home, we didn't talk about that moment. Maybe for him, it was just a forgettable couple minutes of acting the part in the middle of a fun night of hanging out with friends. For me, it was a turning point.

From here, nothing else was gonna be the same. I knew that I was into kissing guys—and especially into kissing Darren.

A tiny part of me fantasized about him inviting me to his bed for the night, but I wasn't expecting it. That meant I wasn't really surprised when he just waved good night and headed to his own makeshift bedroom.

It was weird to feel stung by that, right? It was a sham, after all. I knew damn well. But fuck, I'd realized now that I didn't have the kind of boundaries I thought I did. Instead of separating *kissing him for other people's sake* and *kissing him to see if I'm into guys* from *kissing him because I want him*, it was all kind of blurring together.

It felt like an artificial wall had just been plopped between us, and it was cutting me off from him. As I lay in bed, staring at the very real wall that kept us apart, I imagined that I could hear his breathing as he drifted off to sleep.

I couldn't back off now, that much was obvious. It was playing with fire, but I wanted more.

1 2

DARREN

"You'll never believe everything we had to do last week to get the plumbing situation sorted out." While I connected wires in the new box, George sat on my toolbox nearby and vented.

I didn't really mind. It made the work go faster when someone else took my mind off the mundane details of what I was doing. I'd made a few mistakes earlier in my career, but now, I was good enough not to electrocute myself by not paying a hundred percent attention.

"Yeah? It was a mess, huh?"

"Pipe burst in three places. What the hell?"

I winced. "Coordinating that's not fun."

"You better believe it." George went off on a tangent for a few minutes about all the subcontractors who had screwed him over on this particular job, and I let him do that while I double-checked my work. I'd taken the morning to do it right.

As long as no more plumbing issues cropped up, this house wasn't going to be a danger to anyone anymore. Thank God we hadn't found old wiring in the walls or anything, or it would have been a huge job. As it was, one sloppy contractor had cost the home-owners dearly.

"Hey, by the way, another job for you. Place around the corner. One of the homeowners' buddies. There's a couple of them selling some real fixer-uppers."

"Ah, when is it?" I closed the box and started gathering up my tools.

With a huge sigh, George reluctantly levered himself off his seat so I could put them away. He leaned on the wall instead. "Next Tuesday, we're gonna get in there. He thinks it's got aluminum wiring."

"Ah, shit," I mumbled. I'd made it through the week without having to explain where I was going to George, but it looked like we were about to have that special moment now. "I'd love to, but I'm gonna be away next week."

"That's all right. No sweat. The Monday after?"

I blinked a few times. I hadn't expected the homeowners to be flexible. Usually we had to show up at the time and place we were told, or they'd find someone who was available. Especially a city this big, with enough other guys to choose from. "Huh? I mean, yeah, I'll be back then."

George just smiled at me. He'd taken a chance on me when he agreed to hire a young-looking guy like me without a lifetime of dealing with quirky Brooklyn wiring under my belt. "You're good at what you do, kid. And you're easy to work with. Don't underes-timate that."

I blushed. I hadn't been prepared to handle a compliment. "Uh, thanks."

"And you didn't screw me over on this job like the other guys tried to. I'll tell 'em you're not available until then, and we'll figure out the timeline. In fact, if you'd like steady work, we could talk about hiring you on a more permanent basis."

My heart leapt. Part of me wanted that kind of work—no more scrounging for jobs, and guaranteed working hours. On the other hand, I'd made enough of a name for myself by bouncing between general contractors that I made more than a good living.

"I'll think about it. Thank you for the offer." I offered my hand to shake on it, and we headed upstairs.

"I'll send your invoice through to accounting today," George told me. "So, where you going?"

"Hawaii."

George clapped my shoulder. "Great! I've been looking for a good hotel there. My wife wants to go back to Maui. Let me know how it goes."

"Well, uh," I said with a chuckle, "it's kind of a niche place. I dunno if it's up your alley. I can ask around for recommendations, though." When George gave me a blank look, I knew he was expecting more details.

I hadn't exactly hidden it, but I didn't talk about my personal life. A lot of guys didn't, so it wasn't that weird. "It's a gay resort."

George blinked and then nodded. "Well, I dunno if my wife would be into that, but I can check." He grinned at me. "Actually, one of my wife's buddies went on this cruise thing, not long ago. And one of my guys is gay, you know that? Carl."

I resisted the urge to ask if Carl was okay with being outed to someone else as a conversational talking point. George clearly meant well. "Yeah?"

"Yeah, man." He clapped my shoulder again in that manly way. "No sweat. Hey, you know, Carl got gay-married a couple years back when it became legal. I went to the wedding. My first gay wedding. The food was great."

I bit back my smile. He was clearly trying a bit too hard, but I was glad that he wanted to make me feel welcome. That explained his eagerness to out Carl to me. A lot of people loved talking about the gay weddings they'd been to since it was legalized. "Oh yeah?"

"Yeah, poor guy. Ended up getting divorced again not long afterward. I guess they kinda rushed into it. That's the beauty of it. America. We're all free to be equally unhappy!" He laughed loudly.

Suddenly, I didn't find it nearly as funny as him. I made myself smile anyway. The last thing I wanted was a reminder of how damn fragile love was. Especially given the situation I was rushing headlong into, with Adam and Xavier and everyone. "Yeah? Sorry to hear that."

"Oh, he's a lot happier now. As long as he don't hit on any of the other guys, they don't mind. That's no problem if we hire you." Another shoulder-punch.

I smiled at George. I did genuinely appreciate that, too. "I'll keep it in mind."

"I'll try to give you a good salary. A good guy is hard to hold onto —as Carl knows," George chuckled heartily.

This was turning into whiplash of the highest degree. I kind of hoped he'd drop it soon. At least I was on my way out of the house now, picking my way around the crew who were around. "Yeah. Thanks for the offer. I've gotta figure out my schedule after I get back."

George knew I was in pretty high demand. No wonder he wanted to scoop me up as his own. "No sweat. You have fun on your gay beach."

With that, I was out of there and on my way home. The job offer was almost at the back of my mind, because I suddenly had so much to plan for.

I had to pack tonight—I'd put that off for way too long. That meant doing laundry first thing, so I'd probably just stop by home long enough to grab the laundry and go get that going. While sitting with it, I could write out a packing list.

Briefly, I wondered if I should add my dignity to that list, but it was way too late for that. Embarrassing as it was to be the guy there who couldn't even get a real boyfriend for a free trip, I was locked into whatever the hell this was with Adam.

***

I was kind of glad that Adam turned out not to be home when I got back from the laundromat with my hamper of dry clothes. I was sweating and out of breath and a complete mess.

Not that I cared what he saw me looking like—he'd seen me come home from work in this state plenty of times, especially over the summer. But it wasn't an attractive look for someone you had to fake interest in for the next week. The least I could do for him was look the part.

I'd spent nearly this whole week remembering in great detail how he'd kissed me in front of all my friends. In particular, I'd spent some time in the shower remembering exactly that.

If we got out of this with our friendship and good roommate status intact, I was going to be a lucky guy. Making Xavier give up on taunting me with his bigger, better life was just a bonus.

"Supper," I told myself. "Get your ass in gear."

Adam tended to work as late as his boss wanted him to, and I didn't blame him. Steady work was always worth bending over backwards for. And when one of us got home earlier than the other, we tended to put supper on for us both.

While I cooked, I hummed under my breath as the reality hit me: our vacation was nearly here. The weirdest vacation I'd taken in my life, but also the furthest away by far. I hadn't been out of the contiguous states before, and here I was flying all the way to Hawaii.

If I tilted my head and looked at the situation just right, my luck had changed for the better. Now to hope it stayed that way.

When Adam came back home, he was actually grinning as he walked through the door. I did a double-take. "Good evening to you, too."

"Hello, lover!" Adam proclaimed with one of those trademark obnoxious grins. "May I say how fantastic—no, how *delicious* you look and smell? Either you or supper. I can't tell."

Oh, God. He was in a mood, wasn't he? I rolled my eyes at him. "You won't get much love if you keep that up."

Adam pouted as he strode to his room. "You wound me."

"Not as deep as I'd like to," I idly threatened, trying not to laugh at him. It would only encourage him.

"Oooh." Adam turned that into an innuendo. "How many inches deep, again?"

"Shut up," I laughed, but I already knew I'd lost. In Adam's world, he didn't seem to want to be the first to flinch away from the gay joke. If I chalked his behavior up to that, it all made sense.

I didn't dare hope for anything else. Straight guys were unavailable—end of story.

When Adam came out again, he was dressed nicely. Was he actually taking my advice about dressing up better regardless? I hadn't seen him in cargo shorts since his thrift store shopping day, and he always seemed to be in a nice button-down shirt.

If it weren't for his constant joking around, I might believe my roommate had been taken away by aliens and switched for a man who actually had fashion sense. He wasn't dressing like a Wall Street guy by any means, but he no longer looked like a college kid here on spring break who'd just wandered off a plane.

"Supper smells good, though. Thanks." Adam grabbed utensils to set the table. "Sorry if I'm pissing you off."

I stared after him for a moment before deciding not to question it. If he'd decided to be a little nicer to me every day for whatever strange reason of his own, that was a win. Hearing *sorry* from him was pretty fucking rare, but if I commented on it, he might flee like a shy woodland creature. "You're welcome."

"I've got chewing gum for the flight. Last time I took a plane, my ears damn near burst out of my head." Adam beamed at me again. "And I'm all packed. You wanna see?"

"I'll help a bit, but I trust your new and improved fashion sense," I told him, waving my hand. Dressing the part wasn't as important as he seemed to think it was, but I didn't blame him for wanting to fit the stereotype. "You've got your costumes?"

"You bet." Adam grinned and flexed his biceps and pecs. "And my costume body."

I desperately tried to ignore him. Lord, I was going to faint if I saw him do that without a shirt on. I'd utterly failed at getting laid before we left, and with nothing to take the edge off, his teasing was going to get to me that much more.

And to be honest, I didn't even mind it that much. Being sexually frustrated around Adam beat throwing myself at the nearest guy —a la my history with Xavier. At least I felt good about myself, however much Adam teased and bantered.

"You looking forward to it?" Adam asked as I brought plates of pasta to the table and sat across from him. I tried not to think of it as a date-like setup, but with the dish of water and floating candle I'd added to the table, it felt oddly romantic. Especially when he'd carefully arranged the utensils instead of flinging them onto the table like usual.

"Yeah." I had plenty of reservations, but it wasn't stretching the truth to say that much. "Yeah, more than anything."

"Great." Adam flashed his bright grin at me, and I couldn't help but let that tide of optimism carry me away. "Everything will be perfect, then."

Oh, how I hoped he was right.

ADAM

I wasn't great at reading people, but I was starting to understand how to tell how Darren was feeling. Spending a lot of time around him was no doubt helping with that, but also—unlike how I felt about most people, I wanted to know whether he was doing good or not.

"Nearly on board," I said cheerily as I rolled my carry-on bag along behind me. We were walking down the gangway to the plane, having gotten through the worst of the airport experience.

Darren had grown more and more quiet over the last couple hours, and I was starting to worry. He wasn't having doubts about me, was he? Or the trip? I was going to do everything I could to make him feel like he'd made the right choice in walking away from Xavier.

Oh, wait. Maybe that was what was on his mind.

"You want the aisle or the window?"

"Aisle," I said. "Then I can grab extra drinks when the cart goes by." I winked. "Do we get free drinks?"

"We do, but God help me, you're not going to get drunk on the plane," Darren told me sternly.

I grinned. "What trouble could I possibly get into... Okay, I see your point."

At least Darren was livelier now, and as I stowed my bag and waited for him to take his seat, I ogled the seats nearby. "Oooh. This is fancier."

"Told you it was business class."

"Yeah, but this is like... *really* fancy." I hadn't envisioned this. I'd had no idea what to expect at all. Apparently my taste in getaways was luxury. Good to know, if useless—no way in hell was I traveling again anytime soon after this.

"Shh. The louder you talk about how fancy it is, the more obvious it is we don't fit in," Darren whispered.

I grinned at him. "Really? The gay dudes in beachwear don't fit in with the dudes who look like they're gonna be making Powerpoint presentations the whole way there?"

Darren chuckled and rested his head on the side of the aircraft. "Oh, it's gonna be a long flight."

"I'll make the time fly by," I promised.

"That's what I'm afraid of."

I laughed as I settled in and found my seatbelt. Before I could even buckle up, the flight attendant was stopping by. "Can I offer you Champagne or orange juice?"

Since *both* didn't seem to be the right answer, I opted for Champagne, trying not to get giddy about the free booze. Darren rolled his eyes at me and took orange juice.

"What?" I whispered when she'd left. "This is sweet!"

"You're not trying to be adorable, are you?"

I blinked at him a few times, trying to decide how to take that comment. It definitely wasn't meant to be an insult. Was it a compliment, or was he just practicing for the week ahead? Did it start now? "It just comes naturally," I settled on and finished my flute of Champagne as fast as it would go down.

"Whoa, cowboy," Darren laughed as I set the empty plastic glass on the arm of my chair and grinned at him.

"Okay, now that you're talking to me, tell me what's got you all clammed up."

Darren squinted at me. "I wasn't clammed up."

"You so were." I adjusted my seat backwards and forwards. "Whoa, this is great."

Darren hit the button to bring my seat up and sighed at me. "I see what you're doing. You just want to make me talk so you don't do embarrassing things."

"Is it working?" I went back again. With no one sitting behind us yet, I didn't feel bad about doing it.

Despite trying to give me a stern look, Darren was fighting back a smile. I could tell because the corners of his eyes crinkled and his top lip started to disappear under the bottom. "Fine. Yes."

I zinged my way back up and beamed at him. "Great."

"It's Xavier. I'm gonna be seeing him soon, and... you know, despite this whole plan... he *did* come out better than me. I've got a nicer house now, sure. It looks cute on Instagram. I sound like I have my life together. But do I really?"

I raised my eyebrow. "Steady job," I ticked off my fingers.

"Contracting. Actually..." Darren trailed off and shook his head.

When I waited pointedly for him to explain, he sighed. "One of my companies offered me a full-time job."

"They still call you steadily. It counts," I told him firmly. "And getting offered a job means they really like you. So yeah, steady work." I raised another finger. "Place to live. Not the best roommate, but you could have six roommates in a tin can in Manhattan."

He raised his hands near his shoulders in a shrug and didn't argue.

"Food, bills paid, friends who care about you." With five fingers ticked off, I waved my hand in his face. "Talk to the hand. Did I do that right?"

"That's not even—" Darren burst out laughing, which was exactly what I was hoping for. "Dude."

I smirked at him and folded my arms. "So what if you don't have some catty little thing trying to prove he owns you? Whatever. Ain't nobody got time for those mind games, girl."

"You're picking this up scary fast," Darren muttered. He finally ran his hand down my arm. "But… thanks."

It was an intimate gesture—more than a friend might do, but then, I wasn't really familiar with how gay guys acted with each other. Last weekend, everyone dancing with each other had seemed so comfortable and touchy compared to what I was used to.

Being a part of that—of *this*—was something special.

"I'm nervous as hell to walk around in glorified Speedos and a sailor's hat," I told him with a grin. But he'd picked the outfits, and I trusted his eye. "And I'm worried I won't fit in, and they won't wanna hang with the awkward basically-straight guy. But you know what? Fuck 'em. At the end of the week, we go and have fun in the sun with our water sports of the clear blue type, and beaches, and all-you-can-eat buffets."

Darren's smile slowly grew as I talked. That nervous, self-conscious man I'd been waiting next to at the gate for the last hour all but disappeared. "Yeah. Even though we won our place there…"

"Oh, hell no, you aren't getting insecure about that," I informed him. "You won it fair and square. If you're the only winner, that actually makes *you* special. Everyone will wanna rub off on you and get a bit of your luck. Or rub one off on you." I winked. "You're lucky either way."

Darren grinned at me. "You know what? You're right. I've got you on my arm—that makes me the luckiest guy there."

For a moment, I couldn't breathe. It was like nobody else on the plane even existed. I couldn't quite figure out what he'd said at first, and then whether he was serious. But no, I *had* just heard him say that.

"I'm serious," Darren added with a smile when it had clearly been a few seconds and I didn't respond. "You're hot as fuck, and I'm proud to have you there with me. Doesn't matter what anyone else thinks we are, you know? Fuck 'em all."

I let out my breath and laughed, casting around frantically for a joke to break up the seriousness of the moment. It was all so much to take in. *Too* much. I couldn't remember the last time anyone had said they wanted me around, let alone that they were proud of me.

"Yeah," I managed weakly, just so I had something to say. "Fuck 'em all. Just tell me to keep out of the room first if you bring a guy back."

Darren snorted at me. "I won't toss you out."

"Oh, I thought you were gonna finish that sentence differently." I pretended to pout. "I was wondering what I did wrong."

"I doubt you'd want me to," Darren snorted. That look was back in his eye again—the one that said he felt like he deserved to be used by Xavier. Whether or not Xavier knew it, that was how Darren had seen it, and it had obviously done a number on him. God, I wanted to twist off the prick's… well, prick.

The seatbelt sign came on and I buckled up, then took another glass of Champagne while it was going past. This time, Darren took one too, and stopped me before I sipped. He held out his glass in a toast. "To new beginnings."

That was a cryptic toast if I'd ever heard one. I wasn't even gonna try to make sense of it. "To new beginnings… and happy endings," I smirked just when he was drinking.

He choked and clapped a hand over his mouth as he coughed, barely keeping his Champagne down. "You bastard."

"That's what I'm here for. Keeping things interesting." I quaffed my drink and settled back.

I felt good. Time to rock this thing.

***

I waited until near the end of the trip to bring up the Xavier thing again. We had a lot of more interesting ground to cover first, like talking about our favorite childhood memories, swapping school stories, that kind of stuff.

It was good to finally get a chance to get to know the man I was living with. We both spent so much time at work, and not always during the same hours, that we didn't get a chance to connect like this very often.

But the more we talked, the more I saw that sly sense of humor, and Darren's unflappable good-natured attitude. I couldn't seem to wind him up, because he'd always find a way to puncture a hole in what I said and do it with a smile.

It really shouldn't have been that hot.

"So, you think you'll meet a new boyfriend while you're out here?" I offered him a light smile, trying to ignore how I felt about it. The topic made my heart heavy, but it might cheer him up.

"What? Me? No," Darren said with a short, sharp laugh. "I can't find one when I'm desperate in my own home turf, let alone on vacation."

"A little holiday fling?" I winked. "A vacation romance might make you feel better."

Darren shook his head. "Is it weird to say it'd feel like cheating? Even though we're not together?"

I blinked a few times and then swallowed. The more he did this, the more I was starting to feel like it was an actual relationship, and I wasn't sure I could handle that. "Not weird, no," I finally managed. "We gotta convince everyone else it's real, after all."

"Yeah." Darren avoided looking at me for a few moments, rubbing his nails like he wanted to polish them. "But no. I don't know. I might take a year or two off dating, work on myself."

"What is there to work on?" I might not have asked this question had we been totally sober and on the ground, but the atmosphere between us felt easy. It was like we were in a bubble of our own, outside of time zones and normalcy.

We could say whatever we wanted here, and it didn't feel real.

Except *that*. I couldn't tell him that.

"I feel like maybe Xavier's all I deserve. I mean, I've failed at finding anyone else, and he found a new boyfriend in, like, two days."

I shook my head. "Dude, that is *so* the wrong approach. Even I can tell that."

"Why?"

I folded my hands and hoped I didn't sound as drunk as I felt. God, altitude made that Champagne kick in fast. "Because… It's quality, not quantity. Going for boyfriends because you don't wanna be alone is a stupid idea."

Darren looked almost offended for a few moments before his frown softened. He gazed at the back of the seat ahead of him, and then he finally looked back at me. "Yeah. It is. But you have to keep trying, right?"

"Not if you're forcing it. Like with Xavier, it meant something wasn't right, you know?"

Darren nodded.

"I know what it feels like to force it." This was the closest I was gonna get to admitting it. "Sometimes, I… I've been with girls, and I'm not really into it, but I wanna get off. For a one-time thing, that's all right. You both know you're using each other. That's why Netflix and chill was invented." *Not for cuddling with the line cook at the local diner. Good thing I'm drunk or I might start blushing.* I cleared my throat. "But dating? No. What do you want from dating?"

"What do I want?" Darren looked like he hadn't thought about that. "Uh, a boyfriend?"

"And then?"

Darren narrowed his eyes. "I guess maybe engagement, or

marriage. I don't really want a church wedding, but legal protections are nice."

I nodded and waved the words off. "But basically a lifetime thing, yeah?"

"Yeah."

"If you'd stayed with Xavier, wouldn't you wake up when you're forty and look in the mirror and realize you've just been *making it work* this whole time instead of... you know, enjoying it? And him? And even yourself?"

Oh, God. I was talking to myself. Fuck.

It wasn't that I wasn't attracted to girls. I knew damn well that I was. But by shutting off part of myself and never acknowledging it to myself, let alone them, I was living half a life. And there was no way to fix that, except to... at the very least, come to terms with it myself. And then try it out and see how it felt. And then maybe come out.

At the very least, I had to be open to finding love in some other form—like Darren. If the two of us had only been really dating? Hell, yeah, we'd be good together. But the real me was never gonna be happy with pretending to be anything, whether that was fake boyfriends or fake straight.

"You're right."

Thank God Darren was staring at his hands again and not my face, because I was pretty sure I looked like I was having an epiphany, or maybe a hands-free orgasm. My jaw just wanted to drop, and my eyes were wide. My cheeks flushed, my palms damp.

This felt like the kind of moment I couldn't ignore. Even tomorrow when I sobered up and got over the hangover, I was going to remember thinking, *I'm not straight, am I?*

"What about you?"

"What?" My voice cracked with nerves and I laughed, dabbing my palms on my pants. "What about me?"

"Do you wanna… you know, get engaged?"

"I figure we see how the week plays out before you ask me the big questions." I smirked at him, but this time, he didn't smirk back.

Darren just looked thoughtful for a few moments. Oh, shit. *Now* he was looking at me. What was he seeing?

I prayed to God he was seeing his obnoxious straight roommate who could never take a moment seriously.

Darren finally grinned. "Smartass," he told me, but I couldn't shake the feeling that he was deliberately saving my pride by not asking more. He closed his eyes and settled back in his seat, clearly planning to enjoy the last hour in peace and quiet.

Which left me wondering what the hell to do about myself, and when, and how, and most of all… with whom?

It was getting pretty damn obvious that I was at least romantically attracted to guys. Whenever Darren said something romantic to me, my stupid knees went wobbly. But dating wasn't just romance —at least, not for me. I'd gotten scared away from doing anything sexual with Ricky, and I'd never even tried to envision myself doing it before then.

Could I do the sex part of it? With another guy? I was clearly not about to find out with Darren, but the more I thought about it, the more I wished I could.

When I tried to think about my type, Darren popped into my head. When I jerked it in the shower and imagined fucking a guy —or, to be painfully honest in a way I rarely was even with myself, imagined *being* fucked by a guy—it was Darren.

Maybe it was a psychological thing and I was finding the nearest gay guy to bond with. Maybe it was because Darren was so damn close, and we'd made out a few times, and there were some weird dopamine or whatever chemicals floating around our brains.

Or maybe it was Darren.

Life could be a hell of a lot simpler if I just had the guts to say anything to him, but for all the bravery I pretended to have when the world got in my face, I didn't feel much of it inside. Deep down, I was a scared little boy who would never be able to admit to who or what I was.

I folded my arms tightly as I leaned back in my seat. If I was gonna do this self-hatred thing, I may as well get a good nap instead. I was gonna need all the rest I could get once we landed.

And a bucket full of luck.

DARREN

Our room at the resort was nice and all, but I had one major problem: there was a king-sized bed. One bed, for the two of us. Well, two problems, really… the other was that I was going to lose my damn mind if I didn't rub one out in the next ten minutes.

An entire day of Adam acting so much the part that it kind of thrilled me how easily he'd fallen into the role was great, but he was also being a cocktease. And I got the feeling that with his wicked sense of humor, he was enjoying it.

I'd called the shower first, leaving him to sprawl on the bed and probably text people photos of the room. I desperately needed to get clean after a day of hauling our luggage to the airport, drinking too much Champagne on the plane, and then sweating our way to the resort.

Clean hair was almost orgasmic at this point. After I scrubbed from head to toe, I took a minute to enjoy the luxurious heat of the shower. It was a walk-in marble thing of beauty with rainfall jets. Even the bathroom counter was huge, with a double sink. There was a separate tub. To me, that said luxury.

And drains that could definitely handle a few loads throughout the week. Then, even as I thought it, guilt snuck into the back of my mind. I was usually pretty good at ignoring it for long enough to jerk off, but it wouldn't go away.

Jerking off to my roommate just felt weird. However much he seemed to be coming on to me, I had to keep reminding myself that this was fake. Otherwise I might start to get a serious crush on him, and I couldn't afford that. He was just going to move on with his life in a week's time. I had to be ready to do the same thing.

Hell, he'd casually asked if I was going to find a *real* boyfriend in my week here. He had no idea how much I wanted to tell him that was the last thing I wanted.

I shut off the water and stepped out, grabbing a fluffy towel to wrap up in as I felt sorry for myself. Here I was, trying to feel miserable at the beginning of a gorgeous week on vacation. If nothing else, we were gonna have fun doing something ridiculous and silly and making Xavier realize what he'd missed out on. How cool was that?

And under no circumstances was I going to do anything dumb relating to Adam. No way.

Was it weird that I was kind of self-conscious? I hesitated to turn the handle and head back out, just because I wasn't fully-dressed. Given what we were going to see each other in throughout the week, that was dumb.

I wrapped the towel around my waist, fluffed up my hair, and headed back out to join him. "The shower's awesome," I told him.

"This bed is even better!" Adam rolled back and forth over it. "Look, I can roll like five times and not even get to the edge!"

I rolled my eyes as I crouched by my suitcase to unzip it and grab fresh clothes. "If you get a concussion and have to lie around in a dark room staring at the wall, I'm not keeping you company."

"That's boyfriend cruelty," Adam lamented. "If I get a concussion, you should bring me soup and read to me."

I laughed and dropped my towel, stepping into my shorts. When I glanced back at Adam, he was staring straight up at the ceiling, his cheeks pink.

To make it less awkward for him, I hurried through dressing as I grabbed the first t-shirt I saw. Once I was dressed, I tossed the towel onto a hook on the wall and crashed on the other side of the bed.

"Are you okay?" Adam asked after a minute. His expression was inscrutable.

That was out of the blue. I blinked at him a few times. "Yeah?"

"I was gonna check on you in the shower if you took much longer."

"Oh," I laughed. "Told you the shower was great. Rainfall head."

Adam grinned. "No way. I can't wait for tonight. Tomorrow. This morning. Whatever the hell time it is. I can't keep them straight."

I nodded. Today was the first day of the party, and it was only early afternoon—but to my body, it was the middle of the night. Maybe the next day by now. Fatigue was already tugging my eyes shut. Everything felt surreal, even more than it had on the plane when I'd still been drunk.

Now I was just tired and ready for bed, but it was only four in the afternoon. No way could I let myself crash now, or this week would be brutal.

Adam scooted closer to me and put his hand on my arm. Who the hell was this guy, anyway? I wasn't complaining, but it was a surprise. Apparently all I'd needed to do for Adam to become a sweetheart was pretend to date him.

"If Xavier approaches, how do you want me to handle it? Because I'm tempted to punch him in the nose."

I grinned and shook my head. "Please don't. That would complicate the situation." Adam mumbled something about it simplifying the situation but didn't argue. "Just act, you know… normal. Without being a dick to him," I quickly added.

Adam snickered. "How'd you know me so well?"

"I'm good like that," I told him. Adam was stroking my arm slowly, like the hair along my forearm had mesmerized him. He'd been doing it for a minute, so I was pretty sure he didn't even realize he was doing it now.

It was also incredibly distracting. His touch was firm and warm, and all too easily, I could envision it elsewhere on my body. It was a lot harder to keep my libido in check when he was acting more affectionate than Xavier had—or any other ex, come to think of it.

"What? You're frowning." Adam's touch slowed, and he rubbed the back of my hand.

I tried not to laugh, but it didn't work. When he raised his eyebrows, I shook my head at him. "Look, it's been a long time since a man touched me like this. I'm trying not to get horny and make everything between us awkward."

Instead of the *eww, gross* or the joking I expected, Adam just smiled, his hand going still on my arm. "Sorry. Has it really been that long?"

"I moved in with you, what, six weeks ago?"

"Yeah, but…" Adam trailed off. "Really? Nobody since him?"

"Since my last pity-fuck from him, you mean?" Oops, there it was —the bitterness I was trying so hard to keep in check. I gritted my teeth, but when Adam didn't roll his eyes or laugh at me, the dam burst. "That's all it was, you know."

"I'm sure he genuinely found you attractive. Anyone would," Adam said quietly. He was still touching me, but I was trying my hardest not to see that as a signal. Adam was oblivious enough to the world that I couldn't rely on the usual flirting signals.

"Maybe, or I was just close by and not ugly." I shook my head when Adam tried to scoot closer. "I knew it was wrong. When we dated, I mean. I knew I didn't feel anything for him deep down, but I… I hoped that would grow. And I was afraid of being alone."

Adam sucked in his breath. He was silent now, but he ran his hand down my arm to lace his fingers with mine. For whatever reason, he didn't mind listening to me whining.

"And after we broke up… Xavier still turned me on. I didn't have any better options. But that's all it was. Cheap. *I* felt cheap." Oh, I hadn't expected my chest to tighten or my throat to close with the emotions I thought I'd buried long ago.

"You aren't." Adam's voice was soft and sad as he squeezed my hand. "What he did to you isn't what you are."

I bit my lip. "Yeah, but I let him." There was no way anyone could talk me out of that knowledge. "And I never told him that was how I felt. He thought it was just intense regret-fueled breakup sex: closure, in its own way, if you're both on the same page. It was no-strings-attached fun."

"And you felt like he was using you?"

There were no better words to describe it than those. I closed my eyes for a few moments and nodded. "My heart got caught up. It does that too easily."

"Darren, none of that is your fault," Adam murmured. "You deserve better. Someone who sees your heart is on your sleeve and respects you."

"I should have figured out that he didn't make me happy sooner and then done something about it." I'd lingered for too long instead, indulging in self-torment by seeing my ex go about his successful life in the day and come to my room at night for easy sex.

It had been all too easy for me, too. Easier than moving out and moving on, picking up the pieces and figuring out what I really wanted from my next relationship. All I had to do was say yes and get my dick out and I got to feel good for the next hour, however much my stomach twisted with regret and guilt that night.

"I'm done taking the easy option," I murmured, rubbing my eyes with my free hand. "Next time, I choose who I date, and I find someone who..."

Someone who gives a shit about me, I'd been about to say. And then, like a thunderbolt, I'd realized that Adam—the unflappable joke-ster who kept everyone at arms-length, the straight guy who'd made fun of Kev's gay hookups while they lived together—was lying on the bed with me, cuddling me because I felt like shit.

What I really meant was someone like Adam.

Adam was stroking my arm again, and I was getting fucking turned on by the light touch of fingers on my bare skin. "D-Dude," I laughed breathily. "What'd I say?"

Adam gave me a grin, but there was a nervous look in his eye as he pulled back his hand. "Sorry. If you're that desperate to get laid..." He gestured around at the room, no doubt indicating the resort that lay beyond.

I shook my head. "I told you, I don't want to. But I don't wanna make things weird between us." No way was I gonna be the one to hit on him first. I'd only validate what guys like Adam tended to think—that we gay guys were just waiting for the first chance to jump their bones. Like straight guys dressed smart enough for that.

Okay, maybe I'd jump *Adam's* bones, but not most straight guys.

"It doesn't have to be weird. Guys jerk off together all the time," Adam said with a casual shrug. "Well, maybe not all the time, but sometimes."

"Are you serious?" No way was he serious. My heart rose into my throat, like it was trying to make a great escape. He hadn't touched me again yet, but he wasn't laughing at me or anything. Was *Adam* coming on to me? Hell, had that been what he was up to these past couple weeks?

"Whatever stops you from having wet dreams in my bed, dude," Adam grinned.

I scowled. I should have known he was just taking a chance to make a joke out of me. "I'm not some desperate horndog. Jesus. I've been trying to keep my distance from you. You're the one who's been making out with me."

"You want me to stop?" Adam challenged, raising his chin in a defiant expression. "Act like any old buddies when we're alone?"

Fuck. I hadn't tried to separate how we acted alone from the public image before, but now that I was thinking about it, I didn't. I wanted Adam, one way or another.

Adam smirked. "I thought not. And I'm not suffering through it. I've… I've been learning a lot."

I raised my eyebrows, my lips parting into a small *o* shape. "Wha… what?"

Now, Adam wouldn't meet my gaze. He cleared his throat and shifted a few times on the bed like he couldn't find a way to get comfortable. He wiped his palms on his shirt, too. Was he really that nervous? That wasn't the attitude of a guy who was trying to wind me up. "I... I've always been curious," was all he said. "But whatever, no pressure. I know there's better choices all over here..."

"Shut up," I snorted. "You're the best kisser I've met."

Adam grinned. "Am I?" That set his ego on fire. "Especially in front of all your buddies, huh? I did a good job?" Now he was just milking the compliment, but not in a way that made me feel bad that he'd turned me on.

"Whatever the hell you're playing at, it's working." My breath caught as I looked over at him. This was the line I'd been struggling not to cross. We'd only come up against it a couple times since the whole plan was hatched—and that one time before, when we'd wrestled on the floor.

Oh, God, I remembered that all too well right now.

"Yeah?" Adam's lips were parted, and they looked extremely kissable. He shifted onto his side. "You actually find me... hot?"

I tried not to laugh. That was a hell of an understatement. "Well, now that you're dressing like you might appreciate a good rimjob, yeah."

Adam giggled and put his hand on mine again. "I don't wanna rush into things."

"You? Take anything slow?" I pretended to be shocked. "I expected you'd have me bent over the bed by now."

Adam's eyes widened and his nails dug into my wrist. Just for a moment, but long enough that my body flushed with heat. "That can wait 'til later. We have a week here, you know. Not exactly no-strings-attached—and if you don't feel good about it, we stop."

I smiled to myself. I already felt better about him than I ever had when I was with Xavier, but he was sweet for worrying. Every bit of him was attractive in ways that I couldn't make sense of. "Yeah."

We were both quiet for a few moments, gazes flickering between each other's eyes. I realized how damn close he really was, and how easy it would be to kiss him.

Adam licked his lips slowly and swallowed, looking at my lips and then back to my eyes. His hand ran up my arm to rest on my elbow.

He *wanted* me to kiss him.

And, God help me, I wanted to kiss him, taste him, touch him, and give him the best orgasms of his life.

I closed my eyes and gave in.

ADAM

What the hell was I doing?

Not only had I just admitted that I wasn't straight, but I'd pretty much asked Darren if I could help him release his sexual frustration for the next week.

In all my half-baked imaginings of how this conversation would go, Darren had laughed and reminded me that I wasn't all that. He could do so much better than me, but here he was smiling at me, acting like he genuinely liked spending time with me. Holding me like he would a lover.

Kissing me like he was going to fuck me slowly and tenderly.

I whimpered quietly at the thought and pressed my mouth harder against his, grabbing the back of his head. I was so fucking turned on just knowing what was coming—even if I had no idea what that was.

Something sexy. If we both got off and felt good afterward, I didn't care about the details.

"Adam," Darren gasped when my hand tightened in his hair. "That gives me dirty ideas."

"What, like…" I trailed off, imagining his head bobbing over my crotch, my dick between his lips. Oh, I liked that idea a lot. "Yeah?" I gently released him and stroked his cheek.

I wasn't going to take advantage of him. He could be sleep-deprived, not thinking straight. And he'd just gotten emotional about Xavier. Sticking to something quick and easy, like jerking each other off, was a way better plan. If he didn't hate me in the morning, we could figure it out from there.

Darren looked disappointed for a moment, but then he kissed my lower lip gently. "Tell me what you're thinking."

"That these sweatpants are awfully pointy somewhere." I grinned, fully aware that I wasn't wearing underwear. I'd changed in an awful hurry, after all. All I had to do was shift the way my knees pointed and my problem became obvious.

"Oh," Darren gasped. He actually seemed to like the sight, because his hand drifted towards his own crotch. He rubbed himself slowly as he looked me up and down. He still looked nervous, though. Like he expected it all to crash down at any moment.

If only I could show him how deep inside me the buttons he was hitting were. So fucking deep I hadn't admitted them before. This was everything I'd wanted and then some, and we hadn't even done anything yet.

"Kiss me," I whispered, trying not to sound like a damn virgin.

He smiled and did just that, his lips warm and soft. Eventually, I couldn't stop myself—my hand wandered south, too, and I rubbed myself through the thick fabric of my sweatpants. Nice, but I needed more.

Darren's hand rested on my bare stomach, making me gasp. My

shirt had slid up, and I hadn't known I was so sensitive there. All it took was the lightest touch trailing toward my waistband and I whimpered his name, trying not to feel self-conscious about the way he was making me melt with every damn thing he tried.

"You're hot," Darren whispered. "No matter what you wear. I looked at you before that—that night on the floor. But I never really *saw* you until then."

I knew exactly the one he meant. I grinned up at him. "Something about seeing me under you awakened a fire in you?"

"Oh, yes," Darren growled. That tone wiped the smirk off my face and made my cock twitch as my whole body throbbed with pleasure. I wanted him to show me all the things he'd been fantasizing about that day to make him get a hard-on like that.

"I'm glad you asked me," I murmured. "I'm the worst gay on the island, but God, do I wanna learn how to blend in."

Darren's hand was under my waistband now. He twisted where he lay on the bed so he could run his fingers down across the patch of curly hair, and then… his fingertips were closing around the hard shaft.

I swallowed my whimper and turned it into a short, sharp moan.

"You're learning pretty damn fast," Darren whispered.

I moaned. "Instinct. Desperation to get laid. It's been way too long." Just in time, I remembered my light fiction-weaving about having dates who actually slept with me. Since he'd moved in, I hadn't actually had a successful home run. And then there was the utterly failed attempt with Ricky.

Although I was nervous, it felt like the right moment to try. My gut instinct wasn't just trying to shut me down—it was hollering for me to be bold.

So I reached out and rubbed his leg, searching for his dick. It didn't take long to find the swell against the fabric of his shorts. I tugged gently on them, and he shifted to help me get them down.

There was his cock—exposed to the open air, hard and thick. I took it in my hand and stroked slowly, getting used to the weight of it. *It's like slamming another button I never knew I had*, I thought, marveling at how good it felt for me to stroke another man's cock. I loved watching his expression shift as he caught his breath and moaned.

"Oh, fuck," I gasped. He'd recovered his composure enough to tighten his grip on me. He was stroking in a firm, confident rhythm now, like he wanted to be in charge.

I couldn't disagree. I flopped on the pillows as he sat up next to me, still fondling his cock, but not trying to maintain a steady rhythm. Not when he was doing such incredible things as he jacked me off—twisting his wrist and rubbing his thumb across sensitive spots that made me squirm.

It was all I could do to keep stroking him. I felt clumsy in comparison, but he didn't seem to mind that I was clearly going to get there first. My strokes finally slowed down as I found myself needing to grab his shoulders. "Darren. Fuck. That's good."

"You like it?" Darren grinned, leaning down on his elbow to kiss me.

Yes. Kissing was what I'd been missing. I gasped into his mouth, kissing him with all the energy I had left, letting him sweep me away on a tide of pleasure I'd only ever imagined before.

My orgasm snuck up on me. One moment, I was gasping for breath, my muscles tightening, my brain shutting off every other response besides *yes* and *I need him*. The next, everything gave way at once and I gasped, thrusting up into his hand as I damn well covered myself in a hot, sticky mess.

He must have been horny as fuck, because as soon as he let go of me, he kicked his shorts off and stroked himself hard and fast.

I fumbled to lift my t-shirt to my chest, baring my stomach. "Come on me."

"Are you sure?"

I hadn't known I wanted it, but now all I could picture was his cum landing on me. Him marking me as his boyfriend—if only fake—for the week. Something inside me needed that. Just like when he'd grabbed me at the club and glared at the guy who wanted to hit on me, I wanted his every ounce of attention on me. I wanted him to see his juices streaked across my smooth skin.

"Please," I gasped. One look at the hunger in my eyes made him reconsider asking me twice.

Darren swung his leg over me to straddle me, his hand pumping up and down the pink shaft. He grunted, his hand curling around my bicep as he leaned down for a kiss.

"That's it, baby," I whispered, fascinated by it—and by how much I loved it. What the hell had I been missing my whole life? "Wanna see you lose control."

Triumph flooded me when he couldn't hold back a second longer. He grunted and threw his head back, kneeling back. That gave me the best view of all, from underneath, as his load spilled from the tip of his shaft. The first jet nearly landed on my shirt, and I hastily yanked it further up, but his aim improved as he stroked himself until the last of his mess had joined my own.

"Think you're gonna need that shower now," Darren chuckled, his voice deep.

I grinned, my heart soaring as I sat up carefully. Oh, man. "I think you're right." I ambled to the shower, looking behind me quickly enough to catch a glimpse of him checking out my ass.

Though I left the door open as I showered, he left me in peace until I got out, fresh and clean and wrapped in one of those luxurious towels.

It quickly became apparent why. When I walked out again, I found him fast asleep. I grinned, considering whether I should wake him up. But the flight had been hell. If we had a long night and an early morning, that wasn't the worst thing in the world.

When I turned the lights off and joined Darren in bed, he stirred. "Hmm. Sleeping?" he murmured. His voice was quiet and rough.

"Yeah. You're already halfway to passed out." I grinned and fluffed up my pillows as I settled down.

"You liked that, though?"

It took me a moment to realize he meant our sexy encounter, not the shower. "Yeah! Dude, that was awesome." With the lights off and real blackout curtains—that was how I knew it was a luxury room—I couldn't see him. It made it even easier to spill my guts to him. "I tried to hook up with a guy before."

"Oh?" Darren shifted, probably turning toward me.

"I got too nervous," I mumbled. "Just cuddled."

Darren caught his breath. He didn't laugh, though. If he was grinning at my dumb ass, I didn't have to know about it. "That's so sweet. Why get so nervous?"

No way was I going there. If we started this conversation, we'd be here all night. My brain made Darren's relationship history look neat and tidy. I was never going to figure out all my issues, and once I opened that Pandora's box, I was just gonna feel like shit about them. Darren didn't deserve to hear that sorry monologue. He deserved someone less… well, less broken than me.

"I better get to sleep," I said instead.

"Mm," Darren hummed. Then an arm slid over my shoulders, and Darren's breathing was closer to my ear.

Just before I drifted off to sleep, I decided I liked this. All of it. The package deal. Darren *was* the package deal. If only I was the kind of guy eligible for it.

I liked waking up with my face pressed into someone else's arm. It just took me a moment to realize why I needed to sneeze.

Darren's arm hairs were tickling my nostrils. *Oh, shit—*

Too late. I sneezed so hard that it felt like I'd just had the wind kicked out of me. One of my ribcage muscles wasn't too happy about the sudden, violent sneeze, and it wasn't the only one. At least I was facing away from Darren, but the sudden sound jolted him awake.

"Jesus!"

"Sorry," I mumbled, pushing his arm from my neck down to my torso. "You tickled my nose. Don't those get caught up in your wiring?"

Darren let out a breath as he lay flat again and let go of me. "Sure, blame me. I try not to drag my arms along live wires, so… no."

"I dunno, you had yours around me," I murmured with a grin and turned to face him. This was the moment we'd figure out exactly how awkward the rest of the week was going to be.

Darren was just smiling at me. "You *are* a live wire, aren't you?" he agreed. "But worth the risk."

Damn it, he was going to make me blush. I pushed the covers away and jumped out of bed—which required some awkward squirming to get to the edge of the bed first, since we'd wound up right in the middle. It was light outside, but it looked like morning. "Fuck. How long did we sleep?"

"When was the last time you slept in?" Darren covered his yawn with his arm.

That was a good point. I got mostly enough sleep these days, now that I wasn't racing from job to job, but even so… "Yeah. Point taken."

"And we missed a night on the plane. Someone was too busy drinking all the free Champagne that came within sight."

I grinned. No way was I gonna pass up that opportunity. "You better believe it." God, I felt a hundred times more awake than I had when we'd arrived.

And it wasn't just that. Now that I'd at least told Darren a part of that huge secret I'd kept for so many years, my chest was lighter. A huge lie was gone. I hadn't told Darren that I wanted him, not just any guy, and I hadn't told him how long I'd been curious… but I'd told him something.

It was a start.

And Darren was still acting perfectly comfortable and happy around me. It hadn't gotten weird like I'd feared. He was just affectionate, and damn, that felt nice. I'd been comfortable teasing and joking around with him, and being myself… and now it was like I'd let down one more wall, only to find that it was nothing at all.

"You know," I said, finally heading over to sit on the edge of the bed, "I liked last night."

We'd made a habit of not talking about what we did afterward. That had to stop. Otherwise, he'd never feel like he could tell me if he felt like I was using him. I didn't want that.

"Yeah?" Darren's smile was cautious.

"I wanna do it again sometime."

"Mmm." Darren seemed hesitant to outright agree. He yawned and stretched, avoiding my gaze. That was more the attitude I'd expected yesterday, but he'd been so nonchalant about it all until now... What the hell had gotten into his head while we slept?

I wasn't going to push the issue yet. "We've got a week. We'll talk later."

"You're thirsty, huh?" Darren grinned at me. "I never knew."

Really? Apparently I hadn't been too obvious when I grabbed him and kissed the daylights out of him in Friction. I was starting to wonder if Darren was just as oblivious as me. Maybe all guys were, regardless of their sexuality—gay, straight, bi, undecided.

Undecided about some things, yeah. I wasn't undecided about the fact that I wanted him. I flopped onto the bed next to him. "God, yeah." My stomach rumbled, reminding me that I hadn't eaten since the plane. "But you know what I want even more?"

Darren laughed. "Holy shit, that was loud. Breakfast?"

"Got it in one!" I bounced to my feet to find a change of nice clothes from my suitcase. "They've got a buffet breakfast, right? And we've gotta explore the place and find it first."

"I'm sold. Let's go."

DARREN

We were nearly the first at breakfast. It was actually a bit of a surprise to see anyone else awake, and judging from the startled expressions of everyone we encountered—all three of them—they felt the same way.

It didn't take long before I'd served myself up a plate of breakfast foods. Fried eggs, hash browns, a bunch of meat, and French toast. I loaded up with toast and grabbed a mug of coffee from the carafe. "Should we go meet people?"

Adam looked nervous. He'd shadowed me through the buffet, and he stepped a little closer to me as I made this suggestion. "Sure."

"Just relax," I said with a smile. "Be yourself. Okay, mostly yourself."

That made Adam crack a grin, at least. "Oh, fuck off." He straightened up. "Someone very knowledgeable told me before I left the room that I look the part, thank you very much."

"There we go." I winked. "Better." I nodded toward the nearest table and smiled. "I'll be over there. Coffee's over there."

"Coffee!" Adam did an about-face to head for the carafes while I laughed and went for the table. Already, the guys were pulling out chairs for us and greeting me.

The three of them had come together, all from the north of England. Their accents were a bit hard to understand, but I loved hearing it.

"Aha. So you guys are even more screwed up than we are, time-zone-wise," said Raymond.

"Yeah. You should see how long the flight was."

"Ours was… eleven?" I looked at Adam, who was approaching the table. "From New York City, both of us."

Raymond brightened up. "I thought I recognized the accent. I've been there."

I liked meeting tourists. It was always nice to hear what other people thought of your city. "Yeah? Did you like it?"

"A lot like London, but Manhattan has a better street layout. Nice and logical." Jerry made a grid shape with his fingers. "Good luck wandering around in London."

I laughed and took a seat with my plate. "I guess everything over there is so old it's all windy and twists and turns."

"Cabbies have to take a special test, learning all the names of roads. Takes years to study," Timothy said. I wasn't sure I'd caught their names right, but luckily, Adam approached with his own mug of coffee and plate.

Timothy, Raymond, and Jerry, I reminded myself. I took the chance to get them straight in my head. The more names I remembered, the easier it would be to make friends at parties later. And it looked like we were all going to be early risers, or perhaps late to bed, depending on how our body clocks adjusted.

"Have you been here before?" Jerry asked.

I smiled. "No. I've heard about it, but never. I won tickets, and now I'm suddenly... here."

"Oh, bloody brilliant, mate!" Raymond beamed and high-fived me. "We've been coming for four years now. This is the fifth one."

"No kidding? I heard from friends about last year, but I didn't know it was such a big thing," I admitted.

That turned out to be the right thing to say. Adam and I were able to eat breakfast, just nodding and smiling a lot while we were treated to a history of the event, the faces we'd likely see, some of the big dramas from years past, and which rooms were the best.

"Make sure you grab deck chairs early," Raymond advised, leaning in as if he had to whisper it confidentially. The rest of the cafeteria was still mostly empty, but a couple other guys had now wandered in. "They'll fill up fast. And don't leave them unattended!"

I swapped looks with Adam. "I'm prepared to wrestle for the best spot."

"I'll hold the video camera," Adam responded without missing a beat. I grinned as the others laughed, but this time, part of me wondered how serious he was.

Now that we'd crossed that line in the sand between our public façade and the private situation... where did it stop? Did he really think I was that hot? Or other guys? Was this an awakening moment, or was he just a horny straight guy who wanted to know what it was like? Adam did seem like the kind of guy who wouldn't be picky if he was feeling horny.

It wasn't long before the other three guys headed off to claim chairs—apparently it was that hotly competitive—and Adam and I finished our coffee.

"Let's get deck chairs," Adam urged me. "People are starting to wake up."

I laughed. "You're ready to snooze in the sun already?"

"I plan to do a lot of not-working on this trip, and the sooner we start, the better." Adam clapped me on the back. "Let's go."

With some gentle pressure from him, we grabbed towels from the reception desk before heading down to the main pool. The place was big enough to have three, but it was obvious from the balcony above the courtyard where most of the action was—most of the deck chairs were clustered around the main pool.

A little thrill of excitement ran through me. I hadn't actually taken a day to do nothing at all in quite some time. This could be the perfect excuse. And Adam would get to meet other guys casually throughout the day, so he could relax and not look quite so much like a twenty-one-year-old on his first spring break trip.

"Got the sunscreen?" I elbowed him. "And you'll need a swimsuit."

"Okay, let's grab chairs first. Then one of us waits with them while the other changes." Adam scowled. "I ain't losing my spot in the sun to some chair thief."

Holding my laugh inside, I nodded and held the door open for him as we made our way out to the courtyard.

"We've got the best chairs already," Raymond called. The British accent—Manchester accent, I reminded myself—was easy to place. "But over there is second-best."

I followed where he was pointing and nodded, raising a hand. "Cheers, mate."

He gave me a laugh and thumbs-up, elbowing the other guys. Hopefully that hadn't sounded completely stupid, like people trying to talk like they were from New York and ending up somewhere in Boston.

"Okay, I like these," Adam declared, pointing at two chairs. They were close to an outcropping of the tiled deck into the pool, and there was a bar within spitting distance. If anything, they were front-and-center.

I eyed him and smirked. "You'll see all the action here. Almost three-sixty view."

"Perfect." Adam winked back at me. "It's like a field trip. I'll take great notes this way."

"Are you actually studying us?" I laughed, elbowing him. "Dude, relax. You're not gonna get kicked out for having an unpopped cherry."

Adam blushed deep red and dropped into his deck chair. "Whatever. So, what's on today? We don't have any activities or whatever, right?"

"Of course, if they find out, you might be fresh meat," I added, leaning in to whisper to him. "I might have to get possessive and remind them who you came with." Two could play the flirtation game, and now that I knew it wasn't unwelcome, I intended to get him back for his weeks of turning me on just for fun.

Adam fumbled and nearly dropped his phone as he pulled it out of his pocket. "I'm looking at the schedule, then."

"You do that." I stretched out along the deck chair and laced my hands behind my head, grinning to myself. I waved across the pool at the three British guys, who had set up a whole little camp by pulling their deck chairs together.

"Dude, it's a pool party today." Adam glanced around, and I could see what he was thinking: that explained how many people seemed to be coming down here early, or perhaps not having slept at all. "Right here."

"Excellent." I beamed. "What's the theme?"

"Um, this is the… the nautical one."

I could tell what Adam was thinking again, because he'd blushed so much when we'd picked costumes. The sailor costumes were our skimpiest.

"It starts after lunch, doesn't it?" I asked innocently enough. "You've got a few hours before you have to look the part."

Adam cleared his throat. "Yeah." He kicked his sandals off and stretched out on the chair. "But everyone else is already dressed."

It was true—although it was just mid-morning, most of the guys showing up were already in cute sailor stripes or even hats.

"Go change," Adam ordered me. "Sun's coming around this way. You'll want your swimsuit on soon."

I smirked. "You just want to get into that tight little thing yourself. While you're sitting front and center, so the whole pool can admire you…"

Adam shoved me. "Go change, now." He was trying not to laugh, though.

I snickered and went back to the room, taking a moment to fix my hair in the mirror before I changed into my suit. I'd chosen the more modest of the two—a navy pair of trunks that left little to the imagination. Adam's was white with navy stripes, and even more revealing. But despite his nervousness for the past few days, Adam couldn't seem to wait to get it on.

That man was full of contradictions.

By the time I got back, Adam was chatting with our neighbors. Even I was surprised at how fast the deck chairs were filling up, but now that I thought about it, there were only a few hundred deck chairs for a few thousand guests coming to party the day and night away. Maybe Adam was right about grabbing one early.

"Your turn," I told him, trying not to reveal how fascinated I was. Was he going to follow through or chicken out now?

Adam tipped his chin up at me with a grin. "Back in a minute." The way he sauntered through the pool area and back to the hotel, he seemed to be aware that he was already drawing eyes.

And why the hell did I want to grab him and plant a kiss on him as soon as he got back, anyway? I didn't want anyone misbehaving with him, sure… but it was just plain old jealousy. There was no escaping admitting it. Adam was starting to explore now, and I wanted all of those experiences to be with me.

Nobody else… me.

"Hey!" That was an all-too-familiar voice that cut through the air.

Fuck. I hadn't expected him to be here already.

I forced a smile as I turned and found Xavier striding toward me. He had a more modest pair of knee-length swim shorts on, but he'd added a straw hat on a string around his neck.

"I had no idea you were coming until the guys at Bubbles told me!" Xavier swept me up in a hug, and the familiar smell made my heart ache for a moment—not that I wasn't with him, but that I'd been dumb enough to stay *with* him when seeing him had given me this same sense of dread *before* we broke up.

But I was over it now, I reminded myself.

Xavier didn't seem to notice any awkwardness—but then, he never had. For all Adam acted oblivious, he spotted cues way more than he let on.

No, I wasn't going to compare my current fake boyfriend and kinda-fling to my ex-boyfriend. That was a bad idea on so many levels.

"Yeah, well," I said, pulling away from him. "I'm here."

It wasn't as awkward as I'd expected, until he gave me that look of sympathy and asked, "So how's life treating you?" Like he didn't expect me to have done anything interesting since we'd broken up.

Fuck that. I was going big places—or, if not big, at least medium. If I didn't have another boyfriend for real like him, that wasn't a bad thing. "I'm fine," I said, injecting some cheer into my voice. "Did you come alone?" It was the usual dance— both of us knew that I knew the answer, but I had to pretend not to.

"No, my boyfriend's just off getting his Insta daily." Xavier sipped from his drink, which looked blue and delicious. I could use one right now.

An elbow hit my ribcage as a guy stormed past me, striding up to Xavier's side and hooking his arm around Xavier's waist. There were subtler ways to stake a claim. I snorted with amusement as Xavier's new boyfriend made his appearance.

"You hitting on my man?"

"I didn't know Real Housewives was doing a very gay special," I retorted dryly. That much drama was seriously over-the-top, and I'd seen plenty of drama before.

"No, no, babe. This is my ex." It took all my willpower not to laugh or groan—or both. Okay, Xavier really was that clueless still. How hadn't he figured out that that was actually worse?

The new guy whipped his head around to take me in, his lip curling slightly. "Really?" he asked, and in a word, my self-esteem dropped lower than I'd thought possible.

There was really no need for that cattiness. I'd been friends with exes before they moved out of the city, and I'd met their new boyfriends. All of us tended to get to know each other—if you avoided dating friends' exes or one-night stands, your dating pool would be nil.

I didn't care what he thought of me, I reminded myself. He was irrelevant to my life, and he didn't know me. At this rate, he never would.

And then an arm slid around my waist, and Adam joined me. He pecked me on the cheek. When he stood next to me, it was like he put me back together—the pieces he had to offer me fit into the gulf in my chest. I stood stronger, and I believed in myself just a bit more.

The other guys' reactions sure helped. The new boyfriend looked confused and then annoyed that his hissyfit had been interrupted, and Xavier's jaw just dropped.

It was kind of insulting that my ex clearly hadn't expected me to find myself a boyfriend so quickly. While he was technically right, I'd touched Adam's dick yesterday, so I was willing to ignore technicalities.

I glanced at Adam, and then my jaw dropped, too. He looked *hot*. Tight white briefs with horizontal navy stripes that left little to the imagination, and a body built to wear that outfit. He had a white neckerchief tied around his neck, and—was that a temporary tattoo of an anchor on his shoulder? It was really hard to pay attention to his shoulder when his pecs were drawing a hundred percent of my attention.

"What's goin' on? I'm Adam." He reached out to shake hands, and only Xavier took his hand.

"Xavier."

Adam stared between the two of them and then at me for a moment. "Oh."

New Guy was smirking again, clearly taking that as a sign that I'd told him about Xavier, and pretending he hadn't heard of me in response. His game was so transparent. "Come on. I'd love some more shade." He dragged Xavier off before he could even say goodbye.

I felt kind of bad for a moment because Xavier looked back at me and shrugged apologetically. He was clearly tired of New Guy's shit, but on the other hand... He'd made his bed. He could damn well lie in it. And he'd clearly been surprised that I could manage to find myself a hot boyfriend, so no, I wasn't gonna rescue him from that jerk.

"Did that just happen?" Adam mumbled into my ear. I was busier trying to figure out if *this* was happening, or if Adam was appearing in my dreams now.

"Uhh. That's him, yeah," I managed to answer kind of coherently as I forced my gaze back to his face.

Adam let go of me at last and sat on his own sun bed, folding his arms. It made his biceps do really distracting things. "Is that the new guy? What a prick. I wanted to push him into the pool."

I swallowed my laugh. "That... might escalate the situation."

Adam huffed. "Don't care. He's obviously a jerk. They're made for each other."

If he got to know Xavier, I had the feeling Adam wouldn't be so sure... but then, defending my ex looked really bad. I just lifted my shoulders in a shrug and flopped back on my lounge chair.

Never mind pushing the new guy into the pool—I felt like we'd just been thrown in the deep end. It was gonna be a hell of a day.

17

ADAM

After the little incident with that dick and his new toy dick, the pool party unfolded like a dream I hadn't even known enough about to imagine. Half-naked—or mostly-naked—guys every-where, a lot of laughter, and guys making out in the pool right in front of me without anyone else batting an eye.

It was like walking into the teen fantasies I'd ignored. All those years I'd wanted to be around lots of guys, I'd thought it was because I didn't understand women. According to people like my parents, guys were just "supposed" to be buddies, and girls were unknowable, but you were supposed to pick one and marry her anyway.

Well, that wasn't unappealing, but it was like I'd been cooking with only salt for years and now I'd discovered pepper. I wanted all of it, even if it was so hot my throat burned and I didn't know how to take it in moderation.

I wanted to satisfy the curiosity I'd only barely admitted to, and so much more. I wanted to do the things that I'd fantasized about in guilty moments. I wanted to know what it was like to talk to guys who wouldn't look at me askance for acting a little gay.

If I wanted to do it all in this week, I was gonna have to pick up the pace.

Darren seemed happy to alternate between swimming and basking on the deck chair. After we grabbed lunch and came back quickly enough to reclaim our deck chairs, I left him there to pick up where he'd left off, once I was satisfied that Xavier and his new asshole boyfriend weren't going to come harass him.

Before I could really let go and relax for the rest of the week, it was time to call my parents. I'd carefully calculated the time zones. This made it the right time in the evening to get through to them. Man, how cool was it gonna be to tell them I was in Hawaii? I couldn't wait to hear their reactions. None of us had ever been further than Kansas, except me. Living in Brooklyn was like being on Mars as far as my family was concerned.

"Okay, how the fuck does this work?" I squinted at the paper card and grabbed the hotel phone. The instructions were in small print, but I could just about manage them if I went step by step. No way was I risking a roaming bill. I'd heard horror stories about them.

All I got was a dial tone at first. A few attempts later, I noticed the note on the hotel phone: *dial 9 for outside numbers*. Oh, God, I was showing my roots here. I could count on one hand the times I'd been in a hotel room. I'd certainly never called anyone from one.

I hung up and tried again, a 9 to the beginning of the number on the card. It took two more tries to get the number right.

The fucking thing seemed designed to make me jump through as many hoops as possible. Finally, I entered my parents' phone number and pumped my fist in triumph. My parents would answer the phone for any old telemarketer—an unfamiliar number shouldn't put them off.

I counted six rings before the voicemail kicked in. This was our usual call time. What was going on?

"Hey, guys." I tried to sound cheerful. "It's Adam. Just checking in. Letting you know I'm alive and all that. So, uh, give me a call back when you can? Maybe Sundays aren't such a good day for you, huh? Anyway, let me know how your month's been. Mine's going great." There wasn't a lot more I wanted to say and have recorded on a voicemail message. "Anyway, cool, bye. Love you."

I hung up and flopped on the bed, slightly resentful that it had been made up. I wanted to crawl into the bed now, but if I did, Darren would totally notice the mussed sheets and make fun of me for going to bed in the middle of the day.

The weird, sinking feeling in the pit of my stomach was hard to identify. They often missed my calls, but monthly wasn't too often, surely? I hadn't even told them I was in Hawaii—surely they'd notice the return number and want to know what was going on. Now that I finally had exciting news, of course I wasn't getting through to anyone.

I could always call my old bosses back in Tennessee. Josh and his boyfriend Evan had basically been older brothers once I got over my teen angst and learned how to work like an adult. But what the hell would I say to ask them for help? *Pretty sure I'm into guys, what do I do now?*

Nobody would believe me if I said that. I scoffed and rubbed my face before I adjusted my neckerchief. I thought the outfit looked pretty damn cute. Darren hadn't said anything, but I'd caught him looking at me more than once. I was almost sure he liked it.

The photographer had come over to take a photo of us in our

matching outfits, too. I hadn't minded. I was pretty sure I could do whatever the hell I wanted and not end up outing myself to my parents. They were never gonna find a few random Facebook photos.

Why did that feel so bad, then? Part of me missed the kind of small town where everyone knew each other's business. Being in such a big city—and now thousands of miles away from anyone who mattered, save Darren—should have been liberating, but it just felt lonely.

God. I was in serious danger of spending all my time *thinking* instead of enjoying myself, which was stupid. I pushed myself to my feet and headed back downstairs.

If I was here for a week, I was going to damn well make the most of it.

By the time I made it back to the poolside, someone was sitting on my lounger. I stiffened, glaring at him. I would have been unhappy even if he hadn't been reaching over to touch Darren's arm.

Suddenly, I had the tiniest glimmer of sympathy for Xavier's new boyfriend. It took all I had not to launch myself in there and knock his hand away. Instead, I kept myself to a dignified stroll. I had to act like I was confident that he was mine, whoever tried to pick him up.

"Hey," I greeted and sat next to Darren on the lounger while the other guy pulled away sharply. "Sorry I had to run off."

Darren eyed me and then leaned in to kiss my shoulder. "Everything good?"

I must have sounded stressed still. My shoulders were tense, my neck painful. Thinking about my parents always did that to me. "Yeah, yeah," I waved it off, consciously trying to relax. "It'll be fine. Hey, by the way. I'm Adam." Introducing myself to the other guy was less of a jerk move than telling him that Darren was taken and he could fuck off.

"Manuel." He spoke with a thick accent I couldn't quite place. "Your boyfriend is very handsome."

I grinned at Darren. Had he mentioned me already? In any case, Manuel was clearly acknowledging that I was top dog here, so I liked him more immediately. "I know. I jumped on that as soon as I could. Where ya from, then?"

It turned out Manuel was Portuguese, and he'd flown here with his German boyfriend, who was busy flirting with the bartender.

When I raised my eyebrow, Manuel just grinned. "He can do what he wants, but he comes home to me."

Okay, that was kind of sweet. Even my stone-cold heart melted at that. When I looked at Darren, I found him smiling the same way. At the same moment, I could see how it would be lonely to be single here, among all these couples. Thank God I'd saved him from that fate.

"That's sweet. How long have you been together?"

"Married twelve years."

I gasped. That sounded like a long time for any couple, but gay marriage was so new… "Wait, is gay marriage legal there?" I shot an apologetic look at Darren, hoping that wasn't something everyone was supposed to just know by heart.

Darren just shook his head and smiled back at me. Phew. Safe.

"We got married in Canada. Flew to Toronto." Manuel showed us his ring, and I found myself leaning in to look at it. It was pretty— gold, with inset clear stones. Probably diamond, I guessed.

"Wow. That's some bling."

Normally I wouldn't have given a damn—engagement and wedding rings had always been a thing for girls to show off to each other in the South, but guys wore plain bands if that. Now that I was starting to challenge a few of the ideas I'd been taught, everything was crumbling down at once, and even this fascinated me.

Darren was right—there was a whole new world I knew nothing about, and I wanted to know all of it right now.

"Good bling," Manuel agreed with a hearty laugh. "What about you two?"

"Oh, no, we're not—we're not engaged or anything," Darren stumbled over his tongue to assure Manuel. "No, like, we're new. Newly together."

"I just came out," I added, surprised to find myself the calm one rescuing the situation. "First time for everything, right?"

Manuel stared and then grinned at me. "Wow. Congratulations. Are you happier now? Life will be easier."

It was sweet of him to say so, because I wasn't really sure. "I… I think I am." I glanced sideways at Darren again. "I mean, this trip is great. Spending time with him is good. I don't want to think too far in the future yet."

"When I came out to my parents, they had… great difficulty understanding." Manuel spoke in precise, clipped words that I could tell covered up a lot of history just as effectively as my jokes did. "But they have come around. The world is getting better."

"Good for you," Darren said with a quiet nod and smile. "It is. It's not the same as when we grew up, even. I can't imagine what it's like for you."

"It's good," Manuel said firmly.

"I sure never thought I'd be in this position," I said slowly. For the first time, I started to feel deeply guilty that I was telling everyone this pack of lies. But I needed to tell one lie in order to tell another—and then they all tumbled on top of each other. I wanted to avoid attracting any more to me. "But here we are."

"Cheers to that." Manuel toasted us and I grabbed my empty cup to join in the toast.

"More drinks?" I asked, trying to swallow my protective instinct for long enough to grab drinks from the bar. "Blue cocktails?"

"They have a name, you know," Darren teased.

I waved my hand, but I caught myself before I told him I was too straight to know that. Without that as a shield, I had to actually think about what I'd been about to say, and it sounded... well, scarily like something my parents would say.

Oh, boy. I needed a lot of cocktails tonight. Luckily the bartender took pity on me and let me take four of the blue cocktails away with me. By the time I got back, Manuel had left to rejoin his husband.

"Hope I wasn't cockblocking you," I muttered as I set down two plastic cups and handed over the other two.

Darren looked confused as he took the drinks. "What? Me and Manuel?"

"Well, or anyone else." I glanced around at the pool area, which suddenly seemed jam-packed with attractive men in every version of a slutty sailor outfit it was possible to find.

Darren set down both drinks and took my hands. "Maybe I need to say it again: I don't want to hit on other guys while I'm here."

I bit my lip as I looked in his eyes. He was dead serious, wasn't he? The more he said it, the more I started to believe it. It seemed like a wasted opportunity if I looked at it one way: I should get out of his way and let him flirt with real gay men while he was surrounded by new, exciting guys.

"Unless you want me to," Darren added, almost as an afterthought.

I shook my head. I might not know much, but I knew that the thought of someone else hitting on him made me want to drape myself over him and kiss him with as much passion as I'd found at Friction that night. "God, no. I just thought you might have changed your mind now that you've seen what's available."

Darren snorted with laughter and tipped his head back to sip the cocktail. "The buffet's great, but I'm taking dessert home with me."

I blushed and settled back on my deck chair, making a big deal of adjusting the back so I sat upright instead of lounging flat now. As guys drank more and flirted harder, it seemed like an invitation, and there was only one guy I wanted to crawl on top of me and test the weight limit on this thing.

When I turned back to Darren, he was grinning at me. "You blush so easily."

Focusing on it only made it worse. "Goddamn it," I muttered, flipping him off before I grabbed the cup. "It's just warm here."

"Uh huh." Darren snickered at me and drained his first cocktail before lacing his hands behind his head and settling back to watch the goings-on around us.

I nursed my cocktail. No way was I getting any more alcohol in my system than this for a few hours. I wanted to be fully aware of the situation if anyone came to make trouble—like Xavier's boy-toy, or anyone who thought Darren looked available.

Fine, it was jealousy. I was willing to admit it. But who could blame me? I had the hottest guy here beside me, he'd told me he was desperate to get laid, and I was acutely aware of every glance in our direction.

I was gonna have to take care of that problem for him. The thought made me twitch in my swim shorts, and I had to rein myself in awfully fast. Everyone would see what was going on if I followed that train of thought. Worse, it would look like being around all this bare skin was doing the trick for me. No need to go that far to blend in.

Within the next hour, though, I started noticing staff moving chairs away from the poolside whenever they were abandoned. It started to feel like they were going to shoo us away, and while I might normally stay put and make them ask us to move...

Getting up early was starting to wear on me. I probably wasn't going to make it to suppertime again today without a nap.

Darren's eyes were closed. The bastard was already catching a sneaky nap of his own. I elbowed him. "If you're gonna pass out on me, let's go upstairs."

"Mmm." Darren pushed himself to his feet like he'd been waiting for me to ask.

When he took me by the hand to lead me into the resort, that now-familiar warm glow spread through me. He didn't have to do that, but it was a quiet gesture of affection that meant the world to me. He had me—and I had his back in return.

Yeah, the first day had gone well, all things considered. If only I could have gotten through to Mom and Dad, everything in the world would have been hunky-dory.

DARREN

"You know, I felt your morning wood." Adam was grinning at me as he emerged from the bathroom. "Was that all my fault?"

I noted with a little disappointment that he had a towel wrapped around his waist. We still hadn't seen each other naked—not really. The handjobs hadn't counted, since we hadn't really fully stripped down before or afterward. And I sure hadn't had the chance to admire him.

Last night when we'd changed for bed after the nautical party, we hadn't stayed in the same room to do so. It felt like another boundary we had to work our way up to crossing, but Adam was doing a great job reminding me why I wanted to cross it as soon as possible. He was in another flirtatious mood, wasn't he? Mornings seemed to do this to him.

I grinned right back at him and winked. "I know. I felt your wandering hands when you woke up."

"Oh, I did nothing of the sort," Adam gasped, clutching his heart. Was he picking up my mannerisms accidentally or deliberately?

"Just one squeeze. I think you thought it was your own boner," I informed him, snickering. "You looked half-asleep. Did the shower wake you up? You can speak in sentences now."

Adam turned bright red and huffed his way over to his suitcase. "I don't know. You could be telling tales. I don't remember this happening."

"I know how long it took you in the bathroom just now." I smirked. "Good thing those drains look solid. I'd hate to cause… plumbing issues." Adam turned even brighter red, but I didn't relent. I rolled over to keep watching him as he crouched by his suitcase to throw things around until he found an outfit. "Did feeling up my wood turn you on?"

"Gotta clean the pipes sometime, dude."

I hummed. If he didn't want to bring a hard-on to me to deal with, that was fine. I wasn't gonna make him try out anything he didn't want to. We'd crashed so fast last night that we hadn't tried anything new, and he could well be having second thoughts about all of this.

"White day today," I reminded him.

"I know." Adam shot me a look and then stood up, deliberately and slowly unwrapping the towel from around his waist. That effectively quelled any doubts I was having, but lit something else in my brain instead. I was gonna need a long shower, too, at this rate.

I caught my breath, my eyes shooting right down to his ass. Exactly where he wanted them, judging by the way he bent over to pull his white underwear on.

When Adam turned around again, I eyed his bulge and then looked up at him. "Now if someone hadn't just wasted a perfectly good load…"

Adam laughed and approached the bed, leaning over it to kiss me. "Next one's yours," he promised, his voice low.

Okay, that was hot as fuck. I also still felt like I was in an alternate dimension where previously-straight roommates suddenly decided they liked dick. I loved this dimension, but it was a trip. Every time Adam suddenly found that seed of confidence, he blossomed into a motherfucking rose.

"Good," I managed in return and nipped his lower lip. "Mine."

Adam sucked a quick breath in and stood still, so I pushed myself until I sat up and pulled him to sit down next to me. This time, when we kissed, we took our time to explore. His hand rested on my knee, and he closed his eyes first, so I followed suit.

Before, it had just been sex—or showing off. Now, though? There was something entirely different unfolding between us, and I wanted to be careful with it. I wasn't sure Adam was thinking it through before he tried it out. Tried *me* out, I should say.

Adam finally pulled back and rested his chin on my shoulder. "Do we have excursions today?"

I slid my arm around his shoulders. "Mmm. Yeah, we do, don't we? All the days kind of blur into one when you're on vacation. Is it Monday?"

Adam's smile faded for a moment. "Yeah."

I assumed he was realizing how fast the week was flying by. "Today," I told him, "we stay up late and join the rest of the party."

"Deal," Adam agreed. "Wait. Monday is hiking day, isn't it?"

"Yeah, you're right." I smiled and pulled away from him to rummage through my suitcase for a casual breathable shirt and quick-dry shorts. Then, I laid the white party outfit out for later. It also gave him some breathing room to think about that kiss.

Adam sighed and groaned. "Hiking. I've never gotten the point. It's like exercise, but you're not even getting anything done. You're just walking around."

"Coming from somewhere as gorgeous as Tennessee, I'm surprised." I smacked his leg with my shirt. "You're lucky to have the mountains in your backyard. In New York, we have to drive for ages to get to any."

"No thanks. I'll take the city and a Starbucks on every block," Adam insisted.

The argument carried on through breakfast—where Jerry took my side and Raymond kept talking about something called the Lake District in England, which sounded like the only mountain range he'd seen until Hawaii. A few minutes before the meeting time, we parted ways to find our meeting point.

"Are you sure you've got everything?" I double-checked. "Sunscreen? Water? First aid kit?"

"Hold on there, you boy scout," Adam laughed. "They'll rescue us if we fall in a ravine."

"Oh." The disgruntled noise didn't come from Adam, and it sure wasn't mine. We both looked around, and we spotted the same guy at the same time—Xavier's new boyfriend. Slender and twinky, young and pretty—a reminder of everything Xavier hadn't found in me.

He folded his arms and pretended not to see us, wandering around and looking at the art in the lobby instead.

I rolled my eyes at Adam and tried not to laugh. Clearly, he could dish it but he couldn't take it. Now he was going to be stuck with us all day long.

"Xavier couldn't make it?" Adam addressed him the next time he wandered by anywhere near us.

He couldn't pretend he hadn't heard that. He huffed and turned to Adam, and then shook his head. "No. If you must know."

"Just wondering," Adam said mildly. Someone dressed in a thin rain jacket with an excursion company logo on it was approaching, herding us into a bigger group of people waiting outside for a minibus to arrive.

While we waited, we introduced ourselves to each other, and I overheard New Guy's name—Austin. Typical. Sounded like a dick's name.

"Today's walk is going to be gentle," our leader, Jessie, told us. "But please do stick with the group or let one of us know if you're going for a rest break. I don't want to search the rainforest for you."

I grinned and leaned into Adam. "We might have to have a rest break at some point."

"Oh, I am not getting stung by a mosquito down south," Adam scoffed. "You wait for tonight, mister."

"Fiiine," I teased. "I can wait if you can wait." He'd started it, so I didn't feel bad planning how to tease him all day long.

"I can wait." Adam folded his arms and jutted his chin at me.

We'd see about that.

The trailhead wasn't too far away, mercifully. It felt like no time at all before we got there, stretching and shrugging on backpacks.

At first, I stuck close to Adam, but he was starting to have conversations without turning to me for help and reassurance. I wanted to let him stretch his baby gay wings and fly, so I hung back and found other guys to talk to myself. The group set off at an easy pace, as promised, and I eventually fell in beside Adam once he went quiet.

"You good?" I asked with a smile. He was checking his phone for at least the tenth time since breakfast.

Adam hummed.

"Do I need to confiscate your phone?" I teased.

"No." Adam glared at me and turned to the guy next to him to strike up a conversation.

Okaaay, someone was touchy about that. I made a mental note. I'd let him cool off and talk to him again later.

Now I was next to Austin. He looked around as if searching for someone to talk to, but everyone was already chatting. No escape from me.

"So, how long have you and Xavier been together?" I asked with as polite a smile as I could manage. He might be a dick, but if we could get along, it would make things less awkward if we ran into each other back home.

"A couple months." Wow. He must have found him right after we broke up, then. Where? Austin answered my unasked question. "Met at Friction, and just hit it off."

Of course. I swallowed my sigh and nodded. "I'm glad for him... and you. He's a great guy." Not right for me, but for a guy with more backbone than me. Austin had one, that was for sure.

"Yep." Austin shoved his hands in his pockets. He looked around again for an escape, but no such luck. Finally, after a minute of silence, he spoke up. He sounded gruff, reluctant to engage, but it was gonna be a boring hour otherwise. "So, what do you do?"

"Electrician. You?"

"Interior decoration."

I smiled. "I think I saw some of his Instagram photos. The place is looking great since I moved out. Is that your work?"

"You lived with him?" Austin looked startled.

Oops. Apparently Xavier hadn't told him as much as I'd thought—or Austin wasn't the one trying to cut me out of his life. I gulped and nodded, hoping I hadn't started any trouble. "Almost a year. I saw you finally fixed that awful living room wallpaper."

That, at least, made Austin smile slightly. "Yeah, it had to go."

It felt like the glacier between us had melted just a bit. Enough to get a foothold on it and see over it and connect with him. Maybe, over time, he wouldn't be so defensive.

Adam's arm wrapped around my waist. Apparently he'd noticed who I was talking to. He pointed out our surroundings. "Look at this scenery. Gorgeous." But his tone was flat, and he cast Austin a less-than-subtle glance as I looked around.

I tried not to laugh. Bless him for being so protective. That was all I'd asked of him in the beginning.

By the time I looked back at Austin, he'd managed to disappear into the back of the group and find someone else to talk to. I grinned at Adam. "Subtle," I teased.

"What did that asshole want with you?" Adam grumbled.

I smiled and kissed his cheek. God, he was sweet when he was protective. "I talked to him, actually. He doesn't seem as evil as he did yesterday."

"Hmph." Adam took my hand anyway and walked by my side.

God, this man. He was full of contradictions, and more twists and turns than this path itself had. But, like the lush forest that surrounded me, there was such richness along the way. The ferns dripped with moisture, and the rocks we were skirting no doubt had stories as old as time.

When we finally emerged into sight of the waterfall, everyone gasped in turn. Those at the back of the group hurried to catch up and find out what they were missing.

The hike included enough time for a lunch break, water bottles and sandwiches and tiny pretzel bags, and plenty of chances for selfies.

As we ate, Adam kept looking back at the waterfall. "Damn, that's a lot of water," he finally said.

"Glad you came on a hike to lame old nature? Was it worth waiting for tonight for other activities?"

He stuck out his tongue at me. "I guess."

I leaned in to try to suck on his tongue, but we ended up knocking teeth. I laughed as he cursed and grabbed my shoulder. "Sorry."

Adam grumbled. "No biting my tongue off, weirdo."

"I wasn't planning on biting anything off," I assured him, winking.

"Come on. Nobody's there." Adam hauled me to my feet and pointed at the waterfall when I just blinked at him.

Oh, my God. He wanted selfies? I tried not to grin, but I utterly failed. I was smiling so broadly my cheeks hurt as he found someone, asked them to take photos, and gave them his phone.

We took a few—holding hands in front of the waterfall, kissing in front of it, and then, he did the limbo and stuck his tongue out under it. "C'mon," he mumbled. "Hurry up."

I laughed as a pose came to me and grabbed him by the hair with one hand, lifting the other hand to pretend to be pouring the waterfall out of it.

The guy taking the photo laughed, along with several other people nearby by now, and found just the right position to catch the picture. After he snapped it, Adam straightened up and grunted, clutching his back. "Never doing that again!"

"It was your own fault!" I laughed, but I rubbed it. "You okay?"

Adam waved a hand and scoffed before he took my hand. "I'll be just fine."

As the group got ready to set off back through a pretty bamboo forest, I beamed at Adam and hung back so I could kiss him. "Thanks for taking those photos."

Adam looked like he wanted to say more, but he just grunted. "Yep, sure. Let's go." He checked his phone, scowled at it, and shoved it back in his pocket as he led me along to join the back of the group.

Oh, there was that complicated man again. I wished I knew what was going on in his brain, but half the time, even he didn't seem to know. Not that I could blame him—he had a hell of a learning curve, and he was doing well so far. I was proud of him.

And later tonight, we had a sexy promise to keep. Everything was just getting better and better on this trip.

1 9

ADAM

Holy shit, the gays knew how to party.

I'd gotten that impression before from Kev's stories about the goings-on at Friction and in the rest of the neighborhood—wherever the party spilled over to when the bar closed—but there was nothing like experiencing it for myself.

We'd been dancing outdoors for hours in a huge courtyard with two bars set up on either end. The music was blasting us from a damn good sound system. I'd already been ready to go that morning, and waiting all day only made me want Darren more.

"Is this late enough to stay awake?" I asked once I managed to pull him away from the Californian surfer dudes who were clearly trying to impress him with tales of their extreme sports.

"What?" Darren grinned, bobbing his head to the music. "Are you tired? Have a Red Bull."

I slid my arms around his waist and swayed. "I'm not tired," I told him, looking him up and down.

"Ohhh." Darren's hands went to my shoulders, and he adopted

174

that same expression he always seemed to when I came on to him —a cautious smile, but excitement glinting in his eyes. Like he couldn't quite believe this was happening, and he didn't want to get his hopes up.

I pulled him into me until we swayed in the same rhythm. Just touching him was soothing, and I hoped he felt the same way. At the very least, if not relaxed, I hoped I was turning him on. "What's on your mind?"

"You're right. Let's go back to the room." Darren grinned.

"I'm right?" I pretended to gasp. "Of course I am. I'm always right, you just never want to admit it."

"You weren't right about hiking being a waste of time and energy today."

I scoffed. "Oh, it totally was. We could have been here drinking the whole time."

Darren gasped and then smacked my stomach lightly. "I saw you having the time of your life!"

"Was I?" I caught his hand just before it went to my ass and grinned. "I thought I was saving that for later." Hand in hand, we headed into the resort. The elevator couldn't come fast enough.

Darren winked. "You were saving something for later, if I recall right."

"Oh, I still am," I promised him, leaning in to kiss behind his ear.

He squirmed on the spot and moaned, which was a delightful discovery. Apparently, his body was sensitive... and I suddenly found myself wondering where else on his body I could draw that reaction from.

I'd seen just about everything, after that revealing outfit choice for yesterday's nautical party, but I still wanted to see more of him. I couldn't hide my greed as I let go of his hand. Instead, my hand roamed along his back to cup the back of his neck. Thank God the elevator arrived and the doors opened, because I might have copped a feel if we'd waited any longer.

We stepped inside together, and I hit our floor button and turned to him. I crowded against his front, guiding him up against the wall and holding him still to kiss him a few times. I only planned to kiss him enough to warm him up and make him want more.

Darren gripped my shoulders and dug his nails in, hauling me in to kiss me harder. He wasn't contented with just a few pecks on the lips. He pressed our mouths together like he'd been waiting years for this moment, gasping against my lips when I sucked his lower lip.

The elevator arrived and we stumbled out together, grabbing each other's clothes rather than hands. I wasn't sure which of us hauled which into the room. I was definitely the one who kicked the hotel room door shut, though.

"What's on your hot little mind?" Darren gave me a playful grin as he ran his hands down my sides.

"I'd rather let my hot little hands do the talking."

I'd been waiting for hours to strip him out of his white booty shorts and crop top. Darren had insisted my white underwear and clingy t-shirt would make me look sexy, and sure enough, I'd gotten a dozen compliments. Still, right now it was all feeling like too much fabric. We kicked off our sandals, and then I pulled him to the bed by the belt loop.

"Stand here," I ordered and sat on the bed in front of him. I grabbed him by his hips and pulled him in so I could kiss his thighs, working my way up to the bottom of the fabric one kiss at a time. "I wanna suck you off," I whispered, gazing up the smooth, lean length of his torso to meet his eyes. I deliberately brushed my cheek against his sensitive inner thigh, and the scrape of stubble on skin made him whimper.

Darren nodded jerkily. "I might have to sit down, though. You're gonna make me blow a gasket if I stand up."

"I'd hate you to faint on me and choke me," I grinned. I pulled him down to sit on my lap and ran my hands up his sides to his back again, enjoying the smooth skin under my touch.

Darren caught his breath and closed his eyes, loosely draping his arms around my shoulders. He rolled his head back, and I reached up through his crop top to rub the back of his neck.

"This looks good on you," I whispered and kissed his throat. He moaned in response, his throat vibrating under my lips, so I did it again. It didn't take me long to find out that the sensitive skin on the side of his neck got a good response.

Darren ground against me slowly, moving his hips in circles and lining our cocks up before he started to thrust gently in my lap. All too vividly, I remembered him riding me on the living room floor, and my mind just about short-circuited with how much I wanted it.

I grabbed the hem of his shirt and pulled it off so fast I heard stitches pop.

"Hey!" Darren glared. "Don't rip my crap, dude."

"Sorry. I'll make it up to you." I tried to look cute and batted my lashes, and Darren just snorted and swatted my shoulder.

"Good thing your lips are so pretty."

"Is that a hint?" I licked my lips, exaggerating the movement as I grabbed his ass. "Come on, sit down here." I guided him to sit next to me and then slid to the floor, hitting it with a thud. My poor knees.

"That's a gorgeous sight," Darren whispered as he stroked my hair gently.

I liked the view from down here, too. I grinned up at him and unbuttoned his shorts. "You can grab on if it all gets too much."

Even though I didn't know what I was doing, experience on the other end and instinct led the way. I kissed his stomach and hip, and then let my lips drag along the denim toward the swell of fabric over his groin. I liked how his dick felt in my hand, so surely I'd like the taste, right?

I pulled his shorts down slowly, a distant part of my brain registering that there wasn't a waistband underneath. When his cock sprang free, it smacked me in the chin, and I started giggling.

Darren laughed, too. He bucked his hips to deliberately smack me again, and I laughed even harder as I blew a raspberry against it.

"Oh, my God," Darren flopped onto his back with a strangled noise of amusement and pleasure. "I—I don't even—that weirdly felt good. I've got condoms in my suitcase."

"Perfect." I scooted over and rummaged until I found them, then crawled back, keeping it slow and sexy.

Darren pushed himself up again on his elbows to watch, his eyes dark and fascinated.

"You like that?" I whispered as I reached him again and tossed condoms on the bed. "Put it on." While he did, I knelt between his legs and pulled my shirt off, then rubbed myself through my underwear.

"I love it." Darren had the condom on in no time at all, and I pushed his hands away and back down to the bed. He was all mine now.

My nervousness was suddenly gone, replaced only by the desire to experiment. I kept one hand on his smooth thigh and cupped his hard-on with the other, gently stroking it. When it was this close to my face, I had no choice but to admire it. And for all I tried not to let that thought sneak in, it did anyway: *I bet that would feel good inside me.*

I'd wanted to try it for years, but I'd never gotten more than a minute of fingering myself before the shame had hit. The orgasms were mindblowing compared to plain old jerking off, but it wasn't worth the mental stress.

Now, though, that part of me was slowly being shaken loose. I wanted to feel good, and more to the point right now, I wanted him to feel good. I liked going down on girls, so why would guys be any different? The feeling of making someone come with just my lips and tongue was a point of pride.

I lapped along the shaft slowly, my brain registering the different taste of latex and the slight musky smell. Very different, but equally pleasurable. Yeah, I could totally do this.

I wrapped my lips around the head of his cock, carefully keeping my lips over my teeth, and bobbed my head down to rub his shaft over my tongue. When he got close to the back of my throat and my gag reflex threatened to kick in, I quickly pulled my head up again and repeated.

The motion was easy enough to learn, but the details were going to take some refining. Judging from the way he relaxed and started to moan softly, though, I wasn't doing too bad for myself. At least I knew what I liked to feel, even if doing it was a lot trickier than girls had made it look.

Goddamn, a dick took up a lot of space in my mouth. It didn't leave much room for breathing. And, suddenly, I found out that I cared a little more about dick than I did breathing. *Learn something new every day. I'm gonna have to improvise here,* I thought.

But everything I got right made Darren squirm with pleasure on the bed under me, and in my peripheral vision, I could see him clenching his hands in the sheets. He made the most incredible sounds when I figured out how to run my tongue around the head of his cock before sucking the whole length into my mouth.

I felt sexy, powerful, and in control like I'd never expected.

And Darren felt pretty damn good, judging by the way he started to gasp my name. "I'm getting close. Please—keep going, Adam," he panted.

How could I ignore such a polite request? I found a rhythm I could handle, sucking him into my mouth hard and fast. It turned me on in a way I could barely ignore, but I'd deal with that in a few minutes. Right now, it was all about Darren.

When he grabbed my hair and gasped, "I'm gonna come," I didn't pull away. I just relished the feeling of him thrusting into my mouth and the sound of his grunts, even if I couldn't taste him yet.

His head rolled back and he dug his fingernails into my shoulders, his breathing labored. When he finally relaxed, I was pretty damn pleased with myself.

"I wanna suck you off without the condom next time," was the first thing I told him when I pulled my head off him and took a deep, blissful breath of air.

He grinned giddily at me. "A local group does a mobile testing unit here. We'll stop by tomorrow."

Man, Darren knew everything. I stood up and sat on the edge of the bed, rubbing my knees. That floor time was gonna be a killer.

"Lie down," Darren told me, his voice husky and suggestive.

I smirked. "What if I don't?"

Huh. I was staring at the ceiling now, flat on my back on the bed. He hauled me up the bed by my wrists as I squirmed to get loose, pulled my underwear down, and then he rolled over to straddle me.

Oh, shit. Here we were in one of my fantasies—Darren astride me, holding me down and riding me. Not quite, but I could easily enough imagine it. My boner was rubbing against his ass, and it was an incredibly distracting tease against the length of my shaft.

He let go of my hands and scooted back slowly, kneeling between my legs and rolling a condom onto my dick. Even that much touch made me squirm and catch my breath. The sensation that sparked under my skin from suddenly being gripped so firmly was almost too much.

"Sensitive, huh?"

"Pretty turned on already," I managed, trying to be cool. It really didn't work, though, because I whimpered and pushed into Darren's mouth the moment he sucked the tip of my cock into the back of his throat. "Fuck!"

He moaned around me and laced his fingers with mine, keeping my hands on the bed as he bobbed his head quick and fast. No mercy at all, and I loved it. Sure, I was so turned on I was gonna last about negative-three seconds, but it would be totally worth it.

After a minute, he slowed down and let go of my hands so he could fondle my balls, sliding one palm gently against them as he pressed the other hand to my stomach to keep me down.

I came hard and fast, gasping Darren's name like he'd crashed into my world and taken me apart, piece by piece.

The new Adam had all these desires he didn't know what to do with, and fantasies bursting out that he'd kept under lock and key for so long, and an insatiable need to know more.

What the hell was I gonna do?

Darren grinned and rolled off me. "You look like you just saw God."

"If I did, he has a great mouth." I mentally crossed myself as I said it—some habits died hard.

"Compliment accepted," Darren laughed and pushed himself to his feet.

I felt fulfilled in a way I hadn't expected. Usually, after sex, I was hit-or-miss for cuddling. Sometimes I could handle it, sometimes it annoyed me. Now? I found myself laying a hand on his knee just to make sure I still felt connected. "Where are you off to?"

He chuckled as he eased away from me. "Gonna brush my teeth and get PJs on," he told me. "We're not heading back down to the party, are we?"

"Yeah," I agreed with a smile. "Let's stay in." By now, the party must be wrapping up—we'd been here for hours, after all. I didn't want to put clothes back on—if those could be called clothes, which was debatable—and rejoin people. I was already around the guy I wanted to be with tonight.

He closed the door as he got ready for the night, and that left me with way too many thoughts swirling around my brain. Checking my phone didn't help, either.

No call back from my parents… still. It made me feel weirdly worthless, even when Darren treated me so wonderfully.

After I cleaned up and found a trash can, I crawled under the covers and pulled a pillow over my head. I heard him leave the bathroom first, and then felt the bed give in slightly as he lay down on it. Before long, there was a touch on my back and then an arm over my shoulders.

I grunted and shifted, but I didn't pull away. For the first night since getting here, I wasn't ready to sleep instantly. That meant dealing with the fact that we were in bed together, cuddling, having just had great orgasms again. Once was a bit of experimentation—twice made it pretty damn gay.

Or bi, which was starting to sound like the right word. I didn't have to be fifty-percent attracted to men and fifty-percent to women, right? What if I wanted to date and sleep with men right now? Was I only bi in the middle of a threesome? So many questions, and a man who probably knew the answers was lying right here, but no way was I ready to say these things out loud.

I was barely admitting them to myself. Darren didn't deserve that kind of crap. I was leading him on, using him—because what the hell did I have to offer, anyway? He could find someone smarter, more successful, and more importantly, out. I was obviously too shit-scared to ever be out about who I was. Darren deserved someone better. Someone who wasn't just using him for sex.

Hell, did this mean I was doing what Xavier had done?

I shoved myself even deeper under the pillows and tried to count sheep. It beat talking about my feelings when they were running all over the place. The sheep I was counting were on Red Bull and a line of coke, apparently.

It took all my willpower not to start counting the ways in which I sucked. I had plenty of time for that after I got home to my lonely, sucky little twin bed in the slightly better of our two shitty rooms.

"Good night," Darren finally mumbled, his voice quiet and sleepy. At least I wasn't keeping him up with all this self-loathing, then. That would only be one more reason to feel guilty.

"Night," I mumbled back. I was pretty sure I had a long, restless night ahead of me.

20

DARREN

It seemed like the rest of the trip was going to settle into a routine —sunbathing in the morning, partying after lunch, and fooling around in bed when the heat and the vibes from the dance floor got to be too much to resist. The day after the white party went much the same, except for a lack of excursions.

But just when I was getting comfortable, I woke up on Wednesday to a grumpy Adam. The only thing predictable about his moods was that I couldn't predict them or what caused them. Just because I was sleeping with him didn't mean he was any more forthcoming about it.

I figured sleeping in and grabbing a late breakfast would put him in a better mood. As I chatted with Raymond, though, Adam abruptly stood up.

"I'd better go change. It's the luau today, isn't it?"

"Yeah, but it doesn't start 'til after lunch." I looked up at him and then snuck a glance at his plate. He'd barely touched his food, which wasn't like him at all.

Was he feeling ill? I could see him not wanting to admit to that in front of the other guys. But he hadn't said a word this morning.

"Yeah, but I gotta shower, too."

I nodded and waved. "Enjoy. I'll grab us some deck chairs."

He grunted and strode off, leaving me squinting after him. God, it was getting to be a headache trying to figure out what was going through his head. Even though I'd promised myself I wouldn't, I couldn't seem to stop myself trying.

Raymond gently said, "Everything all right?"

I didn't get the sense he was trying to pry or gossip, so I shrugged. "Not sure," I admitted and forced a smile. "He's the strong, silent type."

"I got that impression." Raymond smiled, and it was actually reassuring. "Perhaps he's having trouble adjusting to the environment. It's gotta be a lot for a guy who just came out."

"You think I should follow him?" Here I was, fretting again. "Make him talk?"

"Far be it from me to offer advice on relationships," Raymond said with a self-deprecating chuckle, "but making people talk rarely works."

That was true. Adam might just double down and make things awkward for the rest of the trip. He knew I was open to listening as soon as he was ready. "I just want to be there for him, you know? He's gone through—is going through—a lot of change. But he's the type to need space to figure things out."

"Then all you can do is enjoy yourself," Raymond said with a smile. "Come on. Let's find deck chairs."

The company was so appreciated. I didn't get the sense Raymond had seen his chance to hit on me, either—he was just being friendly, the way I tried to be when I saw someone else in the dumps.

By the time Adam showed up at the poolside half an hour later, he seemed to be in a completely different mood. Bubbly, outgoing, and not a little camp. "What's up, buttercups?" he greeted cheerily and swished his hips back and forth.

I took a moment to appreciate the full effect: coconut bra, grass skirt, and tiara.

"Goddamn, you look good." I was kind of jealous of his ability to pull anything off. Those abs made any outfit work on him.

Adam smirked. "You know it, girl." Okay, that was a little over-the-top. Raymond laughed, but my bullshit sensor was going off. Whatever was wrong, he didn't want to dwell on it.

"Well, my Hawaiian shirt is just boring in comparison," Raymond joked.

Adam gasped. "A Hawaiian shirt? Are you going as a straight tourist? Tell me you've got cargo shorts. And socks in sandals."

Raymond laughed again and cast me a pleased look, as if saying, *See? He just needed a minute?*

I knew better, but I wasn't going to out Adam in front of him. I just grinned back at him. "He's incorrigible, isn't he? Now that he's got a taste of what it's like to be the center of attention, I can't get him to keep his shirt on."

Adam ran his hand down his abs and batted his lashes. "Darling, these abs were not made for hiding."

He was channelling Billy, or even Kev in a flamboyant moment, way more than himself right now. It made me almost cringe, but nobody else seemed to think much of it.

Whether he wanted me to ask or not, I cared about Adam and I wasn't going to let his defense mechanisms put me off. I waited until Raymond headed for the pool before I gave it a shot.

"What's going on?" I stretched out along the lounger and folded my arms behind my head as I looked over at him.

Adam made a big show of rearranging the grass in his skirt as he sat on the lounger next to me. "What?"

"You're off today," I told him. "Just spill. Can I help?"

Adam hesitated to answer for a moment, weaving a piece of grass between his fingers. "It doesn't matter. We're on vacation, right? To forget about all that shit. I want a drink. You need a drink too? I'm gonna get one."

I grabbed him by the wrist before he could get up, and I sat up to face him. "If you're drinking before lunchtime, at least tell me why. I'm not gonna stop you, but this *I deal with everything myself* has gotta stop if we're doing this."

"If we're doing what?" Adam was tense at first, but he finally relaxed and patted my hand to get me to let go of his wrist. When I did, he took my hand.

I licked my lips. "You know. Whatever we're up to now." It was a pretty safe bet that he thought of it as more than a one-week deal at this point, too. Wasn't it?

Adam's hesitation told me I was on the right track. "I don't know if I can," he murmured so quietly that only I could hear. I took both his hands and squeezed, which gave him the courage to keep talking. He took a breath and let it out before he looked up at me. "It's gonna make everything change."

That was what I hoped. I'd already gone from a miserable existence pleasing other people to a somewhat more stable existence.

Now I had a job offer on the table, or I could keep freelancing—I could see not just a future, but options for it. I wanted any of those futures to be with him.

But I could see how change might scare Adam. "Doesn't have to change all at once," I told him softly. "Just 'cause we're here together doesn't mean it will."

"I hope you're right." Adam chewed his lip and shook his head.

"Are you ready to stop deflecting?" My heart raced as I squeezed his hands, willing him not to storm off. "And stop joking around about it? Whatever it is, if you want, we can go back to the room—"

"Nah." Adam looked around. "Nobody cares enough to listen in." He gave a smile that was distinctly bitter—I recognized it. I'd felt that same loneliness before, when I was hiding the truth of how fucked-up my relationship with Xavier had grown. When nobody had thought to dig deeper and ask me what was going on.

I didn't want anyone I cared about to go through that alone.

"*I* care," I whispered. It almost hurt how true that was. Whatever was wrong, I wanted to swoop in and fix it. Fuck, I'd grown to care so much more intensely than I'd expected in these past few weeks. No wonder I was having such a hard time letting go and letting him be in a bad mood without trying to guess what was going on.

Adam searched my gaze and I held it, hoping he found what he needed there. Finally, he relaxed and sighed, looking down at his lap. "I called my parents on Sunday."

"Okay?" I offered, trying to work out how that made a differ-ence... three days later? Four? I was losing track of the days easily now that I didn't have jobs to keep me focused.

"They left me a voicemail just today. God, they didn't even notice I was calling from Hawaii. Just a thirty-second *hey son, we're good, call back next month.*" Adam swallowed hard, his voice wavering as he crushed my fingers in his grip.

Fuck, I wished I could take that pain away from him. I recognized it all too well. I'd seen it on other friends' faces, and I'd felt it myself when I first came out. My parents had taken years to accept me, and even now they didn't quite succeed. But they tried, which was the important thing.

Adam's parents? I doubted they even wanted to try.

"Shit. I'm sorry," I murmured. "Did you... um, did you ever come out? Or..."

"It's not that they're homophobic dicks," Adam muttered, shifting on his chair and avoiding my gaze. "It's just that... they don't really understand... I mean, I never told them, but now suddenly all my friends are gay, and they don't approve..."

"Wanna head up to our room?" I prompted again. I knew how hard it was for him to show his feelings, and asking him to do it here by the pool seemed like a lot. I'd figured he'd slept a little wrong, or he was insecure about showing up in a skirt. I hadn't realized his life was melting down in front of his eyes.

Adam shook his head fiercely. "No. I want to remember why I'm here, and why I don't care about them being dicks." His grip was still cutting off the circulation in my fingers, which were starting to throb. "I want to stop chasing them. That's all I'm good for—chasing people and apologizing for who I am."

"Awww. Isn't this a tender moment?"

I took back everything I'd thought about Xavier's new boyfriend being kind of okay after all. I could have throttled Austin as he approached, one hand on his hip, a cocktail in his other hand.

Xavier shadowed him, looking vaguely guilty, like he didn't want this confrontation to happen.

Too bad. It was about to go down.

Adam shot him a glare, which Austin didn't seem to notice, and tilted his chin up as he stared at them both. "Yeah, it is." He pulled my hands into his lap, nearly knocking me off-balance, and held on tightly. There weren't many less subtle ways to mark his claim than that.

Thank God. He still wants me, even if it means being out, was all I could think for a moment. The relief was intense. I could work with this.

"You two are so sweet, but hell, you almost make a skirt look good," Austin added, wrapping his arm around Xavier before rubbing his thigh suggestively. "I'm sure you can do better."

I stared, raising my eyebrows. "Better than?"

He just smirked at me, making it clear that he meant me. "Oh, you know. All this faking it."

My heart dropped, and my palms grew sweaty. "Faking?" If Kev had let word slip, I was gonna kill him. "I'm not faking shit, and neither is he."

"I'm sure." Austin's tone made it clear he wasn't at all sure.

Adam stood up and shook his head, letting go of my hands and wiping his hand along his face. "Maybe you're right," he told me. "*This* isn't what I'm here for." He strode toward the hotel.

I scowled. "If you're trying to start shit, fuck off. I don't have time to act like I'm in high school." I stood up to follow Adam, whipping the towels off our chairs.

"Whateverrr," Austin drawled. He turned and strutted off, then paused and looked annoyed when Xavier didn't instantly follow. He gestured to him with a finger in a *come* motion like he was a dog.

Xavier scowled at him and looked back at me. "Dude. Sorry, I..." he trailed off, speaking too quietly for Austin to overhear. "He started drinking early. I think he's pissed at me. I shouldn't have let him come near you."

I wasn't in the mood for his apologies. Not while Adam was on his way up to the room, no doubt upset about much more important things than one dick ex's new dick boyfriend. "This is what happens when you're so desperate to upgrade from your loser ex that you take anyone who throws himself at you." I pushed past him to head to the lobby, my only focus now on finding Adam and talking him down.

I knew Adam, however much he tried to pretend he was mysterious and aloof. For him to leave me with the two of them, he had to be pretty damn upset.

He must have beaten me to the elevator, or taken the stairs. There was no sign of him until I got to the hotel room. I ignored the *do not disturb* sign that still swung gently from the handle, swiped my key card, and tried to push the door open. It opened less than an inch before stopping on the chain.

"I don't want the room made up," Adam snapped. "I put a sign up and everything."

"It's me," I answered. "I'm here to make up with you."

Adam groaned. "You don't need to. I'm not pissed at you. Go away."

I smiled to myself at how petulant he sounded, but it was painful to hear despite any brief amusement I might find in it. Now that I knew what was going through his head, all I wanted was to hug him and tell him he could do better than those assholes who called themselves parents.

He wanted to isolate himself. Maybe he felt like he deserved to. Well, he was fucking wrong. "I'm not going away, babe. If you don't let me in, I can climb the balcony," I reminded him.

Instantly, I heard footsteps. He clearly took me seriously and didn't want me trying it, which made me smile again. However miserable he was, he still cared about me. I heard him mumble something about interfering and not leaving him be, but when he took the chain off and tugged open the door, he was staring at the ground, his shoulders slumped.

Adam had stripped his grass skirt and bra off, and he just stood in his underwear. He looked so damn vulnerable that I wanted to wrap myself around him and make it all better.

I edged past him inside and let the door close before gently putting my hands on his waist. "I don't care what they say. Your parents *or* Xavier's new boy toy—or anyone else, for that matter."

Adam stared at my knees now, his head lifting just slightly. "Even when I'm a dick about it?"

"Especially when you're a dick about it," I told him, letting my hands slide around to his back as I leaned in to hug him. "That's when you need this the most."

The moment my words cracked through his armor, I felt it. His stiff back relaxed, and he hugged me tightly against him, burying his face in my shoulder. He swayed against me here in the hallway of the hotel room, and I braced myself to support more of his weight.

"I'm here for you, baby," I whispered and stroked his hair.

Yeah, I'd made the right call in coming here. If Adam had never felt like he was worth being chased, I was gonna show him differently. I was gonna love him so hard, and not just in bed.

Mine, was all I could think. Mine to hold and protect and help, and to be proud of, and sad with, and to make laugh over stupid shit. As long as he'd let me, I was gonna make him mine.

21

ADAM

I don't know how long I stood in the hallway before I let go of Darren for long enough that he could pull me over to the bed.

It was stupid. Nothing had changed. The only thing that had changed was my own realization of what was going on—or what I'd lost, rather.

"They never really gave a shit," I finally murmured when we were lying on the bed, me flat on my back and Darren spooning into my side, gently rubbing my chest. My eyes ached, and I wished I could cry. I'd managed a few seconds earlier, when I listened to my voicemails while Darren showered. Now, though, I just felt like shit, and I couldn't even cry and get those feelings out.

"They're stupid, then," Darren murmured. "They don't see the guy I do."

"The insecure asshole who can't even stand up for you and do the one job I came here to do?" My gut twisted. "Who can't even fake it when it feels real?"

"You're not an asshole," Darren murmured.

"Might be the first time I've ever heard that."

Darren hummed. "You don't *mean* to be an asshole. But you want your own space to work things out, and you lash out when people threaten that. It's not that you're trying to put others down. There's a difference."

I caught my breath and blinked at the ceiling a few times before I looked at him. I was stunned speechless for a moment, taken by surprise that he'd been watching me closely enough to figure out something about myself that I barely knew.

"That's why I like you," Darren smiled at me. "And you know why Austin said we were fake? Because he's jealous of how much realness he could see there. He and Xavier? That's a fake-ass relationship if I ever saw one."

Finally, I managed a little smile. I turned onto my side to let Darren put his arms around me, shifting until I was sure I wasn't going to put his arm to sleep. "Yeah, he is pretty fake, isn't he? I thought—I thought he'd found out somehow."

Darren shook his head. "I don't think so. He was just grasping at straws." He sounded confident, and I was able to breathe that in and start to believe his words.

I groaned. "I'm sorry I took off. I just couldn't stick around and hear him say anything that might... that would remind me of my parents." I couldn't look him in the eye again, so I focused intently on his collarbone. As I always did, I touched what I liked to see, so I found myself tracing it gently with a finger. "I couldn't even stick around and chew him out. I'm only an asshole to the people I like. How fucked-up is that?"

Darren shook his head. "I'm not gonna believe you, however much you say it."

I blinked and finally looked up at him, frowning as I tried to work out what he meant.

"You can tell me you're a jerk however much you want," Darren told me softly. "I'm only hearing someone else's voice telling *you* that, and now I bet I know who. Just because you believe it doesn't make it true."

My throat felt tight for a minute. He was right—my parents had told me how ungrateful, lazy, and stupid I was, and how I needed to be different. Every time I'd tried to change myself, it hadn't worked, though. Join baseball? That was suddenly too girly. Football? I was gonna get a concussion and end up even more stupid. Get a job? I was too rude to customers to keep it. Get fired? I was just lazy.

It had been a year since I'd moved out, and even now I still heard them telling me how I wasn't going to stay moved out for long, and how I was too lazy to work on a real ranch.

"Fuck them," I whispered to myself, my hold on Darren tightening. "They're disowning me slowly instead of having the guts to do it all at once."

Darren nodded slightly, cupping my cheek. "I'm sorry, hon. It looks like it to me."

"I didn't even come out to them." I bit my lip and looked down, and he let me avoid his gaze again, even if he kept stroking my face and hair gently. "But they always knew."

"Parents do sometimes. They're supposed to love you no matter what. If they don't, that's on them. It's not your job to change into someone who they say deserves their love."

The words were finally getting through, like they were laser-targeted to zap each insecurity I had. I closed my eyes to let them really sink in. "You're right. Yeah. That's what I told Kev, pretty much."

"Let yourself believe it, too." Darren kissed my forehead. "You're a great guy, whatever they say about it. Just having you around, my self-esteem has changed. I was at rock bottom before I moved in."

He'd seemed pretty down on himself, but I'd figured that was just the effects of breaking up. Even after hearing that Xavier had used him, I hadn't realized it got that bad. "Me?" I cracked a smile. "C'mon. You could do better."

"That's what I'm talking about." Darren huffed a sigh and poked me in the chest. "Quit saying shit like that."

"But..." My brows furrowed. "But I believe it. I'm not gonna fake it 'til I make it."

Darren groaned and let go of me, rolling onto his back. "No, you're too honest for that. But maybe it would do you some good."

I could see his point: pretending to have a boyfriend had given me the chance to explore who I was without any pressure. Maybe pretending to have self-confidence would give me a chance to feel it, for once.

"I've been telling you since before we got here: I only want *you*," Darren added. He was the one avoiding my gaze now, twisting his hands together on his stomach. As he played with his fingers, he cast little sideways glances at me here and there. "I don't know what that means for us, going forward. Or after this week. I just don't want it to be over like that." He snapped his fingers.

I flinched, the cracking sound making me recoil. Maybe because a little part of me still expected a slap around the cheeks, and to be told to get myself together and stop being so *girly*. Men dealt with their feelings by punching things, not cuddling.

I drew a breath and let it out. "We can worry about that after we get back," I told him, trying to fake a little of the confidence he wanted me to have.

"So what do you want out of the rest of this week?" Darren looked over at me.

I wasn't sure, honestly. "I've gotten so much more than I expected." I offered him a shaky smile. "Suddenly I'm this person who never had the chance to admit to all this stuff I wanted." It was like acknowledging this part of my sexuality had woken up everything I'd been trying to cut off at once: my feelings about my family, my fears that I wasn't gay enough to attract a man like Darren, but also a need that ran deeper than a quick jerk to some guilty gay porn.

Darren's touch on my chest made me catch my breath. Fuck, there went my body again, waking up in response to his touch, warmth stirring deep in my gut—and deeper still, in my cock. Just feeling his broad palm brush over my nipple made me moan, the sound too good to swallow.

"Oh," Darren whispered and grinned. "Someone's sensitive."

Fuck. I twisted my hands in the covers and tried not to react, but when he brushed two fingers across a nipple, my body twitched in pleasure. It made electric pricks of desire run along my skin, my hair standing on end.

"Is this making you want to explore?"

I huffed out a quick laugh. "I've been wanting to fuck a guy for years," I admitted, watching his hand roam across my chest. "I just never had the balls to say it out loud." *Or, more to the point...* I thought. If I was gonna try to say what I wanted, I may as well be honest. "Or be fucked by," I mumbled.

"What?" Darren paused, his hand going still on my stomach as he leaned in closer.

"Be fucked by," I repeated, a lot louder than I'd meant to, suddenly impatient at the halted sensation I'd been so enjoying. "I want you —" I was going red now, I could feel it. I tried to ignore it and play it cool, but it was impossible when Darren's very body heat made me warm all over. "I want you to fuck me. I've never let a girl… you know… pop my cherry, or whatever," I finished in a mutter, trying not to feel insecure at my lack of experience.

Darren breathed out a silent laugh and kissed my shoulder. "I'd love to," he murmured. "But I wasn't gonna ask first."

"Why not?" I looked over at him, swallowing a moan when his palm ran over my nipple again to my shoulder. "What do *you* want from this week? Why not tell me?"

"Oh, you're good," Darren smiled teasingly. He bit his lip as if he was hesitating to answer, but to his credit, he didn't look away. "I just assumed you knew I was up for anything." I frowned questioningly and he shook his head. "I didn't want to, like… I didn't want it to seem like I was taking advantage of you."

I snorted with amusement. "And I've been trying not to take advantage of *you*. I didn't want it to seem like I was using you."

"We should both take advantage of each other, then," Darren said with a grin.

I tried to set aside my other fears—*what if I don't like it? What if he gets impatient with me?*—and just live in the moment. We both wanted this. What was the worst that could happen? Mediocre sex was just one of life's risks.

"Deal," I whispered and rolled onto my front.

Darren chuckled. "No, baby. I'm not doing this if I can't kiss you."

I caught my breath at how damn romantic that sounded. Still, he patted my hips a few times, making it clear he meant it, and I had no choice but to turn over.

Darren slid between my thighs and kissed me. "Much better," he murmured against my lips.

I had to admit, kissing made it better. I gripped his shoulders, adjusting to the weight of him between my thighs, and the way his cock rubbed against me as he rolled our hips together slowly.

Yeah, this already felt good. I was still nervous, but there wasn't that voice in my head telling me it was a dumb idea and I should get out of it now, like when I'd tried to hook up with Ricky. I was just afraid of screwing up a good thing we already had going. That wasn't good enough reason to keep denying us both what we wanted.

He was thick and hard, and I couldn't deny how much I craved feeling him inside me. As he stripped off his swimsuit and my underwear, I found myself eager to feel skin on skin again.

Darren wasn't rushing it, though. He kept kissing me until I was panting into his mouth, and he ran his hands along my body to explore every goddamn sensitive spot he could find. My nipples were like direct hot-buttons to my cock, and he exploited the hell out of that new finding.

"God, you're the jerk here," I mumbled.

Darren chuckled against my lips and ran his fingers around both nipples again. "How's that?" He ground against me, our cocks bumping and rubbing in a pleasurable slide I couldn't get enough of.

"Making me want you so bad..." I whispered. "So bad, baby."

Darren pinched both nipples and twisted slightly—just enough to send a painful yet pleasurable thrill shooting through me.

"Ah! Fuck!" I hissed, arching against him. I squirmed until I could get one leg up far enough to wrap around his waist. The other loosely wrapped around his thighs, but keeping our bodies locked together like this meant I could grind on his stomach.

"I love feeling you get hard against me," Darren whispered, running his fingers down my sides now. "I wonder what it'll feel like when you come with me inside you."

I swallowed my whimper, but only just. These were the words I'd dreamed about someone saying to me, but I'd never had a face to put to the fantasy.

Now that I did, I was burning up with pleasure and desire. "Please," I panted.

"Please what?"

"Fucking hurry up and fuck me." I growled the words at him, bucking against him insistently. "I need you."

Darren smiled at me, still way too fond and patient. "Have you fingered yourself before?"

"Every damn day this week," I grumbled. When Darren stared, I avoided his gaze. "It's a good shower, okay?"

Darren laughed, surprise written over his features. "I wish I'd been there to watch. Don't let me miss out on that next time, hm? That sounds like a great show."

I blushed at the idea of him watching me slide my fingers into myself. "You could… I mean, if you've got lube, I can do it."

Darren almost scrambled for the lube, not even remotely keeping his cool. That made me feel better about how needy I felt right now, at least.

When I had my fingers slick and warm, Darren knelt between my thighs, one hand on each of my knees as he watched me. Just having him so close, witnessing my inexperienced fumbling, made me burn with what I first thought was embarrassment, but pretty quickly realized felt damn good.

"Oh, Darren," I moaned as I let one finger slide into myself and gently moved it in and out. Even this much took some relaxing. I wanted to be good and ready for him so he could pound me into the bed after all these weeks of fantasizing about it.

"You're fucking hot," he whispered, seemingly entranced by my movements. "God, you make me want to do the dirtiest things to you."

"Like fuck me until the neighbors complain?" I whispered. "Fuck me on the windowsill where everyone can see us? Or in the shower until I come all over the wall? On the desk?"

Darren stroked himself slowly, fumbling as he tried to open a condom packet without letting go of his cock.

I hurried up to add a second finger and gasped, my toes curling into the bed. The extra thickness ached at first, but once I adjusted to the stretch, I was back to talking dirty. "You make me wanna bend over and take it, and then give you a turn."

Darren's sharp groan told me he was into this, so I kept going as I sped up the pace of my hand, plunging my fingers deep into my tight hole and imagining that it was his hard cock. At long last, I was going to get to feel this—any moment now. The thought was almost unbearably hot.

"You want to fuck me, too?" Darren groaned. "God, I've fantasized about that since... well, that time on the floor."

I grinned, knowing which time he meant immediately. "On the living room floor, when you could have been bouncing up and down on my cock?" I tried for a third finger and got it most of the way inside before he pulled my wrist aside and poured lube in his hand.

"If you keep talking like that, I'm gonna come any minute," Darren warned, grinning at me.

I mimed zipping my lips. "Not a peep from me, then. You'll have to imagine your own porno soundtrack."

"Cheeky little asshole," Darren smacked my hip, grinning at me as he pressed the tip of his cock against me.

I took a breath, but before I could second-guess myself, the thick, warm weight of him was pressing into me.

When I cried out, Darren slowed down even more, easing into me with the tiniest thrusts imaginable. He was praising me too, in a gentle whisper.

"You're so gorgeous. You're doing so good. You're so tight around me, beautiful."

I tried to relax, clenching the covers under me, and Darren's hand gently rested on one of my wrists. When I inhaled sharply and moaned, he brought his hand away from his cock to hold down my other wrist, too.

"Yes!" was all I could manage as he filled me to the brim with his hard cock and pinned me down, using my body the way I'd only ever daydreamed of. I couldn't believe how fucking lucky I was, or how much it turned me on to see him naked and hovering over me, his knees pressing into the bed on either side of me as he pressed kisses sporadically against my lips.

When he started to move, I just about lost my damn mind. It hurt at first, but he let go of one of my wrists to keep touching me instead. That skilled hand tugging on my cock and nipples, running along my ribs and pressing me flat to the bed, did more for me than I'd even expected.

He was so damn deep inside me, and I loved it.

"This is—this is perfect," I moaned, spreading my legs wider now. I was sure I could handle it now, and I felt good about myself in a way I never had before. I was man enough to take a cock, and to want more. "Harder."

Darren grinned at me, like he'd just been waiting for me to ask. He thrust quicker now, shifting his weight and pulling both my hands above my head to pin them down with one of his own. His other hand slid down to my cock to start stroking me in time with his thrusts.

The sparks that heated up my body were almost impossible to control. I felt him hitting my prostate, and hot damn, I actually loved it. It was a whole different kind of turned-on than I was used to.

I was whimpering unreservedly now, moaning with every thrust as he pounded into me, squirming under his tight hold and thrusting into the fist he'd closed around my cock.

Time itself stood still, and it felt like every part of me was involved here. Like I'd just awoken something in me that I'd stopped acknowledging a long time ago, and now I was all put back together.

All of me loved this, and I knew I was barely going to last any time at all.

"We'd better do this again," I gasped. "I love it too much."

Darren grinned at me. "That's the spirit," he whispered and kissed me. "I love that you love it. You feel incredible. You're doing so well."

"I'm gonna come," I warned him, gasping when he just tightened his hold and jerked me off even faster. "Ohhh, fuck. Any time now—"

He cut me off by kissing me hard, his teeth finding the sensitive lower lip and sucking hard. I felt like he was laying his claim to me, and I loved it.

I wanted to be his.

When I came, it was hard and fast, and I made a hell of a mess. My climax hit me like I'd run into it at top speed, and all I could think to moan was his name, over and over. The way he kissed me, though, I was kind of able to cling to reality—just to him, like he was the center of my world. And right now, he was.

As I finally relaxed around him, I felt him gasp against my lips. My eyes flew open, because I didn't want to miss a minute of this.

Darren was gripping me by the shoulders now, his nails biting into me as he groaned. "Adam!"

"Come, baby," I gasped, still on the outer edges of my own orgasm. I shivered with pleasure at the way he thrust into me hard and fast, the bed squeaking under us with his desperation. "Come on! Fuck me, Darren!"

That was all it took. Darren threw back his head and cried out as he came, his whole body shivering and twitching, his dick pulsating inside me. I was only sorry we hadn't gotten around to the testing booth they had set up here yet, because I wanted his juices inside me.

Today, I promised myself. Like, ASAP. Maybe in half an hour when we were dressed again.

"That's it, baby," I grinned, rubbing his shoulders and back as his thrusts slowed and stopped, and he collapsed on top of me.

We just held each other for a few minutes, our heartbeats slowing and breathing syncing up.

The orgasm had cleared my thoughts somehow. At the very least, I felt less alone, and I hoped he did too. Finally, when he'd slid out, I murmured, "Let's not worry about the rest of that crap. We've only got a couple more nights here."

God, I didn't want to go home. That meant facing reality, and telling other people the truth about us, and… well, separate crappy bedrooms in a crappy apartment. Not the all-inclusive bubble where we didn't have to lift a finger except to touch each other.

I didn't want real life to destroy this.

Darren nodded, unaware of my pessimism kicking in. "We may as well make the most of them," he agreed. "We've got time after we get home to figure out what to do next."

"We've got some assholes to make jealous. And boy, they oughta feel jealous of this," I grinned, patting my ass.

Darren burst out laughing. "You dirty bastard." He kissed me and stood up to head for the bathroom. "Let's get back out there and give them our best post-coital glow."

I caught myself smiling up at the ceiling as I waited for my turn to wash up. That wouldn't take any faking at all. Everyone else would see something pretty damn close to the truth—a happy new couple. The only thing that nagged me was how quickly Darren had avoided committing to doing this again. But that was a problem to think about later.

We just had to fake it for a few more days, get the asshole ex and his new asshole boyfriend off our backs, and then we'd have a chance to be more real than ever before. And that was a terrifying thought.

22

DARREN

"Yassss, kween!"

Did I even know this man? My head snapped around as I eyed Adam. After the amazing sex yesterday, he'd gotten so much more relaxed, but today he was back to this caricature of himself.

I'd been spending all day trying to stay patient. When we'd gone surfing earlier, he hadn't been half this bad. It was only now that we were back at the poolside waiting for the Slip'N Slide party to start that he'd gotten more… well, camp.

Raymond sashayed past with his hands and arms full of cocktails, spilling some over himself, and Adam pretended to lick them off him as Raymond laughed. "Work!" Adam called after him.

I bit my lip so I didn't cringe visibly.

"That almost sounds right," I murmured to him.

Adam folded his arms and settled back again, looking smugly pleased with himself. "He sure thought so."

I hesitated—we'd had such a good day, and was now really

the time to bring it up? But I was going to get painfully embarrassed if Adam tried to out-camp Austin or Xavier in some epic showdown later. And there were surely guys around who might get offended by Adam's... well, clumsy speech at best.

"Did you fall out of the stereotype closet this morning?" I teased him gently, hoping to warm him up to the conversation and figure out where it was coming from rather than just telling him to stop it.

Adam tossed his head. "It was too rigid to contain me."

I was torn between amusement and frustration. If only I could trust that this attitude was sticking around, I might believe him... but he didn't act like this at all in our room when it was just the two of us. It was obviously just a show, and that was what made me eye him.

"None of them are bad," I told him carefully. "It's just... they don't really seem like you."

"Hell, I don't know who I am." Adam shrugged at me. "No wonder you don't."

I got where he was coming from, but I resented the implication that I couldn't tell he was hamming it up. "You're trying it on, I get it. But it's a little bit offensive when you seem kind of like you're making fun of it, you know?"

Adam frowned at me, finally paying attention. "I do? Why would I?"

"Some guys do," I admitted with a shrug. "Especially straight guys. And it feels shitty to anyone who really does act that way, you know? I—I didn't think you were trying to make me feel bad, but..."

Adam rolled onto his side to face me on his lounger. "Oh, hell, no. You don't get to call me a straight guy when it's convenient."

"Huh?" I blinked at him. I knew perfectly well that he wasn't, and I hadn't meant that he was one, but now I realized how it sounded. "I'm sorry. I didn't mean to include you in that. It's just what it makes me think of."

Adam gritted his teeth, furrowing his brow in that way that meant words were coming to him slower than he'd like. "You're not wrong. I—I talked like that at first because I thought that was what I had to do."

"You don't," I assured him. Everyone here had bought it hook, line, and sinker—probably because he *was* one of us. "Nobody expects you to."

"I know." Adam picked up his drink and cradled it against his chest, sipping from it. I let him have a minute of silence to figure out how to phrase it.

I was happy to let him dress up in tight clothes and talk about having just come out, but as soon as he started talking with our mannerisms and slang, I drew the line? That wasn't cool of me. *Whatever you do, let him explore.* That had been my motto all week, but this particularly grated on me. Why the hell was that?

"I didn't mean you, by straight guys," I added quietly.

"Who, then?"

"You ever hear guys on your job sites talking about *the gays*?" I imitated a limp wrist as I sat up.

Adam winced and nodded, his gaze darting down.

"Well, I'm used to hearing them behind my back, saying stuff about me that… I don't even do, but they assume I do." I'd been on more than one job site where that was the case. Now that George had outed me at work, if I were to be really honest, that was where my fear was coming from. "Fuck. Now I'm even worried—I just got a job offer from one of my favorite contractors, but now he knows, he's gonna tell everyone as, like, a talking point."

Adam bit his lip. "And that's what I'm up against, too."

I hesitated and picked up my own cocktail. It felt shitty to even think it, but Adam wasn't coming out as a *fuck you* to his parents, was he? Or had his parents being dicks finally liberated him— made him feel free to be himself? I didn't want to be a pawn in his identity struggle.

I had to trust that he wasn't using me, and I only now realized how hard it was to have that trust in people. *Thanks, Xavier.* Another item for the list of ways he'd fucked me over.

"I was afraid… *am* afraid," I said slowly. "But we should wait until later to figure it out."

Adam shook his head. "When? Tomorrow? The day after, when we fly back?" He chugged the rest of his cocktail and set the plastic cup down.

After a whole day of just being myself around him, fooling around and joking and enjoying ourselves, I didn't want to bring the conversation back to his horrible night. We hadn't even seen Xavier and his new boyfriend since then, but I knew we wouldn't escape the closing night party without running into them.

"Are you thinking about coming out because of you? Or me?" That was the best way I could think to put it.

Adam just stared blankly at me. "I'm pretty sure I've already come out, dude. It's too late to change that."

That just made me feel guilty, and I looked down.

"Hey." Adam caught my hand. "Dude, look at me." When I did, he met my gaze fiercely. "I'm fucking glad we did this. Even if it all started as a fake thing, it gave me the chance to see how I liked sex and romance with someone I trusted."

He trusted me? That made it sound almost like he *was* going to carry on with this and come out for me, and... well, let this relationship continue.

I swallowed hard. "I feel like I got the better end of the deal here."

Adam pinched my leg lightly—just hard enough to get my attention. "Hey. If I'm not allowed to talk shit about myself, neither are you," he told me, his gaze even fiercer now. "You don't put down the guy I like, all right?"

I opened and closed my mouth for a moment before meekly nodding. "Sorry."

"I might be playing around with who I am, but..." Adam trailed off, frowning at me. "I'm not doing it to make you feel bad."

"Why, then?"

Adam blushed and looked away. "So, when I said I like you?"

My heart started to race in double-time. I tried to calm myself down and tell myself this wasn't happening, but my heart said *fuck you very much, this is happening* and I couldn't stop it. I hoped he was saying what I thought he was. "Yeah?" I squeaked.

"I want you to see me... like..." Adam gestured around the poolside at everyone else milling around, drinking, swimming, chatting with old friends. "Like them."

I didn't get it. I liked spending time here, sure, but I was here *with* Adam, not them. "Like how?"

Adam grimaced and scooted his deck chair closer until our chairs touched. When he stretched out, he kicked one leg over mine.

That brought our faces close—just inches apart—and he could talk quieter. "So I might not know much about all this," he murmured. "But I want you to see me as an option."

I tried not to smile. "Dude, you're more than an option. You kept asking me if I wanted to hook up with someone else."

"Yeah, but that's just..." Adam waved a hand. "Practical."

And like that, it clicked. He'd thought that he wasn't an option for me, and that was why he'd offered to let me sleep around. And now he was trying to take that back, make himself seem like a catch. Little did he know I'd already caught him. "Honey, no." I gripped his shoulder. "I started falling for you—God knows when. Maybe since we moved in. Maybe since that night on the living room floor. Maybe just since we got here. I can't put a date on it," I said with a shrug. "And I don't want to. It's just grown into this natural thing between us, and that's... beautiful."

"But..." Adam trailed off and then looked meaningfully up.

When I followed his gaze, I found Xavier standing there, his arms folded in front of his chest like he was nervous about being here.

"Speak of the devil," Adam grumbled, pushing himself to sit upright and then stand in one swift motion.

I wasn't entirely sure he wasn't about to punch Xavier, so I scrambled to my feet, too.

As I did, Xavier smiled sheepishly. "Sorry. I didn't wanna bug you two. I just wanted to, um, say sorry if I've made anything awkward."

"Oh, well, that's all better then," Adam said sarcastically.

I squeezed past Xavier to put my arm around Adam's waist. "It's okay," I murmured.

Adam shook his head at me. "It's really not."

"He's right," Xavier said. His arms were still folded, and he couldn't seem to look at either of us. "I pitted Austin against you from the start, and that wasn't fair to either of you."

Oh. Well. I hadn't expected this apology at all. I blinked a few times and then looked at Adam, and back to Xavier. I was so caught off-guard that I didn't know how to answer.

I didn't need to, because Adam was already talking. "You made Darren feel crappy on purpose," he said. "Anyone who loved him for real—even if that love was over—would never do that."

Xavier's cheeks flushed, and he finally looked up at Adam and then to me. "You're right," he said, but he was looking at me and not Adam. "I didn't appreciate you, and I should have let you go way sooner. You've obviously found someone who deserves you, and… I'm glad. I'm gonna try to keep Austin away from you guys for the last couple days. I should have done that already."

My heart felt full and warm. I wasn't sure what I was feeling, but it was a damn sight better than anything Xavier had made me feel before. Whether he knew it or not, that pressure had completely accidentally given me the best thing in my life. I reached out to take Xavier's hand. "Thank you," I told him quietly.

He wiped his eyes, nodded, and strode quickly for the hotel lobby, not looking back.

Adam let out a breath and leaned into me. "Well, the plot thickens."

"I told you he's not an asshole," I murmured. "Just oblivious."

"Sounds a lot like someone else you know," Adam told me, cracking a smile. "I'm beginning to think you have a type."

I chuckled, and then I found I couldn't stop laughing. Adam was so much more than an asshole, but maybe he really was—just a little bit. And I loved that about him.

Unlike Xavier, I never had to worry he was pretending. From the start, he'd never been able to hide it when he faked it, and this sure as hell wasn't fake, if it ever had been.

I felt guilty for having doubted him coming out—even in my own mind. His bisexuality had nothing to do with me. If anything, I should be proud of him, and glad for him, that he felt able to come out now. Even if it was him trying to say *fuck you* to his parents, he wasn't doing it for anyone but him. The more he talked about it, the more I could see that now.

"I don't deserve you," I murmured, wrapping my arms around his waist and burying my face in his shoulder.

Adam snorted. "If you don't, then I don't deserve you, either."

"God, you're stubborn."

"So are you."

"Good thing," I said with a grin. "Takes one to handle one." Wherever the hell this was going, I was starting to feel like we had a chance. As long as Adam was willing to keep fighting his demons, I owed it to him to keep fighting mine.

When we finally let go and he came back with another round of drinks, we tried to cuddle up on the deck chairs we'd pushed together.

Naturally, he immediately slid between the gap in the loungers, covering himself in his cocktail and shrieking. As ice slid down his stomach, he flicked it away from himself, tossing the cup clear into the pool and cursing up a storm.

All I could do was laugh until my belly hurt. God, I loved him more than I ever could have thought possible.

Whoa. Not that word, I told myself fiercely. I *liked* him. It was too soon to tell if it was anything more.

But even in months, Xavier had never made me feel this glow—the one that made me want to wrap myself around him and forget about the rest of the world. The one that made me feel complete, for the first time in a long time.

I chugged my cocktail and showed him the empty cup as he scrambled to his feet, wiping the cocktail off himself with something that passed for dignity. "Looks like we both need another."

"Jerk," Adam mumbled. "Do I look like your manservant?"

I tilted my head. "Yeah, now that you mention it, I've always wanted a hot manservant to feed me cocktails by a pool. I never thought I'd get one with abs like yours, though."

Adam tried not to puff up proudly, but it was obvious that he was drinking in the compliment. He plopped down by the poolside to splash water down himself and clean the blue slush off.

"And I'm drinkless in solidarity with you. You should thank me," I told him, smirking.

"Solidarity, my ass," Adam scoffed, but he was hiding his laugh behind his hand, trying to wipe the smirk off his face. He suddenly splashed me with water.

"Hey!" I squeaked, scrambling off my lounger and trying to hide behind it, but his aim was good. I was the first to give in. "Fine! Fine, defeat!" I held up my hands and backed away from the pool. "I'll get this round."

"I should make you lick me clean," Adam said, his eyes sparkling as he grinned up at me. "As punishment. Or I can come up with other ideas."

I resisted the hard-on he was trying to give me, but only just. It was hard to ignore the prickle of desire that shot through me at the thought of licking ice off his toned body, or better yet, other punishments Adam could give me.

Evil little fucker. He knew exactly what he was doing, and I didn't even have to call him out on it—he was already grinning at me. I walked away quickly while he laughed, and the sound made me smile like a loon.

Now that I knew it, there was no going back. For better or for worse, I was head-over-heels for Adam.

If I wasn't careful, this was gonna get complicated. It always did, in the end.

ADAM

How was it already the last night of our vacation? I'd only just gotten used to this damn time zone, and suddenly we were staring down the flight home.

At least I had one more chance to really wow Darren before we headed home. It had taken a lot of hours online reading articles about how to get a suit fitted, and even more effort finding one at the right price—but I looked pretty damn good, if I did say so myself.

I wasn't the only one saying so. Darren emerged from the bathroom and wolf-whistled at the same time my jaw dropped. Apparently, not only did I like a man shirtless, naked, or in skimpy swimwear, but I liked a man in a good vest. I was learning so much about myself.

"Hot damn," Darren said, a teasing grin on his lips. "I'd better keep you in my sights tonight."

I grinned at him. Compliments from guys had always made me feel good, and I'd never really put together why before now. Duh.

"I look like a hot bi guy?" It was the first time I'd used the word, and I wasn't married to it—but it sounded way more like me than *straight* did.

Darren's grin grew. "You do, baby." He looped his arms around his waist and growled. "Especially bi my side."

"Oh, God," I laughed. "No dad jokes."

"If you'd rather I told daddy jokes… I've got plenty up my sleeve."

"Nooo."

"Watersports?" he teased. "I can make those jokes rain on you…"

"You're such an asshole," I waved him off with a laugh, but he wouldn't let go. "I didn't mean for any of this to happen! No jokes, please," I exclaimed. Still, I let him hug me and laugh. He was so sweet when he was relaxed like this.

"Fine. I'll be strictly serious." His lips twitched into a grin. "Even if it's fun to introduce you to new kinks and watch you blush."

I rolled my eyes. "Don't make me shun you tonight."

"I would never let you." Darren kissed my cheek and let go before he took my hand. "Ready to go show those assholes what a real relationship looks like?"

Is he saying we're in one? Or we could be? I smiled giddily and let him lead me out of the room. "So ready." If we could out-love Xavier and Austin, I'd be happy. Somewhere along the way, I'd picked up another goal, too. Or maybe I'd had it from the start: I wanted to make Darren happy.

As long as I was doing that, I felt good. And I could pretend this week would carry on forever—the easy life, sitting by the pool in the morning and fucking like animals at night.

No talking about the future, no figuring out what words like *boyfriend* meant to us, no stress about my family or his friends or any of that. Just the two of us, alone together.

It was nearly impossible to ignore the fact that this was the last night, though. Everywhere I turned, guys were saying goodbye to each other in case they didn't see each other again tonight. Even the damn banner up in the lobby reminded us that it was the closing party.

As long as I don't lose my damn glass slipper. I shook my head at myself, but I couldn't stop feeling like this was all too good to be true. After midnight I'd turn into a pumpkin or something, and reality would come crashing back in.

"I'm getting shots," I told Darren with a grin. "Red Headed Sluts?"

Darren laughed at me and just shrugged helplessly. "If you're offering…"

I leaned in and murmured, "Almost as fiery as I am for you—but nowhere near as slutty." I left him with that to think about and wandered for the bar, which was getting crowded even this early.

I recognized some of the guys there, so I struck up a few conversations while we waited to be served. It moved faster since nobody had to worry about payment, but even so, nobody was working at Manhattan bartender speeds.

When I finally got there and ordered four shots, Raymond came to lean next to me with a friendly smile. "That sounds like a good night or a bad one. I can't work out which."

"Hopefully good," I answered and clapped his shoulder. "It was awesome meeting you." Oh, God. Now I was doing it too—the whole sappy goodbye thing. And there was no way in hell I could afford to come back next year on my own, so it was a real goodbye.

Raymond hugged me instead of shaking hands, and it took me a moment to relax into it. I kind of liked that these guys hugged so much, but a lifetime of carefully avoiding touching men wasn't unlearned in a week. God, it was going to be weird to go back to my job and life in Brooklyn where I didn't see guys dry-humping each other at the breakfast bar.

"Make the most of tonight, huh?" Raymond grinned.

I toasted that and balanced the shots in a square in my hands. "You only live once."

"Too right."

I nodded and headed back to find Darren, still nervous about leaving him on his own for too long. Austin seemed to relish the opportunity to play mind games with him.

"Hey, babe," Darren greeted without even seemingly thinking about the nickname. It only made my heart hurt more to wonder whether that was going to go away tomorrow, when we were back in our old routine.

When he no longer needed me, would he just ditch me the way everyone else did?

Darren looped his arm around me as he kept talking to some pretty boy who could keep his paws off my man, thank you very much. I set down the shots on the high table in front of us and downed one without a pause.

He grinned and took one to do the same, and then gasped. "That's actually… pretty good." The other guy wandered off—probably because I glared at him while Darren was catching his breath.

"Isn't bad," I agreed.

Darren eyed me, but instead of asking what was wrong, he just toasted me with the second shot. "To a great week."

"And to the guy who made it all happen," I responded and downed my shot, enjoying the burn down my throat. That reminded me of something we had yet to talk about.

Darren snorted. "Oh, that was just dumb luck."

"I'm pretty sure I have all the luck here," I told him.

Darren smiled, but it was a sad expression. I hadn't expected that. "I think you're right. You ready to dance?"

"I dunno about dancing." I still didn't feel like I could look half as sexy as the other guys here, but I was determined to cheer him up another way. I leaned in and murmured, "Hey, so. I got a text from the testing booth. Everything's clear."

"Was it worth being leafletted?" Darren teased me. They'd seen a chance to educate a clueless guy—and they were right, to be fair. I had never been sat down and taught all the things I could catch. My school's sex ed had basically been *don't do it, you'll die*, and I'd stuck with condoms because I didn't like the idea of fathering a kid without knowing.

I kissed his jaw. *If I never get a chance to fuck him again, I want to try it without a condom. I wouldn't trust just any guy.* "And you did too, huh?"

"All negative—" Darren broke off, his eyes widening. "Oh. You're thinking…?"

"Just keeping you in suspense for tonight," I told him with a smirk. "So you remember whose room to come back to." I cast another dark glare after the cutie who'd been hitting on him.

Darren's smile slowly grew. "That's a jealous look if I ever saw one, mister."

I scoffed. "No. Go dance. I don't need to be jealous. I know where you live."

"You do," Darren grinned. He pecked my lips and headed for the dance floor while I smiled to myself and found someone to talk to. I still kept an eye on Darren, but he could take care of himself.

It was me that was way out of my depth here.

Unfortunately for me, the only thing that was more predictable than my bad moods was the fact that they kicked in at the worst times.

Now was one of those times. I'd joined Darren for a few songs, but I'd pulled away to find drinks and sit down for a while. Just people-watching was the best part of being here, but it quickly became the worst part. All it took was that part of my brain that loved to compare myself to other people. What a fucked-up evolutionary response. I didn't need to be a better spear-wielder than anyone else in the modern world.

"Oh, who's the last one up against the wall?"

Fuck. Austin had come for me, not Darren. I hadn't seen him coming, I was so busy watching Darren to make sure nobody was dancing too close to him. Not that I was jealous. Just protective, now that we'd both had several drinks.

"Being up against the wall can be pretty fun. Not that you'd know that, apparently," I shot back with a smile at Austin.

Austin just glowered at me. He was wearing tight shorts and a literally painted-on tuxedo.

"Not getting enough attention?" I knew it was a bad idea to provoke him, but I couldn't resist. He'd had a week of needling me and Darren in vulnerable moments. "Had to come over here and try to start something?"

"Eww. I'm not starting anything with *you*." Austin wrinkled his nose and leaned in to hiss, "I've seen your Facebook."

I looked blankly at him, trying to figure out what that even meant. "Okay?"

"You're not even a real gay, are you? I saw photos of you kissing girls."

I scoffed, trying to quell the rising fear. Somehow, I hadn't expected anyone to actually do detective work on me. "No guy here has photos with girls, that's for sure. No girls allowed, is that it?"

"It's guys like you who give us a bad name, you know." Austin stumbled and I reached out to grab his elbow, but he swatted my hand away. Clearly, he'd already had more to drink than I had.

"Like me?" I raised an eyebrow. "Not the ones falling-down-drunk before midnight, making an ass of themselves, surely?"

"Fuck off," he hissed and leaned in. "You're just dipping your toe in the water, admit it."

I wasn't going to take the bait. I might have gotten pissed at him earlier this week, but now? I just saw how sad he was, and it made me almost feel bad for him. "I like the water just fine."

"Fence-sitter."

I grinned at him. He had nothing on me, and he knew it. He was grasping at straws. "I bet you're gonna say it's sluts like me who spread fatal diseases now, huh? Get a new line," I told him. "One that isn't more stale than you."

Austin snarled at me. "You poisoned my relationship."

By now, a few guys nearby had noticed what was going on and

were giving me concerned glances—or drinking in the drama, I couldn't tell which. I just sighed at him. "You did that all by your idiot self."

Still, I'd had quite enough to drink for one night, because the room spun as I ignored him and headed into the crowd to grab Darren. Time to stop being a wallflower and enjoy the only man I wanted to be around.

Darren took one look at me and wrapped his arms around my waist. "Did one of the power dick couple find you?"

"I look that rough, huh?"

Darren squeezed me and didn't answer, so I sighed. My gut sank now that I felt safe to let my guard down. "Yeah. He said some shit about me being bi, and fence-sitting. Nothing I haven't heard before." Never aimed at me, though, I had to admit.

When I pulled away to look at Darren, his brows were knitted together, and a thunderous expression crossed his face as he looked around. Angry actually looked pretty hot on him. I ranked it third on my list of favorite expressions—underneath contented and jealous. No, I preferred seeing him horny, too. But this turned me on just as effectively.

Wait, he was talking. What was that?

"How many drinks have you had?"

"Uhhh. A few. Enough. We could get out of here now."

Darren's lips quirked into one of those sexy, mysterious little smiles. "Uh huh. Let's stick around and dance."

I pouted. "Are you going to be a gentleman?"

"Yes, like it or not." Darren rubbed my back and kissed my neck, and I had to admit I liked that, too. "Not sleeping with you when you're drunk as hell, man."

"We might not get another chance."

Darren pulled back and frowned at me. "We will."

I couldn't believe him, though. I never wanted to take people's word for it. Reality would come bite me in the ass otherwise.

"Kiss me, then." I smirked at Darren. "You know that creepy little twerp is watching."

Darren grinned and pressed his lips behind my ear. "See? I goddamn *knew* you were an exhibitionist."

I ground against Darren, finding my beat to the music. Alcohol made it easier to dance, that was for sure. "Maybe I am. Maybe I just want you to kiss me."

Darren's lips found mine, and his hands wrapped around my shoulders. He swayed with me, his tongue darting across my lips until I moaned and closed my eyes.

Yes. Like that.

When Darren stopped kissing me, I pouted and tried to keep going, but Darren pulled back. "Are you sure you're okay?"

I scoffed. "I was better before you stopped kissing me. He doesn't faze me. I've had bigger bullies." Like my parents, I wanted to say, but I just barely stopped myself. I was trying not to let that bitterness ruin this week. "I just wanna enjoy tonight," I murmured. "Last night here."

"Last night," Darren echoed solemnly and rubbed my back, kissing me in a series of gentle pecks on the lips. "Slow-dance with me." He slowed his pace, making me slow down, too.

I rested my head on his shoulder as he pressed his lips into my hair.

"I've got you," he whispered, and I let go of everything I was holding onto—the fears and regrets, the anxiety about tomorrow and next year and the rest of my life, and how it was gonna work out when all the lies we'd been building up came crashing down.

In his arms, here and now, I was safe.

24

DARREN

The flight home seemed much longer than the flight to Hawaii, even though it was an hour shorter. Maybe because Adam started the flight so hungover he didn't want any Champagne. But I didn't get the feeling he was being so distant just because of his hangover.

We'd danced last night until the small hours, and then we'd just crashed together. No sex—definitely not after drinking so much—but the cuddling had been so worth it.

The hangover, not so much. I'd have encouraged him into less drinking and more dancing in retrospect.

It was a long damn flight for Adam to stew. Sure enough, he started to unwind again after the first hour or two and chat to me.

"Man, I can't wait until Kev opens his souvenir."

I thought it was sweet he'd bought his former roommate souvenirs, but I'd never asked what they were. From the way he was smirking, I wasn't sure I wanted to know. Still, curiosity won out. "Oh?"

"They had these wooden penis-shaped paperweights with the Two Palms logo on them." He grinned to himself. "He'll love it. Did you get anything?"

Like I needed a reminder that nobody really cared I'd been gone for a week. "I got keyrings for all the guys at Bubbles. Hopefully I got enough."

"Parents or anything?" Adam cleared his throat. "I never really asked what the situation is."

I shook my head. "Dad moved to Connecticut with his secretary. Mom remarried, and the new guy doesn't like me. My stepbrother's some fancy high-earning surgeon. Electricians aren't really in the family tree," I summed it up. It had long ago lost any sting for me.

Honestly, I was glad I didn't have to sit around being insulted for what I chose to do. I didn't make as much money as he did, and I had to spend a lot more energy finding work, but the work I did was every bit as important in its own way. Every time I found a short that could have caused a fire, I could be saving lives and I'd never know it.

"Oh, shit." Adam frowned. "Well, fuck that noise."

He wasn't shy about cursing up a storm even in business class, and it made me grin. I'd been embarrassed on the way out, but now? Fuck it, as Adam would say. Life was too short to worry about seeming like we fit in. We'd spent the last week trying to do that. We only had a few more hours to enjoy luxury-class travel.

"It's okay. I see Dad sometimes for Thanksgiving or something, but they try to use me as a go-between." I rolled my eyes. That had gone real well last time. "So, if we wanna talk unhealthy relationship models…"

Adam cracked a smile. "I dunno. Mine were a united front, and that wasn't great."

"It sounds like it." If he wanted to throttle Xavier and Austin on my behalf, I felt the same about his parents. No doubt they'd hurt him more than one dick ex could anyway.

"They were, you know… pretty strict." Adam pulled the footrest out so he could stretch out in his seat. "The more time passes, the more I realize maybe it wasn't that normal."

I tried to bite my tongue and not interfere with his growth process. "Mmhmm?"

Adam just stared at the back of the seat in front of him for a minute before he looked over at me with a casual shrug. "Anyway, I just won't call them for a while. See if they notice." His tone was casual, but his smile was a little too stiff.

I wished I could take away that pain. I suddenly felt selfish for having been worrying about our relationship all flight when he had stuff like *will my parents disown me?* hanging over his head.

"What's it like for the rich people of the world? Enjoying your glimpse of it?"

Oh, God. Like a bad penny, Austin was here and leaning on the arm of my seat.

I'd spotted him at the gate, but I hadn't thought he'd have the balls to come up from economy to this section just to harass us. I was just glad I was sitting between him and Adam, so Adam didn't try anything reckless. I wouldn't put it past him to throw a punch and get the flight grounded somewhere in… God, where were we? The Pacific? California? I didn't want to know how far away we were from home.

Lucky for me, I didn't even have to come up with a witty retort of my own. A flight attendant was already on the way.

"Excuse me, sir. I'll have to ask you to remain in your assigned seating section." She wasn't speaking in a tone that left room for argument.

I offered Austin an obnoxious smile and shrug. "I like any world that doesn't have your face in it."

He huffed and turned on his heel to storm back while she rearranged the curtain and apologized to the passengers seated nearby for the disturbance.

"It's kind of weird to be gloating about sitting somewhere he can't come ooze his horrible attitude around us..." I couldn't quite feel bad about it, though.

"Fuck it," Adam chuckled. "Whatever gets him out of our faces. I don't think Xavier's talking to him." Adam grinned. "From something he said to me at the party last night when he was trying to start a fight, I think Xavier's embarrassed to be around him now."

It clicked then. "That explains why they weren't sitting together when I saw them at the gate." I hadn't brought it up with Adam since he hadn't been in a talking mood.

Adam stared at me. "They weren't? No way. You think we actually broke them up?"

I wanted to feel guilty about it, but I couldn't bring myself to. I'd tried to reach out to Xavier and Austin and they'd still thrown it back in my face. "Maybe. And there he was, trying to break *us* up. Karma, I guess?"

"Good job, karma. About time you got to work," Adam muttered.

Still, Adam had lost that glow that had made him sparkle during our week away. He'd carried himself differently—with more brash confidence. Maybe he'd been faking it so he felt like he fit in among an unfamiliar crowd, but it had looked good on him, too.

Was that all over?

Later, I reminded myself. A plane wasn't a good place to sort all this out. Instead, we needed to get some sleep. We were changing time zones, so by the time we landed it was Sunday. And what with getting home and unpacking, doing laundry, getting groceries, and getting an early night…

Our vacation was well and truly over.

The lights dimmed in the cabin, and I sighed as I pulled my bed out and rearranged my lap blanket so it covered me. At least we were together here. Adam was lying on his side facing me.

It took all my confidence, but I groped around under the blankets until I managed to poke a hand out and find Adam's, close to his head.

Adam took my hand and squeezed it quietly. That little gesture reassured me more than anything else, even if the gap between our seats was too far apart to really cuddle or make the best of it.

When Adam spoke up again, his voice was quiet. "My parents were pretty damn strict with me, I guess."

"Mmhmm?" I wanted him to know I was listening, and I hadn't somehow drifted to sleep immediately. Good luck with that on a plane.

"They smacked me around a little. I was kind of an asshole, though. I know that'll surprise you." Adam chuckled.

I refused to laugh. I knew what he was looking for: some kind of approval that it was okay, even funny. No way. I wasn't going to make him feel like he'd been in the wrong. "I'm sorry."

"Nah, it's not like that. I mean, Kev definitely had it worse."

"It's easy to justify anything in the world if you compare it to other things," I told him quietly. "Stop comparing and start looking at it as its own event. Or events."

Adam was quiet for a minute—long enough in Adam time that I wondered briefly if he was asleep. But then he pulled my hand to his cheek, and it was damp.

Instantly, I teared up too. I couldn't stand seeing him in pain, and not being able to curl myself around him and take it all away made it even harder. But I sensed that there was a reason he was talking about it here, where I couldn't make a big deal of it. I tried to respect that and keep my distance, even if I choked up as he wiped his cheeks.

Finally, Adam spoke again. "No, you're right. They used to say a lot of stuff, too. You were right that they told me I'm dumb, and lazy, and… you know, all that stuff. But I guess I'm not."

I wished there were some way I could show him what I saw in him: the hard worker, the loyal friend, the guy who hid his pain with a smile and kept on going if someone else needed him. All I could do was murmur, "Mmhmm," again, and squeeze his hand tightly.

"And if they were wrong about some things, maybe they were wrong about everything." Adam cleared his throat. "That makes it easier to ignore all the shit they said, you know? Just realizing they've been trying to distance themselves for all this time. Were they always trying to turn me straight?"

"Wouldn't put it past them," I muttered.

"Yeah." Adam sighed quietly, the sound almost disappearing in the constant white noise of the air blowing down from the vents above, and the hum of the engines outside the plane window that vibrated through the chassis. It was a strangely comforting sound, though. It gave me something to focus on other than how much I wanted to throttle Adam's parents for being such assholes.

"They pretty much kicked me out in the end. Told me to go to boot camp or get a job and leave the house, but… I didn't wanna enlist just to avoid myself, you know? Last thing I need is to hurt anyone because I don't have my shit together."

I nodded, the words hitting me like a punch to the gut. I'd said nearly the same thing to Kev only a few months ago, and yet here I was—blundering into Adam's life and risking breaking his heart. Somehow, I'd jumped from dating one roommate to another with barely enough time to catch my breath in between.

It was enough to make me wonder if I had deep-seated issues of my own. Maybe I had problems with commitment. Could I blame my parents?

I cracked a smile and sighed, rolling around to try to find a comfortable spot on the seat. I was already tucked against the side of it to be as close to him as possible. "I know what you mean."

"Dude, you've got your shit together," Adam said, sounding bemused.

I was a little afraid to tell him the truth. I didn't want him to think differently of me—to realize how unlucky I always seemed to be in the end. Maybe he, too, would end up being on the wrong end of that luck.

It wasn't that I blamed myself for my parents' divorce, or for Xavier's lack of interest in me, or for the string of boyfriends who'd been similarly emotionally unavailable and distant, or for the constant stress of managing my own work and the inevitable clients stiffing me or contractors breathing down my neck.

"Sure I do," I laughed quietly, fluffing up my pillow and rearranging the thin plane blanket over my legs. Though Adam craned his neck to look at me, I avoided his gaze. There was no way I was getting into that general feeling of failure that had permeated my life. Even when things were going well, it never lasted.

Instead, the plane soared on through the sky, bringing us ever closer to the resumed monotony of our regular lives as I fell silent. I shifted and pulled the blanket tight around myself to make it clear I was trying to get some sleep. Adam respected that silence, but part of me wished he wouldn't.

Why couldn't the good times last?

ADAM

It took me a moment to realize why it felt so strange for my alarm clock to be going off in the surreal, small hours when the light was still thin in the sky. Even in the summer, morning came far too quickly for my liking.

Especially when I woke up by myself for the first time in a week.

I rolled over and glanced over, half-hoping that the thin slice of my twin bed that wasn't occupied by my own sprawling limbs would suddenly contain a warm body to cuddle—specifically, Darren.

Since we both had crappy twin mattresses, we hadn't even talked about it when we'd gotten home. We'd just gone our separate ways, and now I wasn't sure how to... well, get back together. Sharing these beds was out of the question.

Sharing our lives was a great big proposal, and I was only going to end up rambling and horribly insulting him if I tried to ask him about that.

We'd barely said anything on the way back from the airport. Both of us had been exhausted, sure, but it felt way too much like the future for my liking. I'd chickened out of saying anything to him about *us*. All the promises in the world on a vacation meant nothing in the light of day.

I had no idea how to date Darren in real life. A vacation was such a different environment—like a space with just the two of you, away from the rest of your life. Making it work the rest of the time? That was a whole new ball game, and we were crashing abruptly from the lofty heights of that fantasy land.

God, why was I just so bad at life?

"Up and at 'em," I mumbled and kicked the blankets off my bed, slouching over to the clothing rail to grab work clothes. Eight o'clock waited for no man—even a probably bi, definitely grouchy, unquestionably feeling too many feelings for a guy he shouldn't…

I dragged myself through the morning routine—coffee, cereal, shower—with this weird feeling like everything wasn't quite fitting into the right place anymore.

In one way, it felt like I'd never left; in another, I couldn't help but see my world with fresh eyes. The luxury of the hotel room didn't compare to the way I had to overlook the mold in the corners of the bathroom, or the wobbly tap on the kitchen sink, or the crumbling pass-through window of the kitchen.

I was getting too big for my britches, my dad would have said. He'd picked that up from some book he'd read as a kid and he loved saying it whenever he denied anyone what they wanted— even when that was control over their life, or sexuality, or…

No, that was still a box I wasn't gonna open in my head. I was gonna leave it superglued shut until they noticed I wasn't phoning home. *If* they noticed.

After grabbing my lunch, I shoved everything into a backpack as usual, with my water bottle and last week's leftover bottle of Gatorade. The electrolytes made a big difference in the worst of the scorching heat, around noon to three o'clock. Sometimes we started early, but Henson had texted to tell us to show up at eight. He must be picking up supplies for whatever we were doing today.

I trudged to the subway station, my mind a few thousand miles away. The train ride didn't take long, making me glad again that we were working in Brooklyn. Some job sites were further out, and getting a ride there and back or figuring out the bus system was always a pain in the ass.

I pushed my way through the side entrance, which was carefully screened from the street and all the fancy neighbors. The keypad had been installed, though the gate was propped open. We must be getting close to the end of the job.

"Look what the cat dragged in!" greeted Paolo, clapping my shoulder.

"Goddamn." I stared around at the place and half-hugged him. "Man, you guys are rockstars." The place looked almost like a different yard. With a good week's work, it was amazing what we could achieve, though a part of me felt weirdly guilty that I hadn't been around to help.

It looked like we were laying out a path running from this gate to the mother-in-law cottage—definitely an Airbnb, with a whole new hedge and privacy fence separating the unit from the back-yard of the main house. Most days, I wasn't privy to the details of what we were going to do. I just did what I was told. It was kind of amazing to see the end result when you had no idea what was happening in the big picture.

In the end-of-summer heat, this was the most pleasant time of day. It was nice to stand around in the shade of the yard for a few minutes, knowing that we'd be sweating buckets later. I lived off huge bottles of water and Gatorade.

"Henson's probably gonna get you an ice cream." Rod joined us and punched my shoulder. "Taking a week off for the good of the team, huh? Look at that tan."

I grinned. "I ain't saying nothing."

"Where were you, anyway? Hawaii?" My expression must have given me away, because his joking attitude turned into surprise. "No shit!"

"A friend won a trip," I waved a hand like it wasn't a big deal. "Needed someone to come along."

"Some friend. I want friends like that," Paolo grinned. "Think you can hook a brother up?"

"Yeah! I wanna get me a free Hawaiian trip." Rod folded his arms.

"Next time there's a raffle, I'll hook you up," I promised. I had to bite back a grin, though. If I didn't fit in at a gay resort, neither of them would. I doubted they'd want to give it a shot even for a free trip.

"This a buddy from before you moved here?" I didn't blame Paolo for asking; he'd worked with me since I first got here, pretty much. Landscaping services turned into snow removal in the winter in this part of the country, and we were two of the few full-time, year-round employees. Many of the rest, like Rod, were seasonal hires.

By now, I could kinda consider Paolo a friend. And here I was, figuring out how to come out to him.

"Nah. My new roommate," I said. "My last one went and moved in with—with his new sweetheart." I rolled my eyes, ignoring the guilt that squeezed my heart when I avoided pronouns. Here I was, being the same coward as always. Kev wouldn't give a fuck if a bunch of random guys thought he was lesser-than for being gay.

Why the hell should I? Aside from liking having a job?

"Damn. That excuses pretty much any sin," Paolo joked with a grin.

Even the word *sin* made my heart jolt. Fuck, I needed to settle down—and get my parents out of my head. They didn't deserve to take up any more space there. However much of a sin they thought it was for me to be happy, I was. Or at least, I had been on vacation. I had no idea whether I could hold onto this now that we were back home.

"Yeah, he can punch holes in walls if he wants," I joked back and turned. The distinctive rumble of Henson's truck caught my attention.

"Here's the man himself. We're supposed to be wrapping up this week," Paolo muttered and snorted.

"Gonna be tight?"

"Tighter than a virgin's backdoor."

I winced and elbowed him as we headed through the side gate to greet our boss.

"Morning, boys." He was in a rare good mood as he swigged his coffee and jumped out of his truck. He slammed the door and gestured at the truck bed, but we knew what to do. Paolo was already moving to open the tailgate while Rod and I formed a line to pass bags of gravel.

"That's some color you got on you," Henson addressed me, squinting. "You just take a week to bake on the beach?"

"Yessir." The first bag of gravel caught me by surprise, but my body was glad for the workout after a week of lazing around and drinking. I caught my breath and redoubled my pace.

"Well, you saved our bacon on this one. And the other boys did, too. They stepped up to fill your boots." Henson nodded. "You see the place?"

"It's looking great, sir," I enthused as I stomped my way to the gate to pass the next bag to Rod. "Can't wait to see it done."

"It better be by tomorrow."

"Tomorrow?" Rod yelped, and then cleared his throat when Henson turned a glare at him. He quickly busied himself stacking up the bags of gravel.

"Money ain't flowing like wine, boy. We're over budget already."

I nodded firmly. "What's left to do? It looks like we're nearly there." I'd sensed a challenge and I couldn't back down now. "We've got two whole days."

Paolo stifled a noise of disbelief and I resisted the urge to roll my eyes. The boys up here didn't know how to handle a hot day. If I lay down for a rest every time it hit a hundred degrees in Tennessee, I'd have grown roots and leaves of my own. We just had to work slowly and carefully through the hot period of the day, that was all.

Henson gave an approving grunt and clapped my shoulder. "That's the spirit. Here. I'll show you what we're doing."

That was a little different. He left Paolo and Rod to unload the truck and I shot an apologetic glance at them, but they didn't meet my eyes. After Henson pointed out the path to build, the last flower beds we were constructing, and the paving stones to go in, he turned to face me and folded his arms.

Uh oh. I was used to this being bad news. I straightened up instinctively, hands by my side, but I was tensing up involuntarily. I half-expected a backhand if I said the wrong thing, or the right thing the wrong way.

"You keep it up this summer," Henson told me gruffly. "I need to find a supervisor."

It took me a moment to realize what he meant. *Me*, being put in charge of anything? I cracked a grin and then hastily straightened my face when he glared at me. "I... *me*? Are you sure?"

"You looking a gift horse in the mouth?"

"N-No. No, sir," I added quickly. "I just..." I looked around the yard and then back at him with a frown. "I'm not that special."

Henson watched me for a few long moments, his expression hard to decipher. His eyebrows were spiky, yet bushy. They looked like caterpillars, and they were crawling down toward his eyes as his frown grew. "I'm not blowing smoke up your ass just 'cause you're fishing for it."

I snorted. "No, of course." Henson, of all people, wouldn't.

"But you work your ass off. You stay late, you stay on task. This week would've gone faster if anyone else had taken a week off. Don't do that to me again," Henson instructed me.

"Sorry, sir."

"Hope the break did you good. I'll be working you like a horse 'til

October. Supervisors need a driver's license, too." It sounded like a random aside until I considered the context of the conversation.

It took me a moment to get the courage to offer up, "I got one." I didn't want to be presumptuous.

"Good." Henson shoved my shoulder and I stumbled. "For fuck's sake, toughen up, kid. Sound and look like you know what you're doing, even if you don't. You're usually good at that."

I swallowed and nodded. How he'd noticed that, I didn't want to know. I changed my stance and threw my shoulders back. "Are you offering me the job in the fall?" I tried to sound like I believed I deserved it. My stomach was doing weird flip-flops, and my brain wouldn't stop reminding me that I was bound to fuck up and lose this chance somehow.

"Next week. I won't put you with these guys for a job or two, give 'em a chance to get used to your authority," Henson told me, waving a hand toward them. "No point in causing trouble."

Holy shit. Next week?

"There's a pay raise, if you need any more motivation to take it. An extra three bucks an hour to start." Henson glowered. "As long as you don't crash my new truck."

"I won't crash any trucks, sir. I'll take the job. Thank you." I tried to keep my sentences short so I didn't start rambling and betraying my shock at even being considered for the promotion.

"Better," Henson approved and stuck out his hand. His grip was almost crushingly tight, but I squeezed back as I shook hands.

A pay raise? Three bucks an hour? That was huge—way out of the pay scale I was in now. Maybe a better apartment, or savings, or better insurance. I couldn't quite think about renting a place without needing a roommate to make it work, but I wasn't so dependent on every paycheck to make ends meet.

Money could buy happiness—or at least name-brand toilet paper, and that was kind of the same thing.

"Thank you, sir," I said again with a pump of his hand and followed him back to the crew.

The other guys didn't ask what we talked about, and I didn't volunteer the information yet. It wouldn't take long before they heard, anyway. Instead, they kept peppering me with questions about Hawaii.

It turned out to be way harder than I'd expected to avoid telling them what I'd done. Lying around by the pool and partying prompted questions on how many hot girls had been around.

"Not many," I admitted with a straight face. I wasn't gonna lie about that. I just didn't wanna tell the truth, that was all. Not yet.

"What kinda lame-ass resort is that?"

I could see my chance. It was here, suddenly—the easy way to say *a gay one*. Come out without really having to come out. Let 'em assume whatever the hell they wanted.

But my fears were right there, muffling my tongue and making me keep my damn mouth shut as I had for so many years.

I felt like shit when the conversation moved on to Paolo's vacation plans. Just like that, my chance evaporated and I was left hauling bags of gravel, raking them out, doing anything to keep my mind off what a damn coward I was. Part of me could reason it was because I hadn't told my family and they should know first, but that was just an excuse. I had no plans at all to tell them.

Darren probably wouldn't back down, I reminded myself. That didn't make it any easier to bring the subject up again. It was dead and gone by lunchtime, like none of it had ever happened. Everyone thought I'd just gone to Hawaii with a friend, and last week, I wouldn't have had it any other way. Now, I wanted the courage to say anything else.

At least my muscles burned, but in such a good way. I'd missed the feeling of tearing into lunch after a hard work day. I was working twice as hard as usual along with the other guys to get the job done by tomorrow.

That gave me every opportunity in the world to shrug off any stupid, inconvenient feelings.

26

DARREN

The front door opened as I pushed myself to my feet and headed for the blanket-door of my room. "Hey."

I got a grunt in response. By the time I was in the hallway, Adam's muddy clothes were on the floor and he was in the bathroom. The shower turned on. He left the bathroom door open, but clearly he wasn't in a great mood since I didn't actually get any words in response.

"Well, that's great," I sighed and turned away from the bathroom. So much for a romantic reunion after our first day back in Brooklyn.

Maybe food would help. I stepped over his clothes and headed for the kitchen. I'd grabbed a few things on the way home, but not really enough to put a meal together. It was too damn hot in here to wear more than shorts, so I was shirtless. I was not in the mood to cook a stir-fry or anything else that was gonna attack my nipples.

"Ugh," I muttered and grabbed the saucepan to put on rice. Chili it was, then. We had tortilla chips, too. That would work.

By the time I was done, I heard Adam disappear into his room—presumably for clothes.

"That good a day, huh?"

"It was great." Adam didn't sound like he was trying to be sarcastic, but there was no heart in it, either. Uh oh. Had his parents called or something? That couldn't be it. From the sounds of it, they'd sooner notice an earthquake in Mongolia than their own son.

When he came into the kitchen, he had on nice shorts and a shirt, at least—not his usual slobby after-work clothes. I couldn't help a smile. It was good to see him looking good now. If nothing else, this week away had given him the confidence to look at home in his own body.

"Hey, handsome," I greeted with a wink.

Adam snorted but smiled at me. "Hi." He leaned awkwardly in the doorway, his arms folded.

I eyed him for a minute and then headed through to sit at the table. This was gonna be a long conversation, and I didn't want to wind up sitting on the kitchen floor talking about my feelings. "I can't keep guessing at your mood and what you need, man. If you wanna tell me what's wrong, do that. Otherwise, don't just hang around like a raincloud."

"Sorry." Adam looked sheepish, to his credit. Instead of taking the other chair, he slowly approached me.

Every step closer he took seemed to compress the strange, almost alien tension between us. By the time he was in touching distance, my heart damn near thudded out of my chest. But he didn't stop at touching me—he straddled me, the chair creaking and my thighs tingling as he rested his weight on my lap.

Fuck, I was getting hard already. I didn't want us to just start screwing away our problems, but at the same time, I wanted him naked and under me. It was a dilemma that my cock had more solutions for than my brain.

"I just miss you," Adam murmured, his lips close to my ear. He wasn't quite kissing me yet, like there was still a barrier between us. He rested his forehead on my shoulder and shifted until he pressed both hands against my chest. "It sucks, getting back to reality. Especially this reality."

I slid my arms around his waist to keep him on the chair, praying it was more sturdy than the rest of the apartment. "It's hard to go back," I agreed. George had that new job for me to work on tomorrow now that we'd gone through the house and specs. It was a welcome relief after I'd caught up on a week's worth of voicemails and stress all at once.

"What are you saying? That we should? That this is…" Adam trailed off. He was trying to pull away from my hold now.

I blinked but kept my hold around his waist. "What? No. Sit down."

He plopped back on my lap after some ineffectual squirming and huffed. "I just want to know if we're doing this."

"So do I." The tighter I squeezed my hands together, the more I could stop them from shaking. "It's hot sex, but it's more than that—"

"I could use some hot sex, though." Adam interrupted what was supposed to be a romantic speech, a twinkle in his eye. Well, that made me forget all about it.

"Now?"

Adam sprang to his feet, nearly pulling me off the chair since I was still holding onto him absentmindedly. "Oops. Sorry." He grabbed my arm to steady me. "Now."

I switched off the stove. Before I let him take my hand and pull me toward one of our rooms, I planted my feet until he looked at me. "As long as we talk afterward. None of this *sex to solve problems* crap. That's where I went wrong before…" My throat tightened when I realized all the stuff I'd screwed up. It hadn't just been Xavier at fault. I'd let him treat me like that, and I'd never had the courage to demand anything more—anything better.

His expression softened and he reached out with his other hand to cup my cheek. "Of course not." Adam stepped toward me again and pressed his lips against mine. "It's not your fault that he used you."

In that kiss, he said all the things he never seemed to be able to put into real words. It was the kiss of a man who wanted me—not just for an experiment, but who genuinely cared about me. Hell, the way he touched me changed, too. As the tension drained from me, he held me close and I trusted him to do it.

Instead of him sitting on my lap, it was me leaning into him now, wrapping my arms around him and relying on him to be strong. And he was—he supported my weight and rubbed my back as it all hit me. I had someone I could rely on now, and it was fantastic, sure, but also… overwhelming.

I was counting on him not to walk away right when I was letting myself fall.

"Come on, babe." Adam kissed me again and murmured against my lips, "We'll cuddle and talk it out. But you've had a long, hard day…" He was smirking now as he rubbed my back and then squeezed my ass. "You should get the stress out first."

He'd come such a long way in just a few weeks—from being half-terrified of anything gay in his personal space to hitting on me with a friendly, playful grin.

"I have. Sounds like you did, too."

"I got offered a promotion."

I stared at the side of his head as he led me down the hall to my room. "That sounds good, though!"

"Yeah, mostly." He didn't give me a chance to clarify, because he grabbed my shoulder and pushed me through my doorway and up against the closest wall.

"Oof," I gasped, grinning at him as my body tingled from head to toe. "Someone's getting frisky."

Adam dropped to his knees. "Yeah, I am."

"Someone's gonna have to learn the art of foreplay." I grinned as I leaned back against the wall and spread my legs, running one hand up my chest to play with my own nipples.

Adam surprised me by growling a quiet, "No." He grabbed my wrist and pushed it back against the wall.

Oooh. He was exploring fast. I grinned and laced my hands behind my head instead, watching the fucking fantastic sight of the man on his knees in front of me working on getting my shorts down. When he finally figured out how they worked and stripped me down, I kicked off the fabric, my cock already at half-mast.

"You like me being a bit rough, huh?" Adam grinned up at me and kissed my hip—tantalizingly close, but not giving in yet. He kissed my stomach and thigh, too, and I began to regret teasing him. Now he was gonna make a point, wasn't he?

"I love it." I grinned at him. "Just like you like a little wrestling."

Adam grunted his approval. "Always thought that's how you choose who gets to top."

"Wha—wait, *what?*" I covered my mouth with my hand to try to hold in the giggle, but it burst free, like it or not.

Adam glared up at me. "I'm not sucking your dick if you laugh at me while I do it."

"I'm not… It's not…" Another peal of laughter at the idea of gay guys all over the world wrestling escaped before I managed to straighten my face. *"Just putting you in a quick headlock tonight, dear?"* I imitated and then adopted another voice. *"No, mate, let's go for the full Turkish oil match. I'm here to win."*

"You're the weirdest guy I've ever known." Adam was trying not to grin, though, as he stroked me. Each tug on my cock made it harder to remember that I was laughing at him, though. I found myself moaning and writhing against the wall within moments.

"Guess I won that round," Adam whispered. He glanced up at me. "Can I… without a condom? I mean, we were all clear, right?"

"Mmhmm." I couldn't tear my eyes off him. If he wanted to taste me, I had no complaints at all. "Barebacking's cool, too."

Adam grinned. "Perfect." He lapped at the head, looking like he was deciding if he liked a new kind of pastry cream. Oh, I was gonna give him a mouthful to try out.

"You wanna fuck me?" I whispered. "Cause I could use a good dicking down. It's been a long day. And you look like you could use a nice, tight hole wrapping around that sexy dick of yours…"

Adam moaned and wrapped his lips around the tip of my cock, pushing his mouth slowly down on it. He was a little less clumsy than he had been before, and there was way less teeth-to-skin contact.

I could finally just relax and lean against the wall, my nails digging into the flimsy drywall. I didn't care if the distinctive half-moon crescents left evidence later. I felt too damn good to care about anything.

My cock hit the back of his throat, and Adam pulled back quickly, looking as surprised as I felt. "Good gag reflex," I murmured, cupping his cheek. But Adam wasn't stopping there—he took me in again, my whole length engulfed by his mouth.

Fuck, this felt good. My hands cupped the back of his head now as I pushed forward into his mouth, thrusting into the wet heat while I imagined every position I wanted him to fuck me in.

"Mmngh." Adam finally pulled away from me and scrambled to his feet, stripping down faster than I'd ever seen him do it before.

I stared at him as he tossed his clothing away like it had offended him, but before I could think of a smartass comment, he'd scooped me up in his arms and pushed my back up against the wall.

"Oh, fuck," I gasped, trying to wrap my legs around his waist. "Lube's on the bedside table."

He managed to grab the bottle without moving me at all. Finally, there was a benefit to having a New York City-sized room.

He hoisted me further up the wall and pinned me there effortlessly, and I tried not to swoon. I wasn't a tiny guy myself, but those landscaping jobs had given him a solid frame, and he knew it.

Adam's fingers were hard and callused, but they were gentle as he slid two wet fingertips between my cheeks.

"Hey," I gasped and squirmed at the cold.

He grinned. "Sorry. Should've warmed it up, but I can't wait another second for you."

I appreciated that enthusiasm, and I returned it in equal measure. "Yeah? I need you in me, Adam," I panted, my toes curling as he slid his finger inside me. My weight was balanced between his other arm and the wall, but I'd never felt safer.

Adam groaned as he plunged his fingers deep into me, and I tried not to clench around them. I wanted his dick a hell of a lot more, but we were getting there. I just had to be patient, and patience was not my strong suit when I was turned on.

"You sure you're fine to bareback?" Adam murmured as he slid his fingers out and stroked himself. Watching his hand move up and down his shaft, catching glimpses of the motion between our tightly-pressed bodies, was so hypnotic that I forgot the question until he bit my shoulder lightly.

"Hey!" I laughed. "I'm fine. Fine. Yeah. Good. Now, please."

Adam smirked. "You can't even talk and I've barely started." His thickness pressed against me, and then slowly past the ring of muscle that yielded to him.

I enveloped him, pressing my forehead into his shoulder as he whispered into my ear that I was beautiful and sexy and gorgeous. I hadn't realized how much I'd needed to hear those words, and it helped me relax as much as my own practice did.

The ache began subtly—a shift from discomfort to pleasure, and then anticipation as he thrust into me at a slow, steady pace. It was so slow it was almost maddening, which was how I knew I needed more.

"Ready," I finally whispered, squirming in his arms. "Come on."

Adam growled into my neck and sucked on my skin gently. "I was waiting to hear that."

I wrapped my arms around his neck and let myself give in at last —to everything he was giving me, and everything I wanted. Every thrust pushed my arousal a little higher, and my hard cock bumped his stomach before long. I'd never been shy about moaning when I felt good, and I wasn't about to start now; every time he hit deep inside at just the right angle, I whimpered to encourage him to do it again.

Adam was everything I'd ever wanted, in one sexy, smart, and surprisingly sweet package. It scared the shit out of me, but it wasn't just a sex-fueled realization—it was the reality I'd been trying to deny for a whole week of vacation with him.

Now that we were back home, there was no going back to the way it was before.

"Harder," I gasped, and Adam redoubled his pace. He was pounding me hard and fast now. The time for making love was over, and the time for finding new heights was here.

My ass was halfway into the wall before I registered that anything had happened, quickly followed by my elbow.

"Fuck," Adam gasped, sliding out and cupping my ass as he hauled me toward him, and I crashed forward against him. We landed in an ungraceful heap, and Adam immediately squirmed away. "Oh my God. Are you okay?"

"Oof! Fucking fuck!" When I ran a hand along my ass, I'd only gotten scraped—no blood came away on my fingers. My next priority was the wall, and I rolled onto my stomach to take a look. "I am, but... ohhh, fuck."

We'd gone through not just one side of the drywall, but both. We could see through into the living room now through a fist-sized hole, and there was a much larger hole on this side of the wall. Plaster scattered everywhere. Thin, cheap-ass stuff—how the hell it hadn't given way before now was beyond me.

Adam's hands rested on my hips as he knelt behind me. "There's only one thing we can do right now."

"What's that?"

He poked me in the thigh with his cock, and I burst out laughing despite myself. "Are you serious?" Adam just winked and dusted my ass off.

I buried my face in my arms and laughed, but the laugh didn't last long. When he teased my hole with another fresh handful of lube and his still-hard shaft, I abruptly remembered what we were doing. The structural integrity of our home could wait ten minutes.

"Yes!" I whimpered, pressing my forehead into my arms and pushing up onto my knees. I tried to, anyway; he blanketed me with his weight, pushing me into the hardwood floor. Even the chill couldn't turn me off, though. It danced in electric jolts along my skin, tantalizing every damn inch of me.

Barely a couple minutes later, I writhed until I managed to get a hand under myself and then stroked myself at the same merciless rhythm that Adam had picked up again. When I spilled my load, it was across the floor while clenching around that pleasantly thick length. I rolled my head to the side as he kissed my neck.

I didn't care where we were—even some crappy apartment floor —as long as I was with him.

"I love you," I breathed into my arms, but I didn't have the courage to use my voice. I just mouthed it silently, like doing so would make it easier to put my voice to.

It was a huge realization, and it scared the shit out of me. So I kept my lips sealed as he pulled out and straddled me, stroking himself hard and fast.

When his wet, warm load streaked my back, I turned back to take in his smile. I'd do anything to make him smile like that.

"Wow," Adam gasped and rolled off me to lie on his side on the floor. "Oof." He glanced at the hole in the wall and groaned. "And we fucked that up."

"Yeah, we sure did," I laughed. I slid an arm over him and snuggled into his side. "This is pretty cold. Move to the bed, at least?"

"Sure."

"I'll need a little help." I jerked my thumb over my shoulder at my back.

Adam snickered. "I should make you make a run for it."

"You're such an asshole." I tickled his side.

"Okay, okay! You win!" Adam took off for the bathroom and came back with a wet cloth. He wiped me down tenderly, which didn't surprise me any longer.

I knew him well enough to look under his words at what he really felt—and was too afraid to say. Like me, really. I didn't even have the guts to tell him I loved him. Now was not the time.

As we flopped on the bed together, Adam covered his face and groaned. "So now we talk about us."

"Mmhmm." The wall was suddenly the least of my worries as I lay gingerly on my side next to him, fitting myself around him. "Thoughts?"

"I… I don't know if I can do this."

Like that, my heart dropped. Not even like a stone—like an office block up for demolition. All at once, the carefully constructed visions collapsed into the basement, and it felt way too familiar.

Just like Xavier, then.

Tears stung the corners of my eyes, and I looked around for something—anything—to look at and distract myself. It was pretty damn hard to find comfort, but at least not losing my shit around Adam would be preferable.

My eyes settled on the hole in the wall, and the wall's interior. Wires stuck out at odd angles, and drywall had crumbled straight through into the living room, it looked like. Was that my foot kicking through the other wall? Or was my ass really that bony? An elbow? God only knew—in the heat of the moment, I'd barely felt any limb go through it.

Ignoring the ache of the scrapes, I pushed myself off the bed and grabbed underwear to step into, then crouched next to the wall, trying to avoid the worst of the drywall dust.

"Shit," I whispered. The moment I laid eyes on the wiring, I knew it was wrong. Someone had just tied in wires clumsily, and I saw exposed ends. The whole thing was such an amateur job I would never have let that stay for a day, had I been hired to work on a site like this.

"What?" Adam pushed himself to his feet and hopped from foot to foot to step into his underwear. Then, he came up behind me, trying to look around my shoulder.

I didn't even want to touch it, so I carefully leaned this way and that to try to peer up into the wall. "You got a flashlight?"

"Sure." Adam came back with one after a minute rummaging in his room. I winced at his choice of light—the flashlight was metal —but I didn't have one of my own in the apartment, only in the van. This would have to suffice. Cautiously, I stuck it into a clear gap—one of the few without a rat's nest of wiring—and looked around.

"For God's sake," I muttered in disgust when the quick look confirmed my suspicions. "I bet the asshole landlord did this himself."

"You're kidding."

"Nope." I popped the P, speaking slowly to give my emotions a chance to settle down. I might fall into the same damn emotional trap every time, but this was a problem I was very good at solving. "This is a fucking fire risk. Especially with drywall dust every-where and exposed wiring. A little humidity, or a stray spark…"

Adam groaned and thumped his head against my dresser. "You're kidding," he mumbled again, but this time he sounded dejected.

"We're moving out." I turned in my crouch to look up at him. Even looking at him hurt when he'd been so damn clear about… well, his intentions. But I couldn't leave him behind and escape my own feelings.

No way would I do that. That was an epic dick move.

Adam peered sideways at me, still leaning on my dresser. "What? We can't go."

I shook my head. Way too many horror stories started this way. "We don't own the place. It's the landlord's job to fix it. I'll call an inspector, the city will come down hard on him… but… Jesus." I shook my head. "If this is in here, what else is?" I'd already avoided using the outlets in the flimsy wall, just in case—and now I thanked the fucking stars I'd had that much good sense.

"But we just lost our damage deposit." Adam sank down to sit next to me. His voice wavered. "I got a raise, but... this place is affordable."

Even moving to the average one-bedroom together—and Adam had just thrown that out the window, but I was *not* thinking about that yet—wouldn't make it cheap enough for us. "A raise?" I half-heartedly smiled. "That the promotion you mentioned?"

Adam nodded. "Landscaping supervisor."

"Shit, man." That was one bright spot in this day. I smiled awkwardly at him, not sure what to do. If this wasn't going anywhere, I wasn't going to jump on him and kiss him like I wanted to do. I was fucking proud of him. "That's—that's awesome."

"Yeah," Adam blew out a sigh, his eyes still on the hole in the wall. "First step to my own business. But this isn't awesome. God, I don't have enough for a deposit even for a fixer-upper."

George had mentioned fixer-uppers, right? The solution came to me all at once. I drew a breath and let it out, closing my eyes. It was a dumbass idea, and I was going to get my heart broken, but... "Do you want to keep living with me?" That was an easier question than asking about dating.

If Adam wasn't sure he could date me...

"Yes." Adam spoke without hesitation.

Okay. We could make this work. How the hell I was going to cope, I'd figure out later. But I wasn't leaving him in some shitty ticking firebomb. "Do you trust me?"

Adam snorted. "Of course." He nudged me. "Whatcha thinking?"

"I might have an answer. I have to wait until tomorrow to find out. You willing to wait until then?"

It meant stepping into the unknown and taking a huge risk on a guy who was just as flaky as me, but hell… I had to figure out if it was even possible first. Before I got my hopes up, let alone his.

Adam drew his breath in and took my hand, his grip firm. "I'll wait for you."

I scooted away from the wall and gingerly leaned into his side, resting my head on his shoulder. If only I could bring myself to trust his words.

"I'm not asking you to commit to me for life," I murmured. "But I need to know you can either date me or live with me as friends. Don't leave me hanging like Xavier."

"Fuck, no," Adam told me, his voice strong as he wrapped his arms around me. "I'd never use you like that."

I trusted him, too. He might come off as flaky, but as far as I was concerned, his word had been ironclad before. That was all I needed.

Sure, it scared me that he wasn't sure he could do this—whatever he meant by that—but I had to believe we could at least make it work as friends and roommates.

It would be the hardest thing I'd done in my life, but we'd both be physically safe, at least. That was worth it.

"Okay. I'll give this a shot."

ADAM

"End of story: we can't afford this." I was strapped into the passenger seat of Darren's van, one foot propped on the toolbox in the footwell and one hand on the coffee cup that threatened to jolt out of the cup holder.

Darren eyed me, a smile dancing on his lips. "Oh, don't worry. I'm not promising a fancy life." He'd been vague about our plans for the evening when he'd texted me today to say the plan was a go, and to meet him by his job site. Springing the news on me that we were looking at a place to buy…

Well, I'd panicked and sworn a bit. Only now was I able to breathe and talk to him about it, and it was helping. Hearing that it wasn't a million-dollar house, I relaxed. If I were a debt slave, that would severely limit my options, given my income. "It's a fixer-upper?"

"It's a hell of a fixer-upper."

I frowned as I stared out the window and then looked back at him. "Even those are like, half a million."

"Not if we move this far out."

We were so far away from the gayborhood I'd moved to—unwittingly, though Kev swore he'd had no idea before we moved that he was bringing us to the gayest part of Brooklyn—that I had no idea where we were. "Is there even a train nearby?"

"Yeah," Darren said with a chuckle. He looked over at me and then past me as he maneuvered the van into a tight parking spot. I held still to let him do it before I kept pestering him.

"When you say a hell of a fixer-upper..."

Darren grinned. "Yeah. It's not as nice as our place."

Okay, that was a promising start. I stared at him for a moment, trying to blot out the visions of cockroaches dancing over me as I slept. "Right..."

"We'll have a new place to live soon, but unpacking and repacking again? That's gross." Darren bit his lip. "I've been talking to my... my future boss... and the seller can close on this place pretty quick. We might have time to get it habitable first. Otherwise... We'll crash at friends' places, or something. We'll figure it out."

Future boss? That was a question that would have to wait, along with those details. For now, I focused on the important part. "We'd be living here together." When he nodded, I drew a breath and tried to ignore the nerves that churned in my stomach as I asked, "Do you *need* me to do this, or do you *want* me to do this?"

Darren unbuckled and leaned over to put his hand on my knee. "Both." He turned, awkwardly facing me. "Adam, I want you around. Even if you don't wanna date, if you decide I'm not for you, I want to keep you safe. That place isn't safe. It never was, but especially now. I *can* probably swing the mortgage on this place, and the deposit... It'd be a crunch, but I can. No pressure if you don't want to. I just want you to."

I swallowed hard. I hadn't expected my throat to close up at those words. Surely he was joking around—but there wasn't a trace of a teasing smile on his lips.

"Oh." Darren squeezed my knee lightly, and I covered his hand with my own. "Okay then. But… you know I don't have savings."

"I think we can swing it. Let's just walk through the place first."

Okay, we could do that. I wasn't going to get carried away. Right?

I stepped out onto the sidewalk, wincing. The heat still hadn't broken, even in the early evening, and I was sweating almost immediately. When he came around the other side of the van, I took his hand.

Damn it, even if I wasn't sure I could do this, I wanted to try. The fact that he was willing to gamble so much on me said everything about his feelings. I owed it to him to have the courage to at least *mention* him to my own coworkers.

Tomorrow. I hadn't done it today, but I'd do it tomorrow.

Darren squeezed my hand and looked around. He let go when he spotted another vehicle pulling up, shading his eyes and then pointing. "I think that's him there."

"And that's the house?" It was hard to miss—the rest of the houses around here weren't exactly in Henson's range of clients, but there was only one with boarded windows.

"Sorry, but yeah." Darren grinned.

I shook my head. I'd never been scared off by a challenge, especially when there was an opportunity. If it meant my own place to live… fuck, yeah.

"Hey. You must be Darren?" The guy who came up to us in a

blazer and jeans offered his hand and looked between us, as if not sure who to look at first. "I'm Jon."

"That's me." Darren shook hands. "And this is my roommate and… well, possibly partner-in-renovations, Adam."

"Nice to meet you. Fixing up a place together, huh? Wish I could get a best friend like that!" Jon joked. I traded glances with Darren, who was trying not to smile as Jon gestured toward the house. "Let's take a look before it gets dark. The lighting situation inside…"

"Isn't ideal?" I offered. The price better be right for this place.

Darren pulled out his phone, unlocked it, and handed it over to me before accompanying Jon up the path. I followed in their wake, skimming the listing.

Three bedrooms, one and a half baths, formal living room…

And a price that made me stop in my tracks. Okay, it wasn't half a million. Not even close. And we were technically in Brooklyn, he'd assured me. There were no photos on the listing, which made me suspicious, but that was why I had an expert along with me.

I caught up with them and handed Darren his phone while the agent unlocked the door. Darren raised his eyebrows as if to say, *See?*

I shook my head slightly. *We'll see.*

He nodded back, and it wasn't until we stepped inside that it occurred to me that we were talking without words. Fuck. That was such a couple thing.

"George is meeting us in a few minutes," Jon told us.

"Yeah. He said he'd be on his way…" Darren glanced at his watch. "Any time now. How do you two know each other, anyway?"

Jon launched into an explanation of college that I largely tuned out while I took a look around. The place looked stripped to the bones, with plywood floors, a few walls taken down to the studs, and bare bulbs from the ceilings.

Okay. He'd meant a fixer-upper, too.

"Any holes in the floor to look out for?" I asked when there was a gap in the conversation.

"No. That's one of the perks of this place. Structurally, the assessment says it's sound. It's not pretty, but it shouldn't kill anyone walking through it," Jon told us with a grin.

Honesty in an agent? I liked him already. Maybe he figured he had nothing to lose by calling it as it was. We were obviously still interested.

A knock on the door later, George joined us, and the name rang a bell. From the way he interacted with Darren, it confirmed my suspicion—this was one of the guys who hired him a lot. A contractor or something.

"And you're Adam?" George shook hands. "The new roommate, right?"

"That's me."

"I hope a little elbow grease doesn't scare you off." George stuck his hands into his pockets as he looked around.

"No, sir." My phone went off with a text message alert, so I checked Kev's message while the other guys talked.

Look who I found!

Attached was a screenshot of an Instagram post—me leaning into Darren, my arm around him, drinks in our hands. Fuck, I vaguely remembered the official photographer taking that, but it had all felt so distant. Like nobody would find out about it, let alone post it anywhere.

The blue sky, palm trees, and pools in the background were a far cry from the house I was trailing the others through. I sent back a quick *lol* and pocketed my phone to catch up again.

George was busy explaining to Darren the work that would be involved, and even Jon was honest about the situation.

"It's not gonna be easy," Jon admitted. "That's why the price is right."

Darren looked at me and put his arm around my shoulders, physically pulling me into the conversation. "Yeah, we can see that, huh?"

Oh, shit. He's coming out for me. I swallowed my sudden nerves and smiled at the other guys. "Yeah. I've got a little construction experience. I was a ranch hand. All those damn fences that needed mending," I drawled, letting my accent shine through.

"Yeah? This will be a piece of cake for you then," George said with a laugh that we all shared. It obviously wouldn't, but it wasn't out of the question, either.

Neither of the guys acted weird, even with Darren making such a blatant statement. Just having his warm, steady arm around my shoulders counteracted my nerves, and before long I was truly relaxed again.

"Why are the owners selling?" I asked, apart from the obvious: it was unlivable.

"They decided to get into property flipping and then changed their minds. One of them was more eager than the other, apparently." George gave us a knowing grin. "Doesn't look like that's a problem for you guys."

"As long as we get a place to sleep."

Jon nodded and pointed toward the ceiling. "On that note, let's see the bedrooms and the main bathroom."

The stairs looked rickety but felt stable—Jon walked up first and didn't even tiptoe up them, which gave me confidence. Maybe he was right, and it was just an ugly duckling. I could work with that.

I'd never in a million years dreamed of *owning* property—and certainly not here. But that also raised its own questions, like whether Darren was offering that, or if I was just freeloading when he was coming up with the money. The idea of being financially tied to someone who could hurt me using those ties—again —was horrifying.

But Darren wasn't that kind of guy. I'd seen him at his best and worst already, and he didn't have that mean streak like my parents.

"Okay, I think we've seen enough," Darren finally called it when my eyes had long since glazed over. "Thanks very much for your time."

After the handshakes, we made it out to the van before Darren turned to me. He didn't start it up yet. "So?"

I let out a long breath. "If we can work something out between us... ownership-wise... I mean, I can't afford half the deposit on that, even if it is dirt-cheap."

"I think I've got it covered." Darren looked around at the van and back to me. There was a strangely nostalgic look on his face—was that the right word? It was pained, but not unpleasant.

It took me a minute to understand what he meant. "No. Not selling it?" I caught my breath.

Darren nodded. "George offered me a job before we left." Now that he brought it up, I remembered him mentioning it last week. "I wasn't sure if I was gonna take it, but… his company supplies all the equipment. I'd keep what I need to work on this place, sell the rest. Between that and savings, we can swing the deposit. It's just the mortgage."

"And then what about me? I don't want to freeload." I grimaced. "Or to be in debt to you."

Darren shook his head. "You know how much your raise is gonna be?" When I nodded, he smiled at me. "Okay. We'll go over the numbers as soon as we get home. You can pay a little more toward the mortgage. But we'll both be putting a lot of long weeks into this place. In the end, it'll work out pretty evenly."

What with our day jobs, and then coming home to a place like this, I didn't doubt him. "I'll work my ass off doing whatever you tell me to."

Darren took my hand. "I know. But George told me we should probably make an offer tonight. If you want in on this…"

I caught my breath. Tonight? I was vaguely aware that buying a house meant swift action, but since I'd never considered I might do it, I'd never realized how much pressure that would be.

"Let's get home and talk about it," I said firmly. "I'll put on pasta or something." I cracked a smile. "We'd better get used to ramen if we're doing this. That's all we'll be able to afford for a while."

Darren laughed and let go of my hand. "I'd eat rice and beans every day if I was with you… under our own roof." His voice was warm, and the way his smile glowed and he wouldn't quite meet my eyes…

Fuck. He meant that.

"Me too," I whispered as he started the engine, but from the way his smile bloomed into a grin, I knew he'd heard.

The drive was quiet, both of us lost in our own thoughts until Darren found his usual parking spot and took my hand as he headed upstairs with me to the apartment.

"At least I wouldn't have to worry about parking that thing near security cameras again," Darren offered with a grin.

I laughed and shook my head. "Silver linings."

"And it's steady work. Whether or not we do the house, I've been thinking of taking the job anyway." Darren unlocked the door to let us in. "This just felt like a good opportunity."

It only took one look into the living room to remind me why we were doing this. As fearful as I was, Darren was right—we couldn't stay here, and that meant doing something about it in a hurry.

Once I'd started a pot of water boiling and dumped pasta sauce into another pot, I leaned on the counter while Darren sat on the counter opposite.

He was watching me with such concern that I instantly remembered what he'd told me earlier—that he wanted me safe, even if we didn't end up together. Hell, he'd basically come out to his new boss. He undeniably gave a shit about me, and that wasn't something I was used to.

My life was already changing so much that one more change just seemed inevitable. Why not? "I don't feel like I deserve it," I finally said, walking up to Darren and sidling between his knees.

Darren looped his arms around my shoulders and pecked my lips. "Deserve what?"

"You... the house... the chance to go in on it with you..." I shrugged. "All of it."

Darren frowned at me. "It's not the first thing that would have come to mind—buying a house together when we've only known each other for a few months. But needs must, right?"

"Yeah." I rested my hands on his thighs and breathed in deeply. Only now was I realizing how much stress instantly melted away as soon as he held me.

He wasn't letting me go. In fact, he was pulling me closer, and that felt... good. More than good: it felt like a subtle change in the winds of my fortunes. It felt like a new beginning, or a dawning— the first rays cracking through the darkness I'd grown so accustomed to that I hadn't even thought of stepping out.

I closed my eyes and rested my head on his shoulder. "What will everyone think? Buying a house together? That sounds absolutely insane."

"Fuck what they think." Darren's voice was quiet. "We've been focused on that for too long. It doesn't make a fucking bit of difference what anyone else thinks we should do. We know what makes sense for us."

It did make sense. It wasn't the perfect neighborhood, and it wasn't the perfect house, but we could improve it. Together, with help from his boss and our friends, with a lot of love and labor on our parts, we could build something. And if we could do that, we could build our relationship, too.

"You're right," I murmured. I'd spent too much of my life freaking out about what others thought.

It was time to follow my gut instinct, and it said yes. Maybe it was stupid and reckless—my brain was certain of that, actually—but it was also my decision, and mine alone. It was time to open my damn eyes and see the future I could have if I stopped shooting myself in the foot.

Darren was reaching a hand out to me, and I yearned to take it. Wherever the hell this went in the future, it made sense now. That was all one could ever count on, really.

"Call Jon," I murmured as the pasta water bubbled behind me. "I'm in."

28

DARREN

"Are you ready to head out to the diner?"

We'd had a lot of tough conversations over the last day as we figured out how the hell this house deal would work, but none harder than the one I was putting off right now.

We were due to meet our friends and explain everything, but what the hell were we going to say? The deadline was finally here, and there was no more putting it off.

I shook my head. "Not 'til we've had grownup conversations."

"Grownup conversations," Adam lamented. "Can we at least have Lucky Charms while we have them?"

"Bubbles has lots of breakfast options!" I laughed. "You can wait like ten minutes."

"Not enough breakfast for my supper." Adam's eyes twinkled as he headed for the kitchen. "I need second breakfast."

"Feeding you will be a full-time job. We'd better do the kitchen before the bedroom." I grinned and shook my head.

"Then we can camp out next to the fridge. Perfect." Adam seemed genuinely excited by the idea, and I burst out laughing. It wasn't even that funny, but my heart was lighter than I could remember it being in a long time.

I started the new full-time job soon, and George was even going to front me some extra cash for the house. He was just glad I was taking it off his buddy's hands, and that I'd agreed to be on his crew.

I got a more steady nine-to-five job, I didn't have to worry about scheduling and invoicing, and best of all, I got the chance to co-own a house out of the deal. Maybe I'd only stick around for a few years before the situation changed and I went back to freelancing, but for now, everyone won.

That was rare in life.

I never would have taken this leap without Adam inspiring me to do it. Maybe he was a bit reckless, but I could use much more of that attitude sometimes.

"So, I need to ask you something," I finally said as Adam brought me a bowl of Lucky Charms, too. We crashed together on the couch.

I still needed to talk to him again about his fears. I wouldn't let him put it off anymore. Since the great wall sex, it felt like we'd danced around the subject. *I don't know if I can do this* was the last sword of Damocles hanging over the steadily thickening thread of our relationship.

I could live with him as a best friend, but... fuck, it would hurt. My palms were instantly sweaty at the thought of that conversation.

"Uh oh. Last time you said that, I ended up buying a house." Adam feigned shock. "Is this the engagement? Or the baby?"

"Shut up," I laughed, trying not to put too much stock in the way my heart skipped several beats and my fingers tingled at the mention of an engagement.

Way too soon.

"Aww." Adam pouted. "Now I'm crushed." His eyes twinkled, though. "That blush is fantastic."

Sure, argued the rational voice in my head. *Buy a house with him, but it's too soon to get engaged.*

I huffed. "Anyway," I continued, "remember when we, uh… made a hole in the wall…"

Adam stifled his snort. "It's pretty hard to forget sending your ass through a wall, yeah. I'm sure that happened sometime recently."

"Mmph." I had to admit, the marshmallows in this cereal were pretty damn good. I didn't usually indulge in sugary cereals, since they didn't keep me full for a long day of work. "Well, afterward, before I spotted the fire trap wiring, you said something."

Adam's eyes fell to his bowl and he picked out marshmallows with his own spoon. "Mmhmm?" He looked like he knew what was coming.

I started it. I have to finish it. I drew a breath and looked over at him. "You said you weren't sure you could do this." My throat felt tight. "And I never really… asked…"

Adam was quiet, but he looked over at me at last, clearly waiting for me to finish a question.

"Do you want to do this—this whole thing as friends, or as more?" My hand shook—I'd forgotten that I still held a pile of marshmallows in it, spoon midway in the air, and a fluffy heart-shaped marshmallow dropped onto my lap.

Adam pushed my hand down until my spoon clinked back into my bowl, and then leaned in to kiss me. He tasted like milk and sugar, and he smelled like the man I wanted to bury my face into and hold forever. "Yes. Whatever you want," Adam murmured quietly.

"Y-You want to date?" Even starting this huge transaction without talking about our relationship had been risky enough. I needed to know for sure now, before we were so far in we couldn't back out. "For serious?"

"I want to," Adam said, and I set my bowl on the coffee table at the same moment he did. This felt like a moment to let the cereal get soggy in favor of talking to him while we were spilling our hearts. "I'm just scared I'm not gonna be the guy you need," Adam finally concluded.

I frowned and shook my head. "I wouldn't have asked you…"

Adam cracked a smile. "I know. That—ironically? That was what made me realize that maybe it could work. That's why I came out at work."

I sucked in my breath and frowned at him as he looked away again. "And?"

"They were… they were okay." Adam offered a shaky smile. "A couple of them didn't really get why I've *turned gay* suddenly, and I tried to explain bi and they just couldn't understand. But it was a million times better than I thought it'd go!"

I scoffed and wrapped an arm around him. "I'm sorry, babe." God, I wished I could save him from this part of it, but I couldn't introduce him to just the fun parts of our life and culture. What united us more than clothes or musical taste, after all, was the way the world looked at us.

We got off easy, both being pretty much guy's guys. We weren't out of place in a blue-collar dive bar with beers in our hands, and compared to someone like Kev, I knew it could be a lot worse. But ultimately, people who were gonna hate him would hate me and Adam just as much if we let our "secret" slip.

I hated that, and I hated that now Adam was going to have to learn that cold, hard fact for himself.

"But one of them was cool, so I asked him along tonight." Adam smiled to himself. "That's neat."

I nodded slowly. "Is that it?"

"Well..." Adam hedged, and when I gave him silence, he finally sighed. "I need to tell my parents someday. I don't know why that feels like such a big deal." His voice grew sharp-edged. "It's not like they care."

I rubbed his shoulder and pulled him into me, swaying gently. "I know. But sometimes these things don't make sense. Maybe you need closure."

"That sounds like I've died or something." Adam half-smiled. "Maybe I have. The old me, anyway."

I sucked my breath in, trying not to let on how much I didn't want to think about that combination of words—*Adam* and *died*. Tears pricked my eyes regardless.

Adam's expression shifted to panic. "Shit. I didn't mean to... I'm sorry, babe."

"No, it's..." My voice was thick as I wiped at my eyes. "Fuck. I don't know where that... I mean..." I did know where that had come from. Talking with Charlie about his dead boyfriend, just once or twice, had been enough to make me realize how damn important it was to seize every moment you had with your loved ones and make it count. "Just thinking about us not being together is…"

Adam pressed his lips into my hair and pulled me into his lap. I went willingly, cuddling up against his chest. "I know," he murmured, his voice humming through my cheek. He kissed the top of my head and almost crushed me in his hug. "I meant metaphorically, that's all. The old me is gone. I'm going to try to be braver, and… you know. Worth it."

"You're worth it already," I whispered, sending another ugly thought into the universe for the people who'd made him feel like he wasn't. "And if talking to *them* will help you realize they don't see that, and they're not worth listening to…"

Adam sighed and nodded slowly. "I don't want to wait around for them not to call. I'm gonna do it this weekend. I'll keep calling until I get through. Call their damn church and ask for them, if I have to."

I rubbed his chest and nodded, another glow of admiration forming in my chest. He had no idea how attractive that determination was. When he got in the mood to do something, he wasn't going to be stopped, and I loved that about him. "You know what? Whatever the hell they say, you've inspired me to be a better man. That means you're nothing like they say."

"I have?" Adam sounded genuinely confused. "How?"

I smiled to myself and eased away enough that I could look him in the eye. "Because you work your ass off, and you trust that it'll pay off. I've felt like everything is pointless for a while now, and then you swept in and taught me to do the work anyway. And I realized I've been doing it quietly in my career, so why not in my love life?" I wasn't convinced I was making sense, but I plunged ahead. "I want to—to do the work, and trust that you'll be there to catch me."

Adam rubbed my back and arms and cupped the back of my head, his thumb rubbing gentle circles into my scalp. "I'll be here," he promised. "I'm sorry I said I wasn't sure I could do this. I've never doubted that I *want* to… only that I can."

"If you believe in me," I murmured with a smile at him, "I'll believe in you."

"Deal." Adam kissed me softly, his lips warm and tender. Even the way he held me was so intimate that even I couldn't quite believe this was the same Adam. Was this the guy I'd joshed around with while moving in not even two months ago? The guy who'd been so afraid of getting it wrong that he tried too hard?

Maybe, at last, his confidence was taking over. And maybe I could let mine do the same.

"I love you," I murmured, burying my head in his shoulder so I didn't have to see the reaction. My heart thudded with nerves. "I know it's real fucking soon…"

Adam shook his head slightly. "Nope," he said with so much certainty that I pulled back. Did he mean he didn't love me? When he saw my expression, Adam frowned and shook his head again. "I mean, yes. I love you too. And nope, I'm not gonna second-guess it. I'm fucking *done* second-guessing myself, remember? New Adam says that's a waste of time."

I barely processed the rest of it after his oh-so-casual *I love you too*. "Huh?" I squeaked.

Adam smiled at me and cupped my cheek fondly. "I said, I love you. They always said I'd just know." His grin turned mischievous. "They didn't know I'd *just know* a guy, and neither did I… but hey. Life's funny."

I let out a weak breath and flopped against him. *Thank God, I'm not the weirdo he's running away from. Maybe that's what I need to stop fearing.* The thought gave me strength again. I'd never had so many big relationship discussions at once, and here we were. But I'd also never dated someone like Adam, and if I had my way, I never would again. Adam was looking a hell of a lot like my endgame, and I'd never suspected until now.

Adam laughed and rubbed my back again. "Don't waste those perfectly good marshmallows."

I wiggled my ass and then rolled off him, grinning. "I don't intend to."

"Oooh!" Adam grinned and pinched my ass before letting me go.

"Truce on the pillow fight until tonight. And after the cereal bowls are empty," I warned him, pointing at him. "We're already screwed, damage deposit-wise. I will not have us ruining the carpet with milk, too."

"Fine," Adam pouted. "Be a grownup."

"Only until the milk's gone."

Adam grabbed his bowl and shoved a handful of cereal in his mouth, demonstrating some horrifying caveman eating skills, and I doubled over laughing.

Yeah, there were a lot of good reasons I loved him. Didn't matter what anyone else thought—it was down to him and me, and we were going to get this right. Even if we screwed up along the way, as long as we set aside our fears, maybe it could all work out okay.

Maybe, at last, I was done staying quiet and being screwed over. With Adam, I could ask for what I wanted—and I got so much more.

"So you *weren't* dating, but now you are?" Shay, the handsome weatherman who had so eagerly awaited our relationship update, asked.

"Yep." I swallowed hard and glanced at Adam, who looked just as nervous as I did. I wasn't sure I'd done a good job explaining it, because it didn't make much sense to us, either.

"And how is that different from your average relationship?" Shay laughed. Almost everyone around the table in Bubbles was staring at us with confused or amused expressions—sometimes both.

I blinked a few times and looked at Adam. "Well, we..." I trailed off. When he put it like that, there wasn't exactly a lot to confess. It was true: a lot of guys slept together for a while and then realized they were into each other... "We weren't when we said we were, but now we are?"

"And then you bought a house?" Kev grinned. "Sure you aren't getting Lesbian U-Haul Syndrome?"

"Hey," Jared told him as he approached the table with a pot of coffee. The diner owner was listening in as always, then. "No stereotyping here."

Kev snorted and raised his hands. "My bad. Most lesbians don't buy houses after two weeks."

"Most lesbians don't smash through a wall," I mumbled, but everyone caught it.

"You *what?*" Kev exclaimed.

"The wall in your old room," Adam said with a sigh. "The one to the living room."

"The shoddy one—hang on." Kev's eyes glinted as he leaned in. "Exactly how did you manage to do this?"

For some reason, everyone was more interested in the sordid details of wall destruction than they were in our big confession that we'd only been fake-dating at first. I raised my shoulders at Adam in a shrug when he looked at me for help.

"They were banging," Paolo concluded. Adam's coworker had turned up at the last minute, and he seemed surprisingly okay with it all. Adam had mumbled something about introducing me to his buddies, and that had been that. However much I pried, he wouldn't admit that he was coming out for me.

It was charming, worrying, but utterly intoxicating. Adam was finally putting in such an effort to make this work. All I wanted to do was protect him, but I couldn't. Paradoxically, to make this work, I had to ask him to be more vulnerable than he ever had been. And he treated it like no big deal, but I knew it was.

"Maybe," Adam mumbled while everyone wolf-whistled and catcalled us.

"You're all assholes," I concluded, my cheeks burning. "The poor baby gay here…" I gestured to Adam. "Don't embarrass him!"

"Oh, sure. Use him as a shield." Kev's eyes sparkled. "Thank God he finally came out. I've been waiting long enough."

Adam nearly spat his coffee. He choked and coughed, and I patted his back until he could breathe again. "*What?*" he squeaked. "You knew?"

Everyone laughed again as Kev mimed zipping his lips.

"Oh, God." Adam slumped in his seat and covered his face. "Everything I thought was a big deal isn't."

"Sorry to steal the thunder. We can pretend to cast you out if you'd prefer," Kev said cheerily while I tried not to laugh with sheer relief.

I eyed Enrique, the cook, as he hurried past. He must be just wrapping up his shift. Though Jared tried to call out to him, he just turned his head away and skedaddled out the door.

Adam still had his hands over his face, and I decided to give him a moment to recover by eyeing Jared and raising my eyebrows, nodding after Enrique.

Jared shrugged on his way back to the table. "He does that sometimes. So, I wanna hear more about the house," he said and scooted into the other side of the booth, next to Shay.

"It's a dump," I told them with a cheery smile. "But it's looking like our dump. The owners are desperate to forget their mistakes, and we're desperate to get in. We shouldn't be in our holey apartment for more than a month, I think." George was willing to provide references, and the mortgage broker seemed confident we could get the mortgage. Everything was hanging in the air for now, but it had all moved way faster than I'd even hoped.

"That's fucking awesome."

Everyone toasted that with a cup of coffee, and I grinned around at them all. "The only downside is: we won't be walking distance from here anymore."

"Not even close," Adam added with a chuckle. "Not for now."

"You never know," I agreed and smiled. "We might get into property flipping."

"Flip our way to a place nearby," Adam added. "I'm pretty fond of this neighborhood now."

"Me too."

Kev was snickering at us, and I finally looked over at him. "What?" I playfully demanded.

"You're basically finishing each other's sentences, you know." The others nodded along as Kev pointed at the two of us. "I should have paired you guys up *ages* ago."

I scoffed. "I wasn't ready for a relationship." Hell, sometimes I still didn't feel like I was, but Adam made me want to try. He'd been there for me, he'd seen the damage Xavier had done to my self-esteem and heart, and he'd still taken me, bruises or no.

Adam just smiled softly at me. "Good thing I don't give up easily."

I put a hand on Adam's knee. "You wanna head back now?"

"We've got a long day of waiting to hear back from Jon ahead of us," Adam agreed, sighing. Plus, his day of work had been exhausting—he'd told me that they'd wrapped up some huge project impossibly quickly. How the hell we were gonna get through these renovations with whatever spare energy we had... well, that remained to be seen. I hoped for both of our sakes that his new supervisory role, starting tomorrow, took less out of him.

Despite everyone's protests that they wanted more stories from Two Palms, I managed to extricate us from the social gathering with only a few rounds of hugs and kisses and handshakes and back-slaps.

"They're just going to fuck," Shay said with a wistful sigh. "That honeymoon phase."

I blushed and hurried my steps, pretending not to hear.

"Go get 'im!" Kev shouted, and I flipped him off as I fumbled to open the door and hurry out.

Our friends didn't care—they accepted our journey and us without question. I'd gotten pretty damn lucky on every front.

29

ADAM

"Do you want me here?" Darren was fussing over me, rearranging my shirt collar and straightening the blanket on the couch behind me. He'd been fidgety for days, ever since I brought up this plan.

I smiled at him and took his hand before he started patting my hair into place. No need, since it was a phone call. Good thing my parents had never mastered Skype. Landlines wouldn't betray me if I got upset, so long as I could keep a cheerful voice through it all. I was good at that.

"Always," I told him simply. Totally worth it just to see him blush.

Darren let go of my hand and picked up the phone, weighing it in his hand as he looked at me. I could sense the wise words coming a mile off. "Whatever they say, Adam…"

"It's nothing to do with me," I said quietly. "I know."

Darren smiled and wrapped his arm around me. "Bingo. It's easier said than remembered, I know. But that's what I'm here for."

I couldn't put into words how glad I was that he was here without dissolving into mushy, sentimental crap. Instead I just mumbled and leaned into him.

Darren chuckled softly as he handed over the phone. "Okay. Let's get the formalities done and dusted."

It really did feel that way. Surely my parents knew—what with all the hints and suspicions they'd had about me and Kev. And I already knew what their response was going to be. But rather than let this relationship grow slowly even more distant, I might as well cut it short. At least I'd stop worrying about when I'd hear back from them.

I dialed and crossed my fingers that calling on a weekday would startle them into answering.

"Hello? Adam?" Dad sounded confused, and I was in luck.

"Hi, Dad. Is Mom there?"

"Oh, I'm just chopped liver." It might have been a joke had we been any closer, but it felt more like a ritual, too—the way parents should joke around about their parenting roles. It all rang hollow now.

"No, can you put me on speaker with you both?"

"What's this about then?" I heard shuffling and rattling, so no doubt he was going to find my mom somewhere in the house.

"I'll tell you in a sec."

He was quiet—almost too quiet—until the background noise changed. His voice echoed now as he said, "I'm here with Mom now."

"Hi, Mom. Sorry for calling out of the blue." God, every stilted sentence we had to exchange before getting around to the real point of the call was one too many for me. I rushed through it now to get to the point. "I have something to tell you guys. I think you already know. I'm bi."

I heard one of them gasp. Dad said, "By what?"

"Bisexual."

A long few moments passed before Mom finally spoke, her voice wavering. "I'd hoped it wouldn't come to this. I don't see why you need to tell us these things when you're so far away. Too far away for us to help."

"I don't need help," I told her firmly. "I'm a lot happier not hiding away. I'm done hiding, which is why I'm telling you. You can accept it or not—I hope you do, but I have a great life ahead of me either way."

"We need some time to… to think about this." Dad sounded firm. "We've known it was coming, but it's no less of a shock."

"Right." I rolled my eyes at Darren, who only heard my end of the conversation. "I'm sure it's a shock. It surprised me, too." I couldn't help it—I cracked a grin.

"That kind of humor is inappropriate," Mom cut in. "Your father and I will not support this behavior."

"Okay, cool." They didn't have an immediate response for that, and it made me kind of proud of myself. For once, I wasn't cowering, waiting for the verbal or physical backhand. I had done nothing wrong, and I knew it. "Don't bother calling until you've figured out how to be respectful, like you always preached. Bye."

Darren's jaw hung open in a shocked, yet delighted grin. "Dude!" he exclaimed as soon as I hung up. "That was epic!"

"Not as epic as it should have been." I pouted as I tossed the phone onto the coffee table and leaned into him. Like the hole in the wall of this crappy place, they left me with a hole in my heart. Thank

God Darren was here to fill it… and my other holes, too. "I should have come up with some epic speech about how it's okay to be bi, and I don't need their approval, and all kinds of stuff."

"No." Darren sounded confident, and I looked at him as he leaned against my shoulder. "Doing that just buys into their drama and gives them more power over you in its own way. Cutting things off right away like that was perfect."

I was right to follow my gut instinct and choose the smartass route instead of trying to appeal to their better nature, then. Maybe I wasn't as bad as I thought at being around people.

"How do you feel?"

It didn't feel real, honestly. Part of me couldn't believe I'd gone and done this at long last, and another part felt like it was years ago already. Apparently we'd been dancing around it for far longer than I'd thought. "Pissed off that they didn't tell me sooner. I could have saved a lot of soul-searching. D'you know how many Grindr dates I could have had?"

"I think you did well for yourself, anyway," Darren chuckled.

The guilt of sustaining a lie made my insides squirm. I'd done it for long enough with Kev and I didn't want to keep it up. It was time to let that part of me go, if it was just a defense mechanism for the rest of me that I was putting to bed.

"I… have a confession."

"Uh huh?" Darren played with my hair, and the touch soothed me. I didn't feel like I was on trial. It would take a long time to get over those feelings, I was growing to realize.

"All the times I had girls or guys over… well, I didn't. Well, not *all* the times. I hooked up a little, but not as much as I told you or Kev. Sometimes I tried and didn't get lucky. Sometimes I… I almost did, but I couldn't go through with it." I was blushing fiercely now.

Darren didn't laugh at me, though. He just smiled. "I'm glad you told me. Was that with that guy you mentioned?"

"Ricky, yeah," I murmured under my breath. "Yeah, that's him. I wanted to hook up so badly just to see what it was like, but I wasn't feeling it."

"You were pressuring yourself to get it over with for the sake of appearances."

Fuck. If Darren was gonna go analyze my life accurately like this, I wasn't sure if I wanted him to do it more or stop. "Yeah, I guess. I didn't want to be that loser virgin guy who doesn't know how to fuck another guy."

"I can assure you none of that was true," Darren assured me, grinning. "And I don't care how many people you've been with. There's no right or wrong answer to that."

I smiled to myself, my fingers sliding between the gaps of his. "I'm just happy to be sleeping with only you these days. In more ways than one." We'd shared a bed the last few nights, since the now-infamous wall incident, and he'd basically moved into my room. We didn't want any more stuff near that dangerous outlet than was necessary. "It's nice not to be... well, on my own."

"You won't be on your own," Darren assured me. "Not as long as you let me in."

I squeezed his hand and smiled, trying not to grin like a Cheshire cat. It was nearly impossible, though. "And I'm so fucking glad. You know, you're right that this is closure. The more I see how full of shit my parents were, the more I realize... they didn't know shit about me."

I was smart enough to get through closing a deal on a house when I'd never owned property before. And, hell, smart enough to make life work. Who cared about book smarts compared to being able to trust in myself to live life? Not just that, but I liked working hard. I didn't need boot camp to kick my ass—working at the ranch last year had done that just fine. I liked working hard, and I liked doing it alongside this man.

"There's one more thing I want to do." I tried to sound confident, even if I didn't feel like it. For some reason, this had me more nervous than calling my parents.

Darren hummed questioningly.

I silently dialed from my cellphone, my hand shaking as I raised it to my ear.

"Henson here." My boss's voice was curt as ever.

"Uh, hi."

"Not chickening out after your first day, are you?"

I grinned. I was pretty sure now he was more bark than bite if you were a half-decent person. "Not at all, sir. I just had a question about, uh, a favor to ask."

"Mmhmm?"

May as well go for it. "My boyfriend and I are buying a house. I'll need some serious landscaping. If I don't crash any trucks or let the guys run amok before then… could I get a chance to grab leftovers before we trash them?" Sometimes we didn't use everything we'd bought for a job, and though we tried to reuse it on another job, it didn't always work. It broke my heart to see good turf or plants going to waste, even if we paid wholesale prices. "And maybe borrow the truck once or twice?"

Henson sounded grudgingly respectful. "Don't ask and you won't get, huh? Don't see a problem with that. As long as you keep working your ass off for me before you go renovating in your downtime."

"I will, sir," I promised. "Thank you, sir."

"And I don't care who you date, kid. Nobody else will, either, or I'll whip their asses."

My shoulders sank with relief and I breathed out a momentary sigh.

"That all?" In his gruff way, Henson had confirmed what I'd hoped —it really was no big deal.

"Yes, sir. Thanks. See you tomorrow."

"Bright and early," Henson parted with and hung up.

"I'm so damn proud of you. I have three little words for you," Darren murmured, his eyes twinkling.

My heart skipped a beat and I tried not to blush. I felt so stereotypical, but yeah, love had swept me off my damn feet. "Yeah?"

"I've got wine."

I burst out laughing as Darren jumped up and headed for the kitchen. I tried to swat his ass on the way past, but he narrowly escaped. "You asshole."

"You love me!" Darren called from the kitchen.

"I guess," I drawled.

He came back a minute later with two glasses of white wine and a big grin. "Celebration wine. I think we both have some celebrating to do. You first—how was your day?"

Now that I wasn't hyper-focused on the upcoming phone call, I realized what he meant. It had been my first day on the job as a supervisor. In some ways, it was good I'd had this looming over me, though, because I'd barely stressed about that in comparison.

And now that Henson knew, and he'd given me his word that nobody would treat me like shit on the job, I couldn't wait to go back tomorrow.

"It was good. A whole new crew, but Henson's suddenly treating me like a… I don't know, a collaborator." Maybe that was something else I felt more confident about—being more myself on a job site, and being treated like my ideas were worth listening to. Henson trusted me to divide up the work and see that it got done.

I hadn't really come out in flamboyant rainbows on my first day, but I didn't plan to hide it anymore. If anyone asked, I was living with my boyfriend, thanks very much. With Henson at my back, I felt safe at last.

Darren nodded. "That's great. And for my part, George said to say hello to you today when we were going over the paperwork."

"Oh, that's nice of him. Still excited about the job?" To me, Darren selling most of his gear and especially his van sounded like a step backward, but when he'd explained that this was a once-in-a-life-time fixer-upper price and opportunity, I could understand it.

"It'll be good, I think." Darren had a contemplative little smile on his lips. "No more running around town trying to handle everything at once."

"Good. We'll have enough balls in the air soon enough," I started to say, and then snorted when Darren giggled.

"You said balls."

"I knew there was a reason I love you," I said casually, still trying on the words. They felt good, and best of all was the way I felt when Darren put aside his wine glass and flopped on the couch, his head in my lap, smiling up at me.

"You can say that again."

"Say what?" I teased wickedly.

Suddenly, Darren's fingers closed around my nipple.

I yelped and tried not to spill wine in his face, setting it on the coffee table. "Jesus! You've got a mean streak, don't you?" I batted his hand away, even if my body had burned very pleasantly.

"You *love* my mean streak," Darren whispered and grinned. "It makes the wrestling matches that much more fun."

God, I loved it when he was a dick. I laughed along with him. "For the record, I will still wrestle you for top bunk anytime."

The glint in Darren's eyes was my only warning. Before I knew it, he was rolling off my lap onto the floor, grabbing me by the arm to haul me off, too.

There was barely space between the coffee table and the couch, which made it a lot harder not to just throw my weight against the coffee table and break everything on it. He was smaller, and he squirmed away under the coffee table, fitting his limbs around the legs so he could roll out of reach.

I growled and stood up, chasing him to the only open spot of the living room floor before I grabbed him by the waist. "You're not getting off that easily," I threatened.

"I'm getting off pretty easily already," Darren countered, grinding against me as I pushed him down to the floor. "I mean, you keep that up and I'm gonna come in my pants."

I smirked. "I might make you demonstrate that sometime." I was clearly straddling him now, victorious. He wasn't even wrestling back.

Darren grabbed my ass and arched his hips to press his erection into me. It was only then that I realized his gameplan—get me riding him.

I surprised myself at how fucking hot that sounded. I didn't need to be on top just because I was… well, on top. "Yes, *please.*"

"I'm proud of you," Darren winked. "Ready to take any opportunity that comes your way."

I smirked and kissed him. "You've taught me well," I murmured against his lips, but I didn't have the chance to say anything more.

We were lost in kisses, grinding against each other slowly as we found every way that our bodies could fit together perfectly. The whole time, his lips were finding mine, the tip of his tongue dancing around sensitive skin and making me tingle in a way I hadn't felt in a long time.

I needed him with an intensity that should have scared me, but instead, I was drawn to him. Not like a moth to a flame that might burn it, as I'd first feared, but to the moon.

He was my moon, and my stars, and my goddamn runway lights in the night. I hadn't known that I was so badly off-course until I'd found him. Now, I wanted to follow his lead into safety— wherever the hell he took me, I trusted him enough to follow.

I was going to be okay.

3 0

DARREN

Adam had ridiculously long lashes, and his brown eyes were pretty as hell when they peeked through those lashes at me. He didn't even have to ask a question for me to want to say yes.

With those seeds sown, all it took was a quiet, almost shy, "Wanna take this to somewhere more romantic?" to melt my heart.

The glasses of wine were pretty much forgotten now. I had better ways to celebrate in mind—we could come back and grab the wine later.

"Hell, yeah." I did a crunch so I could sit up and kiss him, and then let him take my hands to pull me to my feet.

He moved me around with ease, and I took a moment to appreciate having a ripped boyfriend once again. I hadn't really planned to, but I'd gotten lucky, which was pretty much the story of our relationship. Hard abs suited Adam, and they gave me some great texture in the mornings.

We didn't rush to the bedroom. We had all the time in the world to spend together, after all. Why hurry a good thing?

Instead, I draped my arms around his neck and leaned into him, pressing butterfly kisses against his lips. Whenever he tried to deepen the kiss, I pulled away and smirked at him.

"Little tease," Adam finally grumbled affectionately, his hand slowly stroking from the back of my neck, down my spine, to cup my ass. The way he held me made me feel secure and supported.

I pouted. "Such harsh words."

"I didn't call you an asshole, you know." Adam rolled his eyes. "I don't know what more you want."

I burst out laughing and had to turn my head away. From anyone else, I might have called that grounds to break up. From Adam, I knew he could take as good as he gave. "Takes one to know one."

"So if I'm aware that you're a sexy hunk whose very presence makes me spring a boner…" Adam smirked.

"Damn right you are too." I winked. "Everyone wins."

Adam's expression suddenly lost a little of its teasing playfulness. This time, when he leaned in to kiss me, I let him and I leaned into him. "I'm pretty sure I win most of all," Adam finally murmured, resting his head on my shoulder for a moment before he kissed my neck.

I curled my toes into the floor and ran my nails down his back. "It's not a competition, it's a collaboration."

"Wise words," Adam said, and I loved that his voice was lilting and light again. He backed toward our bedroom, pulling me along with him.

We both chuckled as we passed the butt-sized hole in the drywall. "You should put me through the other side," I told him. "But only after the main breaker's off."

"Party in the dark with candles and total drywall destruction." Adam swooned and pressed a hand against his forehead. "So romantic."

"We have a lot of hot demolition sex ahead of us."

Adam perked up, grabbing my hips and grinding against me before he shuffled backward through his doorway. "You have my attention."

"I can feel it," I teased, squeezing his package. God, it was sexy to feel a man's hard-on through his jeans—especially when that man was Adam, and I was about to have even more mind-blowing sex with him. *I* was the lucky one here.

Adam moaned and kicked the door shut, then winced. We both glanced to make sure we hadn't splintered the frame or anything.

When it looked like we were safe, he let out his breath and laughed. "Can't say I'll miss this place."

"I'll miss a few of the memories," I admitted, my hands wandering up under his shirt. Bare skin, smooth to the touch, greeted me. "But we have lots more to make."

Adam moaned, and I wasn't sure if he was agreeing or appreciating the touch. Either way, he fumbled for my shirt to pull it off. I wasn't so hasty with his, though. I teased him first, letting the pads of my fingers dance up his spine and around his shoulder blades, and then down that muscled back again.

When my hands reached his ass, he squirmed enough to grab his shirt and yank it over his head in one swift move. "Tease," he reiterated.

I tried to look innocent, but too many filthy ideas played through my mind at the sight of that bare chest.

I wolf-whistled and made a swift mental note never to visit him at work, because I was not gonna be able to control myself if he was all sweaty and dirty, too. I even caught myself inhaling, half-expecting a manly musk of plywood and earth and grass. He'd showered since work, so I only got coconut.

It was a disappointment I could live with, because Adam grinned and ran his hands up my chest to play with my nipples. The sparks that flew through my body nearly made my knees buckle.

"Oof!" I bit my lip and dug my nails into his hips, hauling him against me. "Yes!"

"Hours of fun someday," Adam murmured as if to himself, winking at me. He let go and grabbed my hips, grinding against me in slow rolls of his hips. With our stomachs and chests pressed together, the heat that prickled through me only continued to build.

"I need you," I whispered at last. My pants were way too tight, and I had a plan. I maneuvered him toward the bed. It took up most of Adam's room now that we'd pushed both twin beds together. Springing for a king-sized fitted sheet over them both and anti-skid pads for the bottoms of the legs had made it look like one bed, but we still tried to cozy up on one side of the divide if possible.

Adam thought nothing of flopping onto his back, but before he could scoot over to the inside of the bed, I grabbed him and pounced. In one swift move—careful move, since I didn't want my knee killing the mood—I was straddling him, grinning down at him.

"Oh! It's on!"

I giggled like mad and tried to hold on as Adam threw his weight up and against me, rolling me to the side. I didn't let him get his leg on top, though. "You thought I was just gonna let you win? I was saving my energy for the round that matters!"

My very own live wire finally gave in with a huff and grin at me. "Fine. You've got me where you want me."

"Oh, I do." I pecked his lips, wrapping my hands around his wrists to pin them on the bed by his head. "Remember this?"

Adam moaned and squirmed, grinding against me once again. It was getting pretty fucking annoying to have the sensation dulled by the layers of fabric. "Hell, yeah." He licked his lips. "My gay awakening."

"I'm flattered," I teased, even if I didn't quite believe it. I knew he'd had bi feelings before. But maybe this really had been the first time he'd followed through on them. I'd always be flattered that he'd trusted me enough to do that.

We were still playfully wrestling, but I sensed that Adam wasn't really trying to get free now. He was beaming up at me. "You gonna ride me first, cowboy?"

"I'll save a horse," I promised, winking. "We just need to take care of a few matters first."

"Jeans matters?" When I let go of Adam's wrists, he kept his hands on the bed and obediently waited for me to haul his jeans off. "Oh, I agree. God, that's better," he moaned when his dick popped out into the open. "Is that fair, making you ride me first? I can still go on top if you'd rather."

I smirked at him. "I'm greedy. I want you first. I'll give you something to remember next round," I promised, but I loved that he was thinking about fairness.

"Next round?" Adam's cock twitched as I peeled my jeans off and tossed them aside. "Hell, yes."

I grabbed lube before I straddled him again, letting our cocks line up and gently thrusting. The ridge around the head slid across his shaft, and that steady pressure alone was pure bliss.

Adam wrapped one big hand around our cocks, and I grinned. "You've got this situation in hand. I'll get busy with this, then…" I cracked open the lube and squirted it across my fingers.

"That was bad." Adam groaned but laughed at me. His touch was just firm enough to feel good without being too much stimulation. Between my own fingers sliding inside my tightness and his hand around my shaft, I thrust backward and forward slowly at first.

It didn't take long before I needed more. Even as skilled as I was at using a couple fingers, I wanted Adam's cock now. I ached to be filled by him, stretched open and locked together with him in an intimate dance of bodies.

Adam gripped the base of his shaft with one hand and my hip with the other as he pressed against and then into me.

Enveloping him never grew old. As I sank slowly down, my knees shaking, I steadied myself with a hand on his chest.

"You okay, baby? You're doing wonderfully," Adam whispered.

"Mmhmm." It was a tight squeeze, but already I eagerly anticipated the moment I could relax and ride him like a beast.

Adam's voice was almost a croon as he murmured my praises, his hands running across my chest and down my sides. "I love watching you take my cock. It's so fucking hot. You're tight as anything around me. Take it slow, hon."

I smiled at how sweet he was being. "Slow?" I shifted my weight as I set into motion. "That… would ruin the fun." I grabbed his hands and leaned forward to pin them on the bed on either side of his head again as I rode him nice and slowly at first. I didn't wait long to speed up, though.

"Yes!" Adam grunted when I'd found my pace, taking him in as deep as he'd go with every thrust. My hips rolled against his, my cock hard again and bouncing in the air as I worked. By the time sweat beaded my brow and my thrusts slowed, Adam was too damn impatient to wait any longer and he squirmed free, wrestling his way to the top.

I rolled over onto my back and found my knees hooked over Adam's shoulders as he plunged inside me. From then on it was a frantic race to the finish, my body tensing up with pleasure around him every time he hit the spot just right. I stroked myself hard and fast, begging for more as he gave me everything I could handle.

Losing myself was finding him, and when I lost every other thought, he still remained in the center of every thought and the center of my very being.

I came just moments before him, a whimpered gasp spilling from my throat as he growled my name, his nails digging into my thighs.

It was the most natural thing in the world to collapse together, a tangle of sweaty bodies and limbs and unexplained giggles. I felt so good—so light and free and happy—that I couldn't quite believe it.

If Adam fucked hard, he sure as hell cuddled hard, too. His hard body pressed against mine, wrapping me up in his arms and legs as he kissed my face all over. He was ridiculously over-the-top in so many ways, and I loved him for it.

"You know what?" Adam finally murmured when that burst of energy had passed and I was tucked against his chest. "I don't give a crap where we are—even here, avoiding holes in the wall—if we're together."

He'd said he loved me, but it wasn't until now that it sank in. *That* was love with its work boots on, not just meaningless words that people could say if they wanted something from me. It was nothing like what Xavier had ever said to me. Best of all, I knew exactly what Adam meant because I felt it too.

"So damn proud of you," I murmured back.

"For what?"

I smiled. "You've grown a lot as a person over the last few weeks. You're more *you* now. And I'm proud of me, for… well… learning to trust you."

Adam hummed and nodded. "I can agree with that."

My phone went off with an alert, and I had a feeling I knew what it was. I rolled over to grab our phones from the jeans discarded on the edge of the bed, and then kicked the clothing off to leave more space for us. Sure enough, when I glanced at the screen of my phone, my sixth sense was right—it was an Instagram notification that Xavier had just started a livestream video.

Adam and I's relationship might not be perfect forever, but it was ours. I was done giving a fuck what anyone else thought of our image.

I smiled at how damn peaceful it felt to click through the notification and unfollow his profile. I wasn't even a bit tempted to read his latest photos or captions. I was done caring about him, and it was pure liberation. I'd only ever wanted to show off on social media to get back at Xavier, or creep his profile because I was jealous. Now, though? I was out of fucks to give about him—and Austin, for that matter.

"You good?" Adam murmured, glancing up from his phone and snaking an arm around my shoulders like he sensed I might need comfort. For a guy who pretended to be bad at being around people, he didn't give himself enough credit.

"More than good." I put my phone down on the bedside table and stroked his thigh gently. "I just got rid of Xavier. Enough damn attention-seeking live videos."

Adam laughed, but he rubbed my shoulder. "Good job, babe."

I blushed. "For getting over my ex?" I gave him a guilty grin. "Not sure you're supposed to do that by dating a new guy."

"Depends. If your new boyfriend doesn't mind, who cares?" Adam pointed out, tapping his phone on my thigh gently but firmly. "I probably wasn't supposed to experiment with my roommate before I even knew for sure that I was into guys. We broke all the rules, and it worked for us."

That much was true. Both of us had spent too long worrying about what others thought of us in different ways, even if we'd seemed to be living our lives without a care for others' opinions. Truly letting go of that need for validation was heady. All the validation I needed was in Adam's eyes.

"Would you help me set up an account?" Adam smiled sheepishly. "I've never really understood that app."

I laughed and pulled him into me, cuddling up with him as I downloaded and explained it all. Adam wasn't the same guy who was half-afraid of posting photos of himself with guys on social media anymore. Without secrets to worry about, he actually seemed excited for whatever he was planning.

When Adam blushed, I eyed him. "What?" I was trying not to snoop, but he was also conspicuously hiding his phone now.

"I… uh…" He rubbed his chin. "Kinda wanted to start an account to follow some of my new friends, and tell the story of… uh… you know…" When I waited, he finally spilled the beans, but he blushed furiously. "Two guys building a house together, you know? And a life."

"That's adorable." I grinned, my heart already soaring.

"It seems like the kind of thing the world needs more of," Adam murmured, kissing my temple. "Building connections… places… a life together… inspiring other people… you know, maybe we could do tutorials? Help people learn how to do this kind of DIY?"

"I think that's a wonderful idea." Goddamn, this man inspired *me*, but he'd only blush and deflect with a joke if I told him as much. So I just kissed his cheek and rested my head on his shoulder, listening to him muttering profile names as I smiled to myself.

"A new sun rises," Adam finally murmured, and I looked up at him, my heart skipping a beat. Judging by his expression, he'd realized he found the right one, too.

"Every day," I agreed. "No matter what happened yesterday. I love it."

With a tap of his finger, Adam finished registering and put his phone aside. "And I love you."

I closed my eyes as my smile hurt my cheeks. "Yeah. You're not that much of an asshole after all, you know?" I teased, trying to speak around the lump of emotion in my throat.

Adam burst out laughing and pushed me to the bed to wrestle. "You jerk!"

I grinned. He knew damn well that that meant *I love you* in our own rapidly-growing language, but he also had a grin that meant round two was on the way. "Oh, it's on!"

"I let you win last time," Adam claimed, and I gasped.

"Did not!" I'd won last round fair and square, and we both knew it.

"Did too." He squirmed and laughed as he got a knee over me and rolled me over, and I flipped him onto the other bed, but started sliding down the gap between the beds.

"Help!" I gasped, laughing too hysterically to pull myself up. He was no use, though, because he was laughing just as hard.

"No way. I win by default if you leave the ring!"

"The ring's sliding away from me! Rematch," I gasped for breath as I tried to heave myself back up on the bed. We had some very important decisions to make together, and the more we could settle by a good old-fashioned wrestling match, the better.

Whatever the hell anyone else thought, it worked for us, and I wouldn't want it any other way.

EPILOGUE

ADAM, THREE MONTHS LATER

"Oh, shit. Sorry!" I exclaimed. At least Darren's head had only slightly bumped the doorframe this time.

Darren swore at me and laughed, squirming in my arms as I carried him across the threshold. "Jesus, Adam! Are you going to do this every day until the house is done?"

"Every day until it stops giving you a massive boner." I smirked at him as I set him on his feet and pulled him in to kiss the top of his head in apology.

Darren instantly covered his groin with both hands. "I do not—"

"Liar liar, pants on fire." I sidled up to him and planted a big, wet kiss on his lips until he couldn't help laughing.

"Why is my boyfriend like this?" Darren protested to the grim, bare living room.

I grinned. "Oooh, I know this one. Because he's happy to have a real bed at last!"

We'd just finished drywalling in the bedroom, and the floorboards needed scrubbing. It was far from painted and finished, but it was beginning to look like a real room.

To celebrate, we'd just bought a bed and it was waiting for us in Henson's truck to unload. He'd actually been generous with his advice after coming over here last month. Turned out he knew a thing or two about renovations himself.

The place might not be a showroom, but it was going to be completely ours from the ground up when it was finally done. One room at a time, as we found supplies and money, we were fixing it up.

Basic kitchen appliances, a working sink, a shower and toilet, and a bed were all we really needed, but other luxuries like new windows had seriously improved our lives.

Every day was a work in progress as we split up the tasks and spent our few precious hours from getting off work to drifting off to sleep in each other's arms.

And damn, I was grateful for everything we had.

"I've got a chicken in the fridge," I told him. "And wine."

"Oooh. And then we can christen our new bed?"

"First we gotta get the damn thing in the house," I pointed out with a laugh. "And assemble it…"

"Details," Darren waved a hand and grinned. "We can open the wine first."

I eyed him. That hadn't gone well when we'd tried that strategy in order to move boxes from the old apartment to the cleanest, driest room in this place. "Sure we can."

"Fine," Darren pouted. "Bed first. Truth be told, I can't wait to ditch that goddamn air mattress."

The best part of it all was that we had a queen-sized bed and mattress at last, which meant much easier cuddling space.

We'd had our friends come over once to see the place, and none of them had been able to believe the scope of the project we were taking on. We hadn't had a proper housewarming either, but that would wait until the living room and downstairs bathroom at least resembled a normal house.

They were next on the list, and we were gonna find a way to do it. I wanted that goddamn housewarming before Christmas, one way or another.

"And I gotta drop the truck back at Henson's in an hour," I told him. "No wine until then."

"Wow," Darren teased. "How did I find such a grownup?"

I looked around. "Where? Oh, God. You don't mean me?"

"I do, sorry, babe." Darren kissed my cheek and slapped my ass, then strode for the front door again. "An hour to get a few things upstairs… no big deal. Let's do it."

"If we hurry, we can probably replace the upstairs sink taps today, too. The ones we want were finally on sale."

"Oh, keep talking dirty," Darren crooned, opening up the tailgate and jumping into the bed to take the straps off the mattress.

"I'm screwing you into this mattress the moment we get it into our bedroom." I said it in the same lighthearted tone, so it took Darren an extra second to realize what I'd said.

Then, his jaw dropped. "Come on," he urged. "Not a moment to waste."

That had been our life for the last few months, and it probably would be for another year or more before the house was finally good-as-new.

But that was fine by me. Impulse had won Darren's heart, but slow and steady work would win the greatest prize of all: his hand.

We'd talked about engagement already, and he'd agreed that he wanted it—we just hadn't had a chance to think any more about it with everything else we had up in the air. Plus, all our money was going into the house.

Except a little bit I sneakily set aside every payday. By the Christmas housewarming party, I'd have enough set aside for a plain silver band. Nothing fancy yet, but that wouldn't be like us, anyway.

We didn't need a damn thing aside from courage, love, and faith in each other. That much had gotten us this far, and I had no doubt it would serve us well for a long, long time to come.

For now, we might be barely on the edge of Brooklyn, but that didn't matter: I was still the luckiest guy in the whole damn borough.

Dear reader,

Thank you for reading *Live Wire*, the second book in the Brooklyn Boys series!

Once again, this book wouldn't have come to life without the people around me. Fond thoughts always go to K for introducing me to Brooklyn, which planted the seed for this series in my head long ago. My betas, editor, and proofers made this book so much better again, and deserve a lifetime supply of brownies with ice cream. And to every person who has held the flashlight for me: may you always see the light, too.

Last, but not least, my love to the boy, the ever-patient and deft handler of live wires. I don't know how I'd find my shorts without him, much less fix them.

The next Brooklyn Boys novel is *Boiling Point*. Enrique's double life is crumbling around him while Cedar's old life crashes into him, but nothing will hold back true love.

In the meantime, don't forget to check out *Electric Sunshine*

(Brooklyn Boys #1) to catch up on Kev and Charlie if you haven't already! And to find out what happened between Shay and Jared at a speed-dating session back in January, check out the short story "Wind Tunnel" (you can grab it for free by subscribing to my newsletter).

Make sure you follow me on Amazon to hear about Brooklyn Boys and my other new releases, or subscribe to my newsletter to hear about new releases and sales, get sneak peeks at upcoming books, and hear about audiobook releases, event appearances, and other exciting news as it happens!

I also have a reader group on Facebook here if you want to tell me what you loved about this book, see cute bee and flower photos, and keep on top of my upcoming releases with a whole bunch of fun, lovely readers: https://www.facebook.com/groups/edavies

Last but not least: always be you!

~Ed

ABOUT THE AUTHOR

Gay romance author E. Davies grew up moving constantly, which taught him what people have in common, the ways relationships are formed, and the dangers of "miscellaneous" boxes. As a young gay author whose role models were characters punished for their sexuality, Ed prefers his stories lightly dramatic, full of optimism and hope.

Now out and proud, Ed writes full-time, goes on long nature walks, tries to fill his passport, drinks piña coladas on the beach, flees from cute guys, coos over fuzzy animals (especially bees), and is liable to tilt his head and click his tongue if you don't use your turn signal.

For exclusive release notifications and a free copy of my novel Buzz, sign up for my newsletter below!

Newsletter: www.edaviesbooks.com/subscribe

facebook.com/edaviesbooks

twitter.com/edaviesauthor

instagram.com/thisboyisstrange

bookbub.com/authors/e-davies

Freak

Faux

Forever

After series:

Afterburn

Afterglow

Aftermath

Hidden Creek books:

Shelter

Adore

And, of course, stay tuned for more books in the Brooklyn Boys series!